THE FIRST

NATE D. BURLEIGH

PAGE AFTER PAGE PRESS
www.PageAfterPagePress.com

Page After Page Press
The First
Copyright © Nate D. Burleigh 2015
All Rights Reserved

ISBN-13: 978-0692256794
ISBN-10: 0692256792

PAGE AFTER PAGE PRESS
www.PageAfterPagePress.com

DEDICATED TO MY FAMILY AND FANS,
ESPECIALLY MY UNCLE DWIGHT. I HOPE YOU
ALL ENJOY THE NOVEL.

In the US, approximately 4 million live births occur annually. There are 31,556,736 seconds in a year. Babies don't come in fractions, so a convenient rounding off is about one birth every seven seconds.

At 8:27:03 PM, in the emergency room of Salem Hospital, Savannah Staten became THE FIRST.

1.

"**SNAP OUT OF** it!" The female E.R. doctor shook Michael by the shoulders. "Mr. Staten. When did your wife's contractions start?"

Her cold eyes sped his bounding heart.

Doctors are non-emotional by trade, aren't they? But *her* eyes, the tone of her voice, her stricken demeanor. They held more. They held . . . fear. *Aren't doctors supposed to keep their cool no matter what?* The thought passed as he realized she'd asked him a question. What about? *Contractions. She asked about Stella's contractions.*

"Mr. Staten . . . focus." She grabbed him by the shoulders, brought him nose-to-nose and snapped her fingers in his left ear. "Please. You need to focus and tell me what I need to know."

Okay, focus. I can do this.

She let go of him. "When did your wife's contractions start?"

"I don't know . . . a few hours ago!" What the hell did it matter when the damn things started? The blood freaked him out, not the contractions.

The crimson fluid had soaked the front of his dress shirt and splashed across his lap. He'd thrown his tie off in the back of the ambulance while the medics had worked on Stella. The baby was coming, no doubt about it. He'd nearly had to deliver her at the house, but never expected so much blood. The sight of it made him lightheaded. He'd kept his cool and did the best he could.

"We were gonna have the baby at home with the midwife, but Stella . . . God . . . she was in so much pain. Is she gonna die?"

"Calm down, Mr. Staten, we'll have her stabilized in a moment."

Sure, the medical team had everything under control. Yeah, right? He wiped beads of blood tainted sweat from his brow. "Why is she bleeding so much, is that normal?"

"It can be. But that's what we're going to find out. Try and calm down. Let us do our jobs."

Stella whimpered and writhed on the gurney. Her body bucked up and down. The orderlies, doctors and nurses held her by the shoulders and legs.

The doctor ran to the gurney. "She's seizing. I need five milligrams of Valium."

A stocky black woman in blue scrubs bustled up to the group and handed a syringe to the doctor. The doctor swiped it from the woman's hand and stuck the needle into the I.V. taped to Stella's right arm. A few seconds later, the seizure stopped.

"She gonna be okay? Is the baby alive?" Michael wedged himself closer to Stella through the crowd of medical personnel.

"Mr. Staten." The robust nurse grabbed him by the shoulders. "Go sit in the waiting room. The doctor will talk to you after we have everything under control." She turned him toward the waiting area.

"Why won't you talk to me? Someone needs to tell me what the fuck is wrong with my wife."

The nurse shook her head. "Mr. Staten, the doctor needs to do her job. It would be best if you go to the waiting room."

"Fine!" He turned towards the waiting area, and yelled, "It's not like my wife and first child's lives are at stake!" He glanced back. The nurse had her hand up, but didn't look back.

Nothing could tear them apart . . . nothing. Tears ran down his face as he fell into the fake leather chair.

2.

EMMA KNEW HEMORRHAGES happened, but the baby's movement concerned her more. The lump in the patient's abdomen bulged in different places across the four quadrants, stretching the mother's frail skin. Experience dictated with this amount of blood, there should be no movement.

No heartbeat.

The posse of hospital personnel rushed the gurney down the hall. She jogged behind and listened to the young medic's report.

"This is Stella Staten. She's 32 and in her third trimester of an a-traumatic pregnancy. Abdominal pain and severe vaginal bleeding started about an hour ago. BP is 90 over 68, heart rate is tachy and regular at a 180 beats-per-minute. We ran an I.V. of Ringer's Lactate and gave her .5 milligrams of Morphine for pain."

"Does she have a history of pre-eclampsia, hypertension, or gestational diabetes?"

"No. Ma'am." He handed over his notes and dropped out of sight.

The group in front slid around a corner and rammed into the double doors of the operating room. Blood and debris shot out from under Stella's blood-soaked skirt, and splashed against the double doors.

Stella sat up and screamed.

Emma had never seen anything like it in over 1300 deliveries she'd made in her career as an emergency OB/GYN.

Dan, one of the orderlies, backed away from the stretcher and wretched into a basket.

"Thanks Mike." She nodded and smiled at the orderly who slapped the automatic door opener. Deep concern in his eyes took her back as he stared at the heart monitor.

Stella's heart beat like a locomotive, gaining speed with every horrific lump of coal placed in the fire.

"Did you give her anything for the pain?" Dr. Critchell scowled. The pompous Anesthesiologist had caught up with them a moment earlier. Everyone had told her what a nice guy he was, but that hadn't been her experience. It seemed at every corner he had something to whine at her about.

Emma steel eyed the doctor. "She's had Valium and a dose of Morphine. She should be out."

Dr. Critchell pushed Emma aside and she backed into a wall. With the amount of Valium she'd given Stella, along with the medic's morphine, the girl shouldn't have been able to move, let alone sit up and scream.

"Let's get her under . . . now!" He grimaced.

They would paralyze and intubate Stella and hopefully Dr. Smith's magic could stop the bleeding.

Nurses Joanna and Petra, along with two new orderlies, rolled the gurney next to the operating table, holding Stella down. Her banshee's wail filled the room as she struggled. Petra let go and covered her ears. Her gloves smeared blood on her wrinkled forehead and streaked her hair.

Stella leaned over and punched Nurse Joanna in the face. Her nose exploded. Blood flowed into her mouth and down her chin. She pulled a Chux absorbent sponge from the crash cart next to her and pressed it against her face and left the room in tears.

Stella leapt off the table. The I.V. ripped from her arm.

She screamed.

Emma skipped to the side as a spurt of blood whizzed by.

Stella grabbed her belly and doubled over, holding her belly tight as if she didn't want the baby to come. She looked up. Her ghosted eyes circled.

Dr. Critchell bounced over the operating table and slammed a syringe into her shoulder. "This will do the trick." He depressed the syringe.

Stella slumped forward into the waiting arms of the doctors. Emma helped the men hoist her limp body onto the bed.

"Get your contaminated ass out of my operating room." Dr. Smith pointed at the Joanna and motioned toward the door. She left in a huff. "Ever seen anything like that before, Rick?" Dr. Smith tucked the blankets under Stella's legs.

Dr. Critchell shook his head. "Nada." He stuck the laryngoscope into Stella's mouth and placed the tube down her throat, hooked her to the respirator, secured an I.V. drip, and adjusted her medications and oxygen saturation levels until she drifted into a chemically induced coma.

Emma gave a quick summary. She couldn't wait to get out of the room.

"Piece of cake." Dr. Smith examined his surgical equipment and picked out a scalpel, flashing it in the light.

"Well, I'm out. Thank God." Emma smiled.

"Not so fast." Dr. Smith held up a gloved hand and as he tore his eyes away from the scalpel. His baleful stare took in her clean appearance. "Looks like we're shorthanded."

Emma rolled her eyes. She knew the evil smirk he had under his mask.

"You'll need to scrub in." He once again held his scalpel up to the light. One little smudge and he'd have her get him a new one.

"Sure thing. Be right back, boys." She forced a grin. What she meant to say was, 'Screw you both. Have a good night.' Ugh. *When I get home I'm taking the longest bubble bath in history.*

3.

"CODE BLUE, O.R., room three. Code blue, O.R., room three." A woman's voice blared through the hospital PA system.

Michael leapt out of the waiting room chair and jogged down the hall toward the O.R. If the code had anything to do with Stella, hellfire itself couldn't cause the devastation he'd rain on the hospital and its staff.

"Shit." He jumped into a nearby room as several hospital workers rushed past him.

Screams filled the hall. He followed the group. The closer he came to the operating room, the louder the screams became.. When he turned the corner, he jumped out of the way of several people who back-peddled out of the operating room and ran past him back down the hall.

A woman crashed through the double doors. Her eyes and face should've been bright with smiles and news of his first child's birth. The baby should've been swaddled in a warm blanket, yelping her initial breaths of air, pressed snug against Stella's bare chest. Instead, the woman's face looked like it had been through a cheese grater. She rammed into him and the two toppled to the ground.

Strands of flesh dangled against his forehead. Her blood ran into his eyes and down his cheeks. She scrambled to her feet and stamped on his nuts and stomach as she raced away.

He grasped his crotch and took deep gulps of air.

The operating room doors swung back and forth. Blood spatter, coupled with the two windows above, gave the effect of an abstract portrait he'd seen in some magazine Stella showed him. Lights behind the doors flickered. The screams within died down.

Another person burst halfway through the double doors. Michael recognized her as the doctor he'd spoken to earlier. She tripped and landed face first on the cool linoleum. She lifted her head, outstretched one arm and gurgled, "H . . . h . . . elp!"

Michael's eyes widened and his stomach raced to his throat.

Her body jerked back like someone snatched her by the feet and pulled. A wet grunt escaped as the doors crushed under her arms. With every yank of her body, the pressure increased. Her eyes bulged. The grunts and wheezes from her collapsed lungs slowed. Blood vessels burst within her eyes, staining them red.

Michael choked back vomit and dove for the woman. As he slid through a puddle of something vile on the floor, he grasped the left wrist of the doctor. With a quick spin he maneuvered himself into a seated position. His left foot slammed against the door jamb. It felt as if the veins in his neck would pop as he strained against whoever had her from behind.

A Herculean orderly half-crushed Michael's ribs. They pulled together. The pressure of the pull from behind had anchored the doctor between the double doors.

Inhuman sounds escaped her pursed lips. The assailant behind the doors let go. Her head drooped and bounced on the tiled floor. Blood soaked hair flipped over her face and slid across the floor as the men dragged her from the doorway.

Michael sat against a wall and panted.

The orderly backed away from the doctor. "Oh, my fucking God."

At a quick glance she seemed asleep with her arms behind. His gaze settled on a gaping hole in her back. Not being a medical professional he couldn't be absolutely sure what protruded from the wound, but if he had to guess, he'd say . . . her spine. His heart slammed against his ribs. His stomach lurched, he heaved and vomit slapped the linoleum to the left of the woman's dead body.

The doors rocked back and forth in eerie cadence.

A survivor whimpered in the dark.

Quick electronic chirps inside the operating room smeared into a long tone of death. The whine of the machine sent chills up and down Michael's spine. He heard a faint crunch and the whimpering behind the door stopped. *Stella.*

"What the hell was that, Holmes?" The bean pole orderly towered over him.

Michael couldn't find words. He shook his head and clambered to his feet.

"Move away from the door!" a voice commanded from behind.

Michael whipped around.

A large police officer approached. Several hospital security guards surrounded him with their guns drawn.

"Are you hurt?" One of the security guards knelt next to Michael and the perplexed orderly.

"I . . . I don't think . . . " Michael lunged for the door.

The security guard tackled him from behind and pulled him back.

"Stella!" He wriggled against the man's tight grip. "My wife's in there!"

"Give us a minute to assess the situation." The man could've been a pro linebacker for the Seahawks.

Michael struggled under the powerful hands. "Get the fuck off me. *Lord, please let her be alive.*

Several more security guards and police officers showed up and proceeded into the operating room.

"Watch out!" someone yelled.

A muffled voice quivered from inside the operating room. "Where'd it go?"

Deep voiced screams pierced Michael's ears.

Cracks of gunfire set off flashes of light in the windows, snapping through every room and corridor in the hospital.

Linebacker stumbled through the operating room door. His left arm dangled mid-forearm. A bone pierced the skin. Streams of blood ran down his face from a large gash in his forehead and pooled on the floor.

Small legs clung around the man's neck. Infant hands with razor-sharp claws gouged at his face from behind. One reached around and plucked his left eye from its socket. The officer grunted and stumbled to his knees in front of Michael. He slumped forward and cracked his head on the floor.

Red eyes appeared over the man's head. The little ruby circles pierced deep into Michael's heart. He realized what had killed the man. She, his first born—they'd named her Savannah after his great grandmother—leapt from the officer's back. Michael didn't have time to scream.

Savannah's jaw clasped around his throat; her knife-edged teeth shredded the flesh and crushed his windpipe. Michael gasped for air as the world around him darkened. He fell to the ground. His eyes fixated on the rocking doors, through which he saw Stella's left arm. It dangled from the operating table. Blood dripped into a dark puddle beneath.

4.

DR. ALEXA MASON rolled over to find the other side of her bed empty . . . again. She sat up and dangled her feet over the side of the bed. The blue satin slippers sat in their usual spot, perfectly parallel to each other, exactly one pace from the bed. She stretched, stepped into her slippers and shuffled into the bathroom.

She had never cared for trinkets littering the shelves and counter tops. They just looked messy. Since her husband's death from cancer a year earlier, there weren't any shavings scattered about the counter. No goatee hair clippings in the sink. No half-squeezed bottle of toothpaste. She loved and hated the cleanliness. Scattered pictures of the family hung in the hall and living room. Their wedding pictures above the hearth constantly reminded her of what she'd lost. Pictures of their sixteen-year-old daughter Teagan, along with various awards, decorated the cherry oak china hutch in the study. The house décor was simple and logical, just how she liked it.

After she brushed her teeth, she disrobed and stepped into the steam-filled shower. Warm water flowed over her porcelain skin. Colleagues had labeled her 'the Vampire of Room 119', her lab at the university. With the highest I.Q. in the building, she had plenty of ups and downs. Yes, she could refute papers written by other doctors. No, it didn't make her any friends. And no, she would not go to tanning, however many times they asked. Being a natural blonde with fair skin defined her. She'd never had to bleach her hair and certainly would not bow to the whims of her co-workers.

With her morning routine finished, she put on her gray suit and headed out the door. Teagan had stayed at her best friend, Ellie's house the night before because Alexa would not take to the streets with her daughter dressed like a cat in an effort to swindle people out of candy. Frankly, she thought Teagan too old for the pagan rituals of Allhallows Eve, but her friends had wanted to go and she would have never heard the end of it if she didn't let her.

Alexa's charcoal Volvo sat in the near side of the four-car garage, sparkling from the detail work she'd had completed on it the day before. The cell phone in her purse chimed three times; if she didn't get on the road in the next five minutes, she'd be late for work.

Normally she drove to work in silence, but as the traffic was a bit congested she listened to the traffic report on the radio. A jackknifed semi had brought 405 East into Portland to a standstill. She'd have to take the back roads up to the university, something she didn't do on a regular basis as it made her nearly 20 minutes late for work and she abhorred that.

As Head of Genetics Research at Oregon Health Sciences University, going on ten years, she had grown quite infamous in her work. She generally kept a low profile. The fact that she'd been the youngest woman ever to graduate from the university also added to her notoriety.

Her earliest memories all had something to do with her becoming a doctor one day. When she played the game with the little boy next door he'd been sorely disappointed all she wanted to do was listen to his heart and count his respirations.

"Officials at Salem Hospital are tight lipped regarding the details surrounding last night's grisly tragedy but Channel Five News has learned similar events have occurred in hospitals across the United States. Law enforcement is baffled. An inside source at the hospital said at least ten people are presumed dead."

"Oh, my word." Alexa sifted through the plethora of radio station news on her in-dash satellite radio. Each had little or no concrete reporting. Some of the events had taken place in maternity wards or the emergency rooms. In each instance multiple people were injured or killed.

In the thirty minutes it took for her to arrive at the office, she heard droves of news reports with detailed gruesome incidents. But not only at hospitals: birthing centers, homes, backs of ambulances and one movie theater where the slaughter of sixteen people rocked the small town of Bangor, Maine.

She pulled into her parking space and took a moment to let the information sink in. Wow! She'd never seen or read anything this horrific in her entire life. Times like these made her glad she never went into politics.

The constant in the equation surrounding each of these particular incidents had to do with childbirth. This was one puzzle she'd love to put together.

When she opened the door, it bumped against Dr. Silverman's silver Mercedes Benz. Its alarm wailed through the parking garage.

She didn't make a clumsy mistake like that. The news had shaken her up more than she thought. Minutes passed and security didn't arrive, not even to turn the alarm off.

They must be busy.

Gunfire clacked somewhere nearby. Not close enough to have to take cover, but near enough for her to give the parking garage a good once-over before continuing into the building.

Yep, they're busy.

Briefcase in hand, she proceeded to her lab on the fifth floor of the science building. Various people hustled about the entrance and the commotion didn't stop when she got off of the elevator. Her colleagues and other people she didn't know . . . men wearing suits littered the usually empty business area. Nobody had been told not to come to work, a huge oversight by the hospital administrators. They could have at least closed the labs.

Two men walked toward her, swift with purpose. She only recognized one of them.

"Dr. Mason." Dr. Jackson greeted her with a handshake.

"What can I help you with, Dr. Jackson?" His sweat-filled palm slimed against hers. She discreetly wiped it against her pant leg.

Dr. Henry Jackson had the biggest head and the skinniest body of anyone she'd ever seen, like one of the bobble heads her assistant Justin kept on his desk. The senior professor's pristine mannerisms and neat attire gave one the impression he might be British. He even spoke in an old world way, though, she was pretty sure he came from Philadelphia.

"I do not believe you have had the pleasure of meeting Agent Harris from the F.B.I." He emphasized the acronym.

She took the agent's outstretched hand; a different handshake experience altogether. The man stood at least six-foot-four. Perfect black hair speckled with some gray stopped in a thick widow's peak. Thick black eyebrows shrouded his large brown eyes, which scanned her with fervor. Muscles threatening to tear his perfectly pressed suit rounded off his smoldering looks. She caught a glimpse of a gun in its shoulder holster under his suit jacket as he retracted his hand.

"Agent Harris is with the task force assigned to fossick out this mess."

"You mean figure out what's going on with the newborns." She smiled.

Harris cocked an eyebrow. "They say you're the best in the business. This true?"

She reciprocated with a glare. *Who does this schmuck think he is? He should have at least done his homework to see who he's going to be working with.* Two minutes in and she'd already decided she didn't like the guy.

"Come with us, Dr. Mason. I've got something I need to show you." Dr. Jackson led them to the conference room.

5.

SEVERAL MILES DOWN the road at Dallas Hospital seventeen-year-old Tania Erres lay on the hospital bed with her feet in the stirrups. She'd been tough, didn't want anything to dull the pain because she needed to feel her baby come out. The adoption papers were in her mom's purse and the birth would be the only time she'd get to have with her baby.

She had been dating Dallas high school star running back, and 'player' asshole, Trevon Miles. He'd professed his undying love and devotion to her on their third date. On the fourth date she gave in to his constant advances. He didn't use a condom and she'd been bitch-slapping herself ever since.

What was I thinking?

"I'll pull out, nothing will happen, you'll see."

Fuckin' idiot.

Even though the act lasted only a few minutes, the pain would last the rest of her life. A baby? No way in hell. She would put herself back together for her senior year and salvage the gymnastics scholarship to OSU. That's what she thought – then. Now that she'd carried the baby for nearly nine months, her heart ached for the child within her. She'd heard of mothers forming bonds with their babies, but hadn't known it happened in the belly. She couldn't help but love the little imp who kept kicking her in the bladder and making her pee her pants. Once while she was in line at McDonald's with some friends; super embarrassing moment.

"How are you doing, sweetie?" Her mom patted her hand.

Tania's eyes narrowed.

"Don't glare at me, young lady. You're the one that didn't want any medicine."

"Yeah . . . yeah, can I take it back?" Another contraction hit and Tania bit down on her bottom lip. The copper taste of blood filled her mouth. "Holy shit, motherfucker."

"Tania." Her mom scowled.

She didn't know how long the contraction lasted, but it felt like a long time. "That one hurt."

"Oh dear, looks like you bit your lip." The nurse looked at Tania's mom. "Give her some ice to chew, should help stop the bleeding."

Her mom took the cup of crushed ice from the rolling cart next to the hospital bed. She spooned out a heaping teaspoon and held it to Tania's pursed lips. "Do what the nurse said. The blood's dribbling down your chin."

With a second taut glare, Tania took the spoon of ice into her mouth and swished it around. The cold soothed the throbbing pain.

"That better?" The nurse loomed over her.

"Yeah thanks." Tania started to smile. The contraction hit like someone took a baseball bat to her crotch and stomach. "Oomph!" She sat up and almost pulled her feet out of the stirrups.

The nurse clasped Tania's shoulders and pressed her into the bed. "Look into my eyes and count with me. Ten . . . nine . . . eight . . . "

Tania wanted to count with her, but instead she grunted and screamed. When the pain subsided, she slurped another mouthful of crushed ice stuffed into her mouth by her mother.

Dr. Johnson waddled into the room and plopped onto her swivel stool. She wheeled herself between Tania's legs. Tania jerked when Dr. Johnson's cool gloved fingers probed her warm insides.

"Fully-effaced." Dr. Johnson wheeled over to the sink, removed her gloves and tossed them in a red waste basket with a biohazard sign on it. "You know what this means, Tania?"

"Yeah." The dreaded push she'd heard way too much about. She shivered, not knowing if she had the strength left to squeeze something the size of a large grapefruit out of her.

Dr. Johnson smiled. "You'll do fine."

Tania looked at her mother, who nodded in concurrence with the doctor's wishes.

Fuck those idiots who say the push is natural.

Dr. Johnson had her hands on both of Tania's wide-spread knees. "Bear down, like you're having a bowel movement."

"Bowel, what?" Tania grimaced.

Dr. Johnson looked up from between Tania's legs. "Like you're pooping . . . push just like that."

"Mommy." Tania squeezed her mom's hand and pushed.

The baby pushed back.

Tania's stomach rolled. "Not time for your gymnastics tryout yet," she whispered and patted her belly, knowing she'd never get to see or hold her baby.

"My lord." Her mom watched Tania's belly. "Is it supposed to do that?"

"Do what?" Tania looked up. "Move? Yeah mom, it's a baby. Shit."

Dr. Johnson blinked. She turned to one of the nurses standing next to her. "Did you see that?" she said under her breath, but Tania heard her clearly.

"I . . . uh . . . " The nurse backed up her eyes wide with terror.

Dr. Johnson tucked her head as if to get a better look.

A loud pop came from between Tania's knees. Shocks of pain stiffened her legs; she nearly hopped into the stirrups.

Dr. Johnson stood and kicked her chair toward the door. Blood and mucous painted her face. She stumbled back and landed on her oversized rump.

Another jolt of pain zinged through Tania's abdomen. She Screamed, looked down and saw a line of blood blossom from her naval to her left hip.

The nurse hurried from the room.

Several more physicians stormed in, each with the same horrified look at first and then bewilderment.

Dr. Johnson swiped a towel from the nearest cabinet, wiped the blood and goo from her face and placed a handful of gauze across Tania's belly.

"What's happening? Is my baby okay?" Tania searched the doctor's eyes for reassurance. The room inched in on her. A dark-gray haze shadowed her peripheral vision.

Dr. Johnson's eyes widened. Her mouth opened, but nothing came out.

Tania glanced down. Four tiny spikes protruded through the back of Dr. Johnson's hand. The little blades zipped from side-to-side, shredding a hole through skin and bone.

Tania screamed.

Dr. Johnson pulled her hand away, swooned and fell into the arms of an Emergency Medical Technician who had walked through the door moments earlier. He and another medic whisked the doctor out of the room.

Tania clenched the sheets as she watched a little hand retract into her stomach.

Her mother screamed.

Tania wanted to say something to comfort her. But the words didn't come. Instead, she retched and coffee-ground vomit scattered across the floor below the bed. *What the hell are you doing in there?*

Tania's mom moved out of the way and for a moment, stopped screaming.

The rest of the medical professionals in the room had formed a half moon about five feet from where Tania's toes stuck up from the stirrups.

"We've got to get this bleeding under control." One of the EMTs rushed to her side. The man's thick mustache weaved under his nose like a garden caterpillar on a pale leaf. His beer belly bumped her side as he pressed more gauze to her blooming wound. He then fetched a white blanket from a cabinet and placed it over her.

Pressure shoved the baby down. A rip deep within her body split her spinal cord. In an instant, she could no longer take a breath, as if someone had piled a ton of rocks on her chest.

"She stopped breathing." The medic moved around to the top of the bed, he disappeared for a second and when he came back he had some equipment in his hand.

No air.

No air.

No air.

The medic placed a mask over her mouth and pumped air into her lungs. "That better?"

She shook her head. Another doctor placed the chilly stethoscope on her chest and listened. "I think she has bilat tension pneumotharax. I've got to pop her chest." He turned toward the other EMT. "The kits are above your head, toss me one."

"You got it doc." The spindly kid, not more than nineteen, found the kit on a shelf and handed it to the doctor.

Tania flailed her arms like a diver swimming to the surface for a breath of air, too deep to make it to the top without running out.

"I know it's hard, but try and keep calm." The EMT's steel blue eyes, pierced into her waning dark browns.

She read his name tag upside down. *Toby*.

"Get ready for a big pinch." The doctor put his hand on her shoulder.

A quick sharp pain hit just below her right boob. A hiss of air escaped from the wound as the lung re-inflated. Tania still couldn't take a deep breath. Instead, she took in little sips of air, which felt much better than not being able to breathe at all.

The doctor moved around to her other side. "One more and you'll be right as rain."

After the second hiss of air, Tania gasped.

"Steady, take a nice deep breath through your nose." The doctor breathed in deep through his nose and exhaled slowly.

Tania followed his lead, clenched her mouth shut and inhaled through her nose.

"Better?" Toby removed the mask with the bag attached to it and replaced it with another mask. This one had a cool rush of air blowing into her mouth and nose.

She removed the mask. "Yeah, I can breathe . . . but it feels like someone stomped me into the dirt."

Everyone in the room remained silent except the doctor working on her. "It's because you've lost so much blood. You're fatigued. We'll get some fluids in you and you'll be feeling better soon." The room's lights glared off a prominent bald spot near the back of the doctor's head.

"The baby's not moving anymore, is it okay?" Tania still had the mask clenched in her hand.

Toby took the mask and placed it back on her face. "You need to keep this on. Your oxygen saturation isn't too good right now."

"Okay." Her breath fogged the inside of the mask.

"Heart rate is still normal." The doctor flicked some buttons on the equipment next to the bed and she heard the baby's heartbeat. Fast, like dripping water from a leaky faucet hitting a snare drum.

But from what? There's no way this is a normal child birth. Tania moved as much as she could in an effort to get comfortable.

Another nurse and several more orderlies came in to help clean up the mess.

Baldy hung two bags of blood on the stand next to her bed. He grabbed what looked like a huge needle and moved behind her, ushering Toby out of the way. With a quick swipe of something cold across her neck, he came at her with the spike.

"What're you doing?" She flinched.

"We need the biggest vein we can get to push this blood into you fast."

She felt him pinch the skin on the side of her neck. "There, all done."

Toby moved around and took her by the right hand. "See. Not so bad at all."

"I guess." She rolled her eyes.

Several other people in doctor's clothes listened to her stomach, pushing here and there across her belly. Her mother stroked her sweat-matted hair and whispered into her ear, "It'll be okay, looks like the worst is over."

"What's happening, Mom? I don't understand what's wrong with my baby."

"I'm not sure." Her mother's intense gaze at the doctor went unnoticed.

Someone wheeled in the ultrasound unit she'd seen so many times before. A slender man spread the cold goop over the upper half of her bulging belly and skated the probe back and forth, watching the tiny TV monitor at the same time. "Looks like a normal baby to me." He rolled the ball around some more. "Wait. She's moving, I think opening her mouth. What the . . . "

Everyone in the room crowded the monitor.

"Are those what I think they are?" Baldy pointed at the monitor.

"Yeah, I've never seen anything like it." The man conducting the exam tapped the screen.

Baldy's eyes widened. "You think it's one of those . . . "

"Shhhhh." The ultrasound man grabbed Baldy and whispered in his ear.

"What? What do you see?" Tania's mom wedged her way into the group.

"The baby has teeth." The man pointed to the monitor.

"We need to get her out now." Baldy looked at his colleagues. "Is Jake here yet?"

"Who's Jake?" Tania tried to sit up to see what the commotion was.

"Lay back down." Toby held her hand and placed his other hand on her forehead. She went along with it and laid back.

Dr. Baldy patted her knee "He's our on-call anesthesiologist. He'll be here any minute. We're going to give you an epidural and get this baby out of you.".

"You said, she. It's a girl?" The thought of having a girl and giving her up for adoption brought more tears to Tania's eyes and a large lump to her throat.

The man at the monitor smiled and nodded.

"Is she still alive?"

"Yes. But there are some abnormalities. She's got very long fingernails and for some reason, teeth."

"Does that happen often?" Her mother moved back to her left side.

"There are cases of children being born with baby teeth, but they're pretty rare."

Toby packed more gauze on her stomach and smiled. "They'll have you fixed up here in no time. Are you in any pain?"

"Not really. I can feel the pressure, but the sharp pain is gone and I haven't had a contraction in a while. Aren't they going to stitch up my stomach so I don't bleed to death?"

Toby scratched his chin. "They may use the cut to help get the baby out. You know what you're gonna name her?"

Silly boy, trying to change the subject. Tania thought for a moment. "Probably Maleia, after my mother, but I'm not keeping her."

Toby's eyes sparkled. "Maleia's a cute name." He looked over at Tania's Mom, who smiled back.

Jesus, Mom, flirting while I'm in labor . . . figures.

"Hi Jake." The ultrasound man moved the monitor so the young doctor walking through the door could see. "You'll want to take a look at this."

Jake stared at the monitor like the rest of them had before. "Well I'll be." He pulled his tight blond-curly locks into a ponytail and tied it with a rubber band. "Are those what I think they are?"

Dr. Baldy stood and moved back over to the monitor with the other two men. "Yep. Those are teeth my friend." He pointed at the screen again.

A nurse bolted through the door, ran up to Dr. Baldy and whispered something in his ear.

"Really? When?"

"About twenty minutes ago. The news in the lobby is showing this happening . . . "

"Where?"

"Everywhere!" The nurse's worried look panicked Tania.

"We have to get this baby out now!" Dr. Baldy pushed the ultrasound cart to the side. "No time to scrub up. Get the gloves and kit." He told the nurse. Another nurse must have heard because she handed something to him.

"What is it?" Tania's mom stomped up to the doctor. "I demand to know what's going on."

"Mom, what's wrong?"

"I don't know, baby."

"It's routine." Jake slid a chair up behind her.

Tania looked back and only saw his upside down masked face, his eyes tense

"There's nothing routine about this?" Her mom's hands were on her hips, which Tania knew wouldn't end well for those being spoken to.

Dr. Baldy cut in. "We routinely perform a C-section if we haven't seen the baby move in some time. So . . . yes, it's routine in that sense." He turned. "Can I get some help over here?" Toby and the other medic sank into the corners of the room as a nurse stormed between them.

Dr. Jake and the nurse rolled Tania onto her side. A prick above her butt sent a twinge through her spine.

"Ouch." She reached back and rubbed the sore muscle.

"Let me know when you can't feel your toes anymore."

"Why do they call you Jake and not doctor so and so?" Idle chit chat was her defense mechanism for about everything; her go-to routine as they would say in gymnastics.

"Because no-one can pronounce my last name, hell, I have a hard time saying it."

"What is it?" she asked, her interest piqued.

"Southwickendwire."

"That's a mouthful." She flinched from the pressure on her spine.

"Try not to move."

"You're not the one with the needle in your spine."

The doctor chuckled. "Well, can you say it?"

"Southwistishire."

He laughed again.

"Well?"

"Well what?

"Did I say it right?"

"Close, but I think that's a condiment you cook with. How are those toes?"

Toby appeared at her feet, off to the left, staying out of Dr. Baldy's way. "This little piggy went to the market." He wiggled her big toe.

"No he didn't. He got his ass drunk and stayed home." She smiled.

"That means you can't feel Mr. Piggy?" Jake whispered in her ear.

She nodded.

"What about this one?" Toby checked the pinky toe.

"Nope."

"This one?" He wiggled the other foots pinky toe.

"Nope."

"I think we're ready to proceed." Dr. Baldy looked at her and winked.

Tania glanced at the plethora of masked vultures picking at her. But she didn't see her own doctor, the nice old lady who'd been working with her for nine months. "Where's Dr. Johnson?"

Dr. Baldy raised his hand. "Right here."

Another Dr. Johnson?

"Wait. Is she your wife?"

"No . . . no, she's my mother." He laughed.

Various giggles and guffaws came from around the room.

"Is her hand okay?" Tania figured the longer she talked, the longer it would be before they ripped the baby out of her.

"Haven't heard yet. But don't worry about her, she's a tough old bird, she'll get through it." Concern crept back into his voice; he cleared his throat and took a deep breath. "Let's deliver this baby of yours."

A cloth shield across Tania's chest obscured her view of the hospital staff. Everyone seemed to be all 'routine this', and 'normal that'. But she felt like the humongous dick in the room no-one would talk about. Her blood boiled. She hated when people kept her in the dark.

Jake played classical music in the background as he fiddled with his medical equipment behind her.

Tania's eyelids began to droop, but Jake kept talking to her, like one being kept awake after a head injury and she'd seen plenty of those in gymnastics. She would love to stay up, to see her baby born, to hold her and hug her and kiss her before they tore her away forever.

"Okay, we're ready to extract the baby. Her heartbeat is slowing quite a bit, but she seems fine otherwise."

Tania didn't know who had spoken, but figured the male Dr. Johnson since he'd been the guy in charge.

"Just relax. It'll all be over sooner than you can say . . . " Jake stopped . . . his eyes reflected what she could only call terror. As if he'd seen a ghost. She half expected him to run the other way.

The screams started; first from a nurse, then wailing from Dr. Johnson. Jake, who had been tending to her anesthesia from behind, disappeared to the other side of the cloth shield separating Tania from the pandemonium.

Jake stumbled back from the other side and gurgled. "S . . . sorry." His throat gaped. Blood soaked the front of his scrubs. He fell to his knees, then face first into the ground.

Someone pulled the screen off of her. She lost her breath. Blood flowed and guts protruded from the gash in her stomach. Dr. Johnson lay on the floor with the shield over his torso. Blood seeped through the cloth like a paper towel sopping up spilled ketchup.

Someone lunged forward and draped their body across hers. She looked into Toby's compassionate, fearful eyes.

"Close your eyes. Don't watch. I'm sorry." His body shook. His eyes rolled back and a trickle of crimson fluid seeped from the right corner of his mouth. A spurt of blood flew over his back, splashing across Tania's face. He rolled off her and landed on bald Dr.

Johnson's body. A geyser of fluid erupted from a shredded hole in his back.

She turned her head, looking for her mother in an attempt to find some solace amongst the terror. Horrific cries and wails from others filled the room. But they were only echoes as the room fell silent. She heard a crunch of metal on metal and the lights in the room went out.

Through the dark Tania could barely make out her mother sitting in the chair a few feet away, her eyes fixed on something beyond Tania's field of vision. "Mommy! Mommy!"

She couldn't answer and didn't move.

A man's voice boomed through the doorway, "What's going on in there?" Several other men ran into the room.

"Hospital security, Ma'am, can you hear me? Shit. She's not responding."

Tania had no idea who the man spoke too, but a light flung around the room and settled on her mom. In her lap, cuddled against her chest, lay a small naked body.

"She's got a kid in her arms."

"What the hell happened in here?"

Her mom's mouth fell open and a trickle of blood spilled from the corner. Tania tried to scream. The baby wriggled in her mother's lap. It looked to be suckling.

A man in a blue uniform rushed to Maleia's side. He knelt at her knees. "Give me the baby ma'am."

She had one hand on the baby's back, the other dangled at her side. Her eyes had rolled back. The man put his hands on the infant and struggled to pull it away from her.

Tania's heart raced. She lay helpless as the man withdrew the child, revealing a massive gaping hole where her mother's left breast should have been.

My baby . . . my baby.

The infant Maleia turned her head, her mouth still full of flesh from Tania's mother's chest.

As Tania's life dwindled away, she felt love and devotion for the child she would never hold, never coo to, and never kiss.

Baby Maleia tore the ribcage from the man she attacked. Then Tania saw those gorgeous, deep, black eyes.

6.

SAVANNAH RECALLED THE events of the prior evening as she stood anew on the roof of Salem Hospital. Bright lights had flickered and ricocheted off her amber eyes when she'd emerged from the dark place. She'd been quick when she feasted on them, tasting the sweet morsels pulsating within. As she lapped up the crimson fluid next to her latest meal, the hallway congested with creatures—food to her. She finished the chunk of flesh in her mouth and swallowed. Deep within, a war raged against her primal urge to eat the creature under her. At some point and in some way this beast had meant something to her. Yet, none of that mattered as her tiny tummy growled, coaxed, and urged her on to the next meal.

A projectile had entered her left shoulder. The force sent her tiny body tumbling back through the double doors, into the dark room. Her eyes flickered and the room brightened as if someone had turned on amber covered lights. Objects in the room gave off dull silhouettes, but the food, it had a bright red glow. Sometimes the glow dissipated, rendering the meal tasteless. Another large creature came through the door. Life pumped through its glowing vessels. The large orb in the middle is where the flow started and stopped. This sweet piece of meat quenched her thirst and satiated the rumble in her belly.

The piece of meat burst through the double doors wielding some sort of object in its hand. Savannah reacted to the loud snap coming from the object. With blinding speed she avoided the projectiles flying at her. They pinged against the wall behind her, angled up and disappeared. Again and again the object snapped and out came the projectiles. She dodged most of them by crawling up the wall.

With a twist of her hips, she aimed her body at the large-red thumping orb deep within the creature.

She crouched.

Tendons tightened. Muscles tensed. Razor-sharp nails extended from the tips of her fingers. The force of energy she pushed into her legs sent her careening into the object, her muscular infant arms extended. Her nails punctured through its thick front, slicing through like a knife into a Jell-O mold. When she felt the thump, thump, thump of the morsel within, she tore the beating piece of flesh out and stuffed it into her mouth. Rows of jagged teeth sliced the orb in half with one bite. The meat soothed the pangs of hunger. A twinge of prickling nettles drew her attention to her shoulder. Flesh stitched together from where one of the projectiles had hit her.

More noise came from beyond the swinging double doors through which she saw multiple creatures heading in her direction. Sustained for the moment, she scanned the area for a way to escape. Where the two walls met she spotted a small hole. She scampered up the wall, tore the cover off the hole and flung it into the group of creatures making their way into the room.

The cover spun and lodged into one of the unsuspecting creatures, knocking it to the ground. Its orb stopped glowing. Savannah crawled into the hole. Her fingernails and toenails caused flickers of electricity as she scampered through the tunnel. Other orbs came into view through the walls. Some moved, others didn't, but each creature meant prey; a meal ready to be eaten. As she scurried through the dark tunnel the pain in her belly caused a ripple through her system. She needed more food and she needed it now. Prey that couldn't struggle or fight would be the easier kills. Another opening loomed ahead and on the other side the glow of two large entities brought her to a halt.

One didn't move at all, the other had some sort of sound coming from it. A sound she distinctly remembered while in the dark place. The place she had eaten her way out of. Those sounds, somehow they soothed her.

The cover blocking her exit flew through the room and clanked against the opposite wall, startling the creatures. One of them reminded her of the place from whence she had come. Savannah hesitated; puzzled at a strange longing she had to snuggle against the food and sleep.

A loud scream came from the prey as their eyes met hers. The shriek stopped once Savannah's claws dug deep within. The creature gurgled and spat up some of the tasty fluid which Savannah lapped up before she dug deeper into it and removed the thumping piece. That piece had become her favorite part of the meal, her second—the hunt.

7.

AGENT HARRIS STRODE into conference room B as if he'd worked there his entire life. He pulled a chair away from the oblong oak table and gestured for her to sit. Alexa sighed, took his noble offer and sat down. He nudged the chair under her; a bit too hard as the metal rammed against her Achilles tendons. Then he sat and scooted his chair closer to her. Their knees touched and she quickly pulled hers away.

"Sorry about that." His smile lit up the room.

Ughh. One of those chiseled chin good-at-everything good 'ol boys, not the kind of guy that interested her at all. "Not a problem."

In front of them sat a large laptop with a global map across the screen. Tiny red dots blinked. A new one popped up every couple of seconds. The screen looked like it had chicken pox. Alexa knew within a short period of time the screen would be full.

"What are they?" She knew the answer to the question, but wanted to hear it from the F.B.I. agent firsthand.

Harris took a deep breath. "You know already, don't you?"

She nodded.

His eyes went tense, deep with concern. "Each dot represents an event that has occurred. As far as we can tell, the one in Salem was *the first*. The Department of Defense immediately thought terrorists; chemical or maybe biological? We do know they're no longer babies. Whatever happened to them seems to have happened at a genetic level. You're the best geneticist in the United States."

She smirked. "World."

His swift condescending smile irked her. "Dr. Mason, we're asking for your help. If there's any way to counteract whatever's causing these . . . deformities, we know you're the one who can figure it out. You up for it?"

Alexa knew her answer before he'd finished the question. "Something else must be causing the anomaly. It can't be an isolated terrorist attack. Look at the map. It's happening across the globe."

More red dots appeared, slowly filling the screen.

"We figured that much. Or that the attack backfired."

"No . . . " She tapped her fingers on the top of the table with her perfectly manicured, unpolished nails. " . . . this is something else."

"What?"

"I don't know yet. I'll see what I can come up with. I need you to procure a specimen for my research."

"The intel we've collected shows these infants can take a direct hit with a large caliber bullet. And though they bleed a bit, they heal rapidly."

Just like a bunch of bullheaded government officials, shoot first, ask questions later. "So they're able to regenerate tissue." O.H.S.U. scientists had been recreating tissue, specific body parts like ears, noses, and digits, for many years. Regenerative tissue on a live being, however, was a much different matter from recreating tissue in a lab.

"I didn't say that. I'm sure we can find a way to kill them. Even Dracula was killed." He laughed a deep guffaw.

The reference didn't impress her. She read the Bram Stoker novel in seventh grade. Since then she'd been too busy reading text books to bother with much fiction, and she sure as heck didn't take to fawning over sparkling teenage vampires or muscle bound werewolves. Such were the posters in Teagan's room.

She stood and made direct eye contact. "Get me a specimen. I can't do anything without a DNA sample."

Harris ran his fingers through his hair. Alexa's eyes followed up his elbow to the flexed muscles in his upper arm.

Ughh . . . Was he flexing to show off? I hate men that try to impress me with their body; a cock fluffing his feathers. That's all it is.

"Could you get DNA from a piece of flesh one of them chewed on?" His arm lowered and he straightened his suite coat.

"Or feces, urine, spit up . . . anything, as long as the sample isn't compromised. If you do get some chewed up flesh, nothing can touch it after the bite, otherwise our readings will be contaminated.

Though I have a sneaky suspicion we aren't going to see a normal DNA pattern here. Something is happening to these babies on a genetic level of the likes I've never seen."

"Okay. I'll see what I can do about procuring some samples." Harris turned to leave.

"Mr. Harris?" She caught his arm.

He turned and she swore she felt his arm flex under his jacket. "You can call me Ross."

Boys.

"Ross." She accented his name. "I'll need military clearance at the highest level to access some databases no-one has seen in years."

"Will do."

"Oh . . . and Mr. Harris . . . um . . . Ross?"

"Yeah."

"Do be careful out there."

"Will do Ma'am." He gave her a slight nod and sauntered out of the room, the way one might imagine a cowboy making his way into the barren streets for a final shoot out.

Ma'am? Did he really just call me ma'am? Goodness. She didn't know how she felt about that. Of course as a mother her natural instincts sometimes took over. Though other instincts began to flare again, things she hadn't felt since her husband passed away.

Oh God! Love? Lust? Maybe the need to have someone to wake up next to? No . . . a warm smile to make the rest of the day worth living. Not that Teagan's smile wasn't enough. But the smile she wanted would send shivers up her spine and butterflies flitting about her stomach. Not make her want to lash out with uncontrolled hyperboles.

Goodness. She didn't know what she thought.

8.

"I DON'T GIVE a shit what your mom says. Dillon is so much hotter than Brandon." Alyssa shifted from lying on her stomach to sitting up on the bed.

"Are you kidding me?" Ellie's full, pouting red lips twisted into an awkward frown.

Teagan rolled over on Ellie's king-sized bed and stuffed a pillow under her arms to prop herself up. "Chillax you two. I wanna see what happens next."

The trio of teens had only just discovered the show their mothers said was the soap opera of the '90's. Well, Alyssa's and Ellie's did. Teagan figured her mother had been too busy going to medical school at the ripe age of eighteen. She'd heard the story a thousand times and didn't really care. So . . . she wasn't a genius like dear old mommy. At least she had decent grades and might get into U of O with her girlfriends like she'd planned all along. She hadn't anticipated being fucked over by a college guy.

The dick had used her and never called back. Hence the love-in with her BFF's the night after the Halloween party. The three inseparable opposites didn't look anything alike. Ellie's hair bounced with red curls a little below her shoulders. She stood a good foot taller than the other two who would never see anything taller than five-foot-four. Ellie had a slender upper body with a small chest and lanky arms and legs. To Teagan, Ellie belonged on the cover of Vogue and stomping down a fashion runway in Milan.

Alyssa had straight, white-blonde hair she'd tease into a full mess or let it flow down to her sizable hips. Ellie called them "child bearin' hips," though she didn't have a lick of cellulite on her. Being a powerlifter had given her muscular legs and the most rock-solid butt Teagan had ever seen.

She gazed at her own arms. No muscle. Even though she weight-trained at school and went to Zumba twice a week with her mom, she considered herself a regular old plain Jane with average sized boobs and straight jet black dyed hair, her natural blonde hair like her mother's hidden on purpose. Her skin had always been fair and with the black hair, her friends teased her and called her Snow White. Better than the Vampire of Room 119.

When she dated Lyle she'd been blonde. Almost the same color as Alyssa's, but it looked silly when the girls went anywhere together. After she stopped hearing from that ass hat, she dyed it.

"Looks like someone needs another ice cream bar." Ellie nudged Teagan with her foot.

"What?" Teagan turned.

"She's pathetic." Ellie rolled her eyes at Alyssa.

"I'll get it." Alyssa hopped off the bed and jogged out the door.

"Be a doll and get me one too," Ellie called after Alyssa.

"No problemo," Alyssa answered from somewhere down the hall.

Ellie flopped on her belly next to Teagan and scooted over until the warmth of her long body snuggled against Teagan's. It did give a calming effect, like an electric blanket on a chilly day.

"Still pining over him?"

"No. I'm so over him."

"But Tea Bags, you gave it away to him. That's gotta be eatin' you up."

Teagan didn't like the way Ellie said it and she didn't like being called, 'Tea Bags'. A nasty habit Ellie had picked up after hearing the term while being stats girl for the wrestling team. "I'm fine." She scowled. "He wasn't worth it anyway."

"How many times did you guys?"

"I told you. We did it once in his dorm and once at my house a couple of weeks ago, when Mom went to L.A. for that conference." Teagan sighed as the memory of the act flooded her mind.

"Didn't you say you saw him a couple of days ago?"

"Yeah."

"And nothing happened?"

"No. I saw him with his friends at the mall. Dickhead smiled and walked the other direction. Two of his friends turned, looked me up and down and then high-fived him like he'd just scored at the game. I couldn't find a store quick enough to get away from the assholes."

"Sorry to bring it up." Ellie rubbed Teagan's back.

"My mother said that according to research, talking things out is the best way to rid one's self of needless emotion. Something she's a master at. You know, I don't even remember her crying when my Dad died last year. She sat me down and said . . . and you know how she is . . . all science twenty four-seven. She said, 'Death is a part of life and statistically speaking one out of every eighteen men will get lung cancer and twenty-six percent of those men will die from it. Once your father was diagnosed, we knew this could happen.' I couldn't believe her. All I wanted was a hug." She wiped away a few tears dripping down her cheek.

Ellie wrapped her arm around her. "This is all I can do. You've had a tough last couple of years. But look at it this way. We're seniors and soon, we'll be in college and then it's our turn to start breaking hearts."

Alyssa danced into the room. "I . . . for one . . . am going to screw the brains out of as many boys as I can."

"Lyssa!" Ellie slapped her on the rear.

Alyssa handed them both an ice cream bar. "Bitch, please." She rubbed her backside in Ellie's face, grabbed her ankles and began to twerk. "Like you ain't gonna hump anything with two legs and a ding-a-ling?" She kept up the dance.

"Thanks, Miley; now get that fat ass out of my face." Ellie smacked her again.

"That fat ass . . . " Alyssa clenched her cheeks. "...can crack walnuts." She wiggled a couple more times.

Ellie giggled. "Or other things if stuck in the wrong place."

"You're Sick." Teagan sat up so she could unwrap the bar and eat it without melting crumbs all over Ellie's comforter. She bit into the dark chocolate. A sharp pain shot through her head as her front teeth sliced into the vanilla ice cream. "Ow!" She pushed her finger into her right temple and scrunched her right eye. "I think my brain just froze to the top of my mouth."

"Is that even possible?" Alyssa took a giant bite of her ice cream. "No brain freeze here. Guess I win." She pounced onto the bed next to the other two. The girls spent the rest of the evening watching re-runs of 90210, eating ice cream and helping Teagan get over the jerk that broke her heart.

9.

THE SONG "PRIVATE EYES" blared from his iPhone, ending his nap. He'd usually shut his eyes for an hour or so in the late afternoon. Ross rolled over and picked up the phone. Several texts from his superiors stated Dr. Mason had been given the level five clearances she needed from the F.B.I, C.I. A., N.S.A and Interpol. Apparently she's very connected. Now she would be able to leap into her research head first.

His GPS program showed the newborn's whereabouts. Red dots blanketed the screen. Not just in the United States. Each continent started to fill with the dreaded red dots.

A double beep from his cell phone signaled he'd received an email and with it Salem's finest had sent him digital footage from Salem Hospital's security cameras. *Unbelievable . . .* couldn't describe the carnage in the video. The video reminded him of a scene from a horror movie. Reality hit with why he had headed down to the hospital, to get a better feel for the devastation and see if he couldn't bring Dr. Mason a DNA sample. The sheriff's department might have had jurisdiction, but, the F.B.I. owned this one and he had to make his presence known. He would gather all the intelligence the sheriff's department had on the creature they had named, "Baby Staten".

Ross pulled the government-issued black Lincoln Navigator into the emergency room parking lot.

An officer stopped him.

"F.B.I." He flashed his badge.

"Park it over there." The young man pointed to a space next to an ambulance. He clicked a radio on his shoulder. "Sheriff, feds are here."

A series of profanities spewed from the young deputy's radio as Ross pulled into his designated parking spot. Through the double doors of the E.R. strode the sheriff and several deputies. Ross took a deep breath and jumped out of the rig, fastening the top button of his black sports jacket. He'd dealt with many a sheriff's department and wasn't in the mood for attitude.

A large man who looked of Asian descent led the pack. The Sheriff looked as if he'd had one too many beers and slept in his shirt. His goatee fluffed around his mouth as if he'd just eaten a big black cat. The beer belly hung over the top of his service belt, covering the top of his Smith and Wesson .357 Magnum. Ross wondered why he carried such an archaic gun.

"Sheriff?" Ross held out his hand.

"Lawson." The sheriff shifted his belt, hiking it up his waist, ignoring Ross's hand. "Now you listen to me uh . . . " He cocked a bushy eyebrow.

"Agent Harris."

"Harris . . . "

"Agent." Ross glowered.

Sheriff Lawson pulled a long off-white handkerchief from his back pocket and blew his nose. He folded it in half and patted the sweat from his brow under his large cowboy hat. "I got things under wraps here, sent all the forensics to the labs in California. We don't need the feds comin' in here and gummin' up the works. My best detectives are on this thing like powder on a doughnut. We think we got a bead on where the little monster went and my best guys are on it, so don't come in here thinking you're gonna overtake my investigation and bring in your own people. If that's the case, then I'll get on the phone with my good friend Senator Smith and he'll have a thing or two to say, I shit you not."

Ross waited with his hands deep in his pockets. His toes tapped inside his black suede shoes. "Are you finished, sir?" He hoped the tirade had ended.

"Don't ask me if I'm finished, boy. I'll let you know when I'm finished."

"Very well." Ross tapped his toes as he waited impatiently.

The sheriff looked around at his deputies and sighed. "Okay . . . I'm finished."

"I'm not here to take over anything. We've got one of the top geneticists in the world working on this up at OHSU."

"I heard that place is a wreck." The Sheriff's chew smacked the road.

"Yeah, four births in the first few hours and a dozen dead, at least."

"So . . . your . . . uh . . . doctor, he know what these things are?"

"She's working on it. That's why I need tissue samples or any blood samples that you might have."

"Like I said, all that shit went to forensics in Cali to be examined."

"You'll let me know when you get the results and kindly ship us any leftovers?"

A female deputy got on her tip-toes to say something in the sheriff's ear. The massive man towered over the petite girl.

Sherriff Lawson turned. "You might want to come with me Agent Hammons."

"Harris. Agent Harris." *What a moron.*

"Whatever." The sheriff scoffed. "The janitor found something in the hospital venting system you're going to want to see."

"Lead on." Ross unbuttoned his jacket and unsnapped the strap on his Glock.

The group followed the deputy into the hospital and piled into the elevator. Panicked, Ross searched for the license on the wall giving the weight capacity. He found it under the button the deputy pushed with a large B on it. Phew, luckily they couldn't weigh more than the maximum.

The elevator dinged, doors opened, and the group filed into a long narrow hallway.

"The cafeteria's this way." The deputy led them down the left corridor.

Ross's insides churned. What exactly had they found? He hoped something tangible he could take to Dr. Mason. What did she say her first name was? He couldn't remember.

They marched into the cafeteria. The room, polka-dotted with empty tables had a large section of the kitchen cordened off with police tape. Chalk drawings of three bodies on the blood-stained linoleum made him pause for a second. One looked half the size of the others. *Poor kid. Never had a chance.*

A short, paper-thin man wearing a white lab coat strolled over to them. "The janitor found the specimen over there." He pointed at a section of the rectangular air duct system which followed a serpentine path over the kitchen. Part of it had been removed. Next to it stood a large man in coveralls. Ross figured him for the janitor the lab rat had been talking about.

"I didn't want to move it or bag it until I showed it to someone. Damnedest thing I ever saw." The janitor squinted over his glasses into the duct system.

Ross braced himself for what he might find in the metal box.

10.

FLUID RUSHED UP the back of her throat, searing her mouth and nose. Teagan retched and vomited for a third time that morning.

"Do you have a fever?" Her mom tapped away at the laptop on the bar.

"I don't know Mom. Haven't been able to . . . " Again she heaved and couldn't figure out where the fluid came from, surely she'd finished by now. " . . . get my head out of the damn toilet long enough to check."

"Watch your language, please. It's probably the twenty-four-hour 'flu or food poisoning. I guess you better stay home from school. "

"Ya think?" Teagan said under her breath, the stench from the toilet making her heave again. She flushed, stood up and rinsed her mouth out with water. After brushing her teeth thoroughly and rinsing several times with Listerine, she grabbed her favorite comforter and Mr. Simpleton; her treasured stuffed black cat. She curled into a ball on the couch. She'd eaten way too much shit at Ellie's.

"Drink a lot of fluid today. The flu should be flushed from your system by morning,"

"Fine. I think I'll sleep all day. Nothings on TV 'cept those stupid babies."

"Those babies are a genetic anomaly."

"You figure out what they are yet? Where they came from?"

"Not yet, but we're working on it. Since Halloween, every fetus born has . . . for lack of any other explanation, a genetic disorder. We're trying to pinpoint the mutated gene, isolate it and reverse or stop the process. It's very complicated."

"Blah . . . blah . . . spare me the details." Her stomach rumbled again. *Shit!*

"Take care of yourself. I think there's some Cup of Soup in the pantry."

Figures. Her mother never could cook. That particular job had gone to her father. She missed his patented Mexican spaghetti. He made it all Italian-oh to include large sausage meatballs, Portobello mushrooms, and his special ingredient; taco seasoning. She'd tried to recreate the dish, but like her mother, she had two left feet, or hands, when it came to cooking.

"Oh . . . before I forget." Her mom placed her briefcase under her left arm holding the cup of coffee while she opened the door. "That boy called again. He sounds kind of old."

"His name's Lyle. I told you Mom, he's seventeen." If Teagan told the truth (that Lyle's really a twenty-one year old college student) her mom would give some sort of spiel about underage-sex and probably try and get the cops involved.

"Well, I don't want any boys here while I'm gone and certainly not while you're sick."

"Simmer, Mom. I won't be hearing from him again. Ever."

Her mom looked around for a moment. Not at anything in particular. But the vibe was all too familiar. *She's searching for something to say.*

After what seemed like forever, she spoke. "Sorry to hear it, hope he wasn't too important to you."

"No. Not at all." *Just talked me out of my virginity then joked about it to his friends.* Teagan rolled her eyes.

"That's nice to hear. Oh. Also, the president is making an announcement later this morning. You should probably watch."

Yuck. If one thing pissed Teagan off more than asshole college guys, it was politics. She'd had it force-fed to her every day of her life. From the time she woke to the minute her mother walked out the door at 6:35 A.M (sharp) she had to listen to C-Span or to her mother going off on some political tirade. But once she left, MTV or a mundane cartoon became the new topic of the day before she left for school at 7:50.

For her seventeenth birthday her mom gave her a little red beetle bug car, of course, only after she'd proven complete trust with an automobile for an entire year. Even so, she wasn't allowed to have any passengers until she turned eighteen. What her mom didn't know wouldn't hurt her; she picked up Alyssa and Ellie almost every day without her mom's knowledge, why would this be any different?

Teagan rolled over and swiped her iPod off the glass end table next to the plush beige couch. At least her dad had left them with a nice entertainment system. The fifty inch plasma screen TV mounted on the wall had small Bose speakers imbedded above and on either side. The speakers could out-bass any of her friends' three-foot stand up speakers. Her mom didn't mind, because they didn't take up much space mounted into the wall with the rest of the electronic equipment. If she'd seen one wire, she would have made him take it all back. Come to think of it, that same week she went with her father to pick out the entertainment equipment for the new house, was the same week they found out he had cancer.

With a sniffle she squeezed back tears. Those dark tears she'd been holding onto for a year. She'd gushed enough after her dad died; enough to last a lifetime—no more. There would be no more tears for dad, mom, or the bastard at Phi Theta Delta whatever. She'd used up her tear quota for at least the next ten years.

She channel surfed, stopping on a station with the words *'Stand by for an important message from the president'* scrolling across the bottom. The announcers speculated on what the president might talk about.

Boring. She clicked recall on the remote.

"This is a test, right?" She scowled.

Every channel she switched to had the 'Emergency Broadcast System' scrolling across the top. "Ughh." For some reason, this time, with all the bouncing baby shit, the emergency message meant something new and a nest of hornets whizzed around her stomach. Again, she nearly vomited. This thing with the babies was bad, but bad enough to cause a national emergency. *He's just gonna come on and announce the troops are going back to war.*

11.

"SUMBITCH." SHERIFF LAWSON'S jaw went slack. His double chin covered most of his lapel. "Is that what I think it is?" He wobbled over to the janitor and shined his own flashlight on the object.

"I know, it's incredible?" The janitor reached inside the metal ventilation tubing.

"Stop!" Ross grabbed the man's thick arm. "We need the skin for testing and it can't be contaminated by human touch."

The janitor wiped his hands off on his pants as if he thought he could give it another go.

"No one is to touch this but the men in the Tyvek coveralls. They'll bag it and tag it and I'll rush it up to the hospital, since it seems we're short on helicopters." Ross ushered the janitor and several sheriff deputies back a few feet.

"To hell you are." Sheriff Lawson stepped in front of Ross. "You feds ain't gettin' first crack at this. I shit you not."

"Listen, sheriff. This might be our only chance to study one of these creatures DNA Our scientist knows her stuff and with this kind of genetic evidence . . . she might find a solution tomorrow."

"Is this really happening all over the world, like they said on the news?" The janitor wrestled around with something in his pocket. Not a weapon, something else. Perhaps a token of some sort to calm his nerves.

"That's classified information."

Sheriff Lawson frowned. "You shouldn't try and keep people in the dark, federal agent man. It's all over the news. Classified? 'Bout as classified as my left ass cheek." He humphed.

Hard-headed sheriffs; needles being driven into him over and over again. Same thing in about every case he'd ever been on. Except Sheriff Murdock. That one was a fire cracker and will go down in history as one of the best weekends in his life. But this guy, he needed a lesson in law enforcement etiquette. "You don't get it, do you?" Ross looked Sheriff Lawson in the eyes like an attacking animal.

"I get it all right. You ass munches think you can do whatever you want with my crime scenes."

"Listen . . . Sheriff. This isn't about you *or* me *or* the feds. It's about the entire fucking human race. Our women are bearing monsters, not kids. Not babies. If we don't find a cure or some sort of solution, humanity will be fucking lost. So yes! Gimme that thing, it's going to my scientist. She's the best at what she does and the sooner you hand over the evidence, the sooner my scientist can save the world. You okay with that?'"

The sheriff's face blanched. Ross thought if he got any hotter under the collar, he'd set off the fire alarms. With a deep inhale and long exhale, his natural dark skin returned. Ross waited for what was sure to be a colorful rebuttal. Instead, the sheriff stepped to the side. "When you put it that way, I ain't gonna stuff my boot up humanity's ass. Take it. We'll pray your genius can come up with a way to stop this. For fuck's sake, my niece is pregnant."

"Thank you. We all have a stake in this." Ross pulled the latex gloves on and took the bio-hazard bag one of the sheriff's deputies held out to him.

"You sure we shouldn't put it on ice or something?" the Sheriff asked.

"No. I don't think so. Does someone have the tongs?" Ross couldn't take his eyes off of the hunk of flesh in front of him. Somehow, it screamed evolution.

A forensic specialist in a biohazard suit handed him the tongs. He thought maybe he should be wearing one too, but figured if he didn't touch it, he should be fine.

"Like a damn snake skin." The janitor inched forward and watched Ross lower the skin into the bag.

"Or a lizard," one of the deputies interjected.

"Gentlemen." The sheriff held out his stubbed arms. "What we have here is the next missing link. Whatever shed this skin is still alive and probably bigger. But what are we looking for now, a giant baby?"

Ross shrugged. "I don't think so."

The technician zip-tied the bio-hazard bag and handed it back to Ross. "Thanks. Maybe we should be looking for a toddler."

Sherriff Lawson sat on a bench seat at one of the tables. "Now, that makes perfect sense."

12.

ROSS SET THE specimen bag on the lab table in front of Alexa. He'd told her over the phone what to expect. She felt like a little girl waiting for Daddy to come home with a promised double-scoop of ice cream.

Ray had prepped the exam table and she had double checked it, making sure everything remained picture perfect. She even let Ray clip the zip-tie on the hazardous materials bag. But she wanted to be the one to spread the contents onto the table.

When she slowly let the shucked form of a healthy newborn slide out of the bag onto her table a tear welled in her eye. Alexa had never seen anything so beautiful in her life. This discovery held so many possibilities. The regenerative properties of these beings alone could fix injuries and maybe even cure diseases.

"Ray," she whispered, "can you lie it prone?"

"Sure," he whispered back.

"Why are we whispering?" Ross looked between the two of them for a clue, ready to make a joke.

Alexa helped Ray smooth out the carcass on the table.

"This is the way we keep ourselves in check when working with delicate material. It's one of Alexa's *things*." Ray's fingers made rabbit ears in the air and winked.

"Oh . . . " Ross laughed. "...she has *things*, does she?" His hands went up in a mock quote unquote.

"Dozens." Ray laughed.

"Pipe down over there, I'm trying to think." She circled the table, clockwise as per her usual routine when examining doing an examination.

"See . . . things . . . plural," Ray said.

She caught the boys exchanging grins. "Ray. Do us a favor and find some decent coffee, we could be here for some time."

"Sure boss." He scuttled out of the room, dejected.

"Gruesome, eh?" Ross got in her way. Purposefully, she thought.

"Excuse me." She walked through as though he weren't there. Luckily he moved or she would have walked into a six-foot-four inch wall. "If gruesome means beautiful, then yes, it is gruesome." How could anyone could see anything but beauty in this.

"No. Gruesome means, gross, as in disgusting."

She'd looped back around the table. This time, she bumped into the wall. Unwelcome butterflies zipped around her stomach as she looked at him and then quickly averted her eyes to the specimen. She scurried around him and continued her visual once over. The specimen seemed completely intact, like an invisible zipper had opened in the back and the child's insides, skeleton and all, stepped out.

"What do you think it means, boss?" Ray sat the cups of coffee on her desk.

"It means the infants are not infants for long. Traditionally, when an animal sheds its skin, it's either because it needs a newer, harder skin or it's growing. I think we're no longer looking for an infant, we're looking for something larger, possibly a toddler."

"That's what I said." Ross raised his hand in a fist. It surprised her a little when Ray completed the knuckle bump. Out of the corner of her eye, she caught Ross looking at her.

The space behind her ears warmed a little, but she suppressed the blush and didn't return the glance as she snipped a small piece of the de-gloved left index finger from the specimen. With a pair of forceps she set the sample on a Petri dish and handed it to Ray.

He walked away with delicate speed, which she liked to see in her assistants; hurry, not rush. Ray wasn't morbidly obese, but could use some Weight Watchers. He had a pear shape to him; another genetic anomaly to add to her collection for the day.

"What are you thinking?" Ross sat in a chair backwards.

Alexa stared at the backside of Ray as he turned the corner and winced when she saw him stumble. She gave a silent "phew" when he recovered without spilling the specimen.

"Close one." Ross laughed. "You didn't answer my question." He stood and placed his hand on the crook of her elbow, turning her until she had to look at him. "What are you thinking?"

She yanked her elbow from him.

"Sorry about that." He retracted his hand.

Maybe she'd been too harsh? Had she completely forgotten how to be around a man? "It's okay, Ross. You just startled me."

"I'm really sorry."

Ughhh . . . puppy dog eyes. So, lame. "It's quite all right. This is the most amazing find in the history of mankind." She paused, savoring the knowledge. "It's absolute evolution in progress. Maybe life as we know it has come to an abrupt end."

"You're talking about an apocalypse? The End of Days?" He glowered.

"Something of the like, at least it won't be a nuclear holocaust, or the Four Horseman riding down from Heaven raining fire and brimstone. The bible says, '...and a child will lead them'. Maybe these children are here to cleanse the earth?"

"Didn't know you were religious."

"I'm not. I do find the bible fascinating, so I read it once."

"You memorized a passage from reading the bible once?"

"I memorize everything I read."

"Oh . . . you have a photographic memory."

"I guess you could call it that."

"I have trouble remembering where I put my keys." He chuckled.

She appreciated the twinkle in his eye. This guy did enjoy life.

"My husband was the same way." Not just that he lost his keys a lot.

"Was?" His deadpan face hastened her explanation.

"My husband passed away from lung cancer last year." Even to her it sounded emotionless.

He rested against the wall and looked at her, this time with a growing, genuine concern. "I'm sorry to hear that."

She'd never had guessed how emotional he would get. Her pencil scratched the clipboard in her arm. She wasn't writing, just avoiding eye contact. "It's okay, we're dealing with it. Isn't the president addressing the nation soon?" She had to change the subject.

Ross pulled up his sleeve and looked at his watch. "Yeah, in about fifteen minutes, Do you have a break room with a TV in it?"

"Down the hall, but we can go to my office and watch it on my laptop. I think that would be more comfortable. There's a couch if nothing else."

"Will you make us popcorn?" He grinned.

Idiot. The office didn't even have a microwave. She walked past him down the hall. Soon they would know the government's take on the situation. The thought both frightened and excited her.

Ross settled in the crook of the couch. "What do you think he'll say?"

"Historically the government panics at the first sign of anything which threatens the infrastructure. In this case it wouldn't be the cyber infrastructure, but the fabric of humanity itself; our DNA." She closed the door, set her laptop on the coffee table and clicked on her CSPAN link. "I think they're in a panic and will probably do the wrong thing."

"Let's hope not." He had his arm spanned across the back of the couch.

"Do you mind?" She looked at his arm.

"Sorry." He placed his hands in his lap.

Better. She sat down and turned on the television. Then she felt a bead of sweat travel down her scalp and trickled down her back. *Oh, no.*

A woman's voice came over the air, "We are moments away from President Obama's address to the nation regarding what some are calling, 'the most catastrophic event since the bubonic plague or the Spanish 'flu'."

Alexa glanced at Ross.

He watched the monitor, eyes glued to the screen, and twiddling his thumbs. She didn't have any nervous habits that she knew of, but his seemed normal for someone in his situation. She'd think nothing more of it.

13.

TEAGAN'S STOMACH ACHED. She held her belly, hoping the pressure would stop the churning. *I shouldn't have choked down those Nachos last night. Knew the sour cream smelled like ass.* Now she'd have to listen to some nonsense politics all day long because the only thing she could find on television was about the bouncing baby whatever. She figured she had some investment in the whole thing, since they hired her mom to fix it.

The President stepped to the podium. For an old guy, Teagan thought he was cute. His dusty-gray suit tapered nice to his wide frame and thin waist.

"My fellow Americans, in times of crisis, we as a nation must take it upon ourselves to put a stop to tyranny whether it be foreign, domestic, or other. We are in crisis. That is fact. Homosapien life as you and I know it has come to a standstill. Every child born since Halloween night has been, for lack of a better word, mutated.

"Now, our nation's top scientists are working diligently to put a stop to whatever has altered our newborns. We can only guess that it is at a genetic level. That being said, desperate times breed desperate measures. Thousands, maybe tens of thousands of these children have been born in past days across the globe. By our calculations, at the rate they are killing off humans, these infants will repopulate the planet in a matter of months.

Therefore, I met with congress and the Joint Chiefs of Staff this morning and it is with a heavy heart that I declare martial law. And it is my unfortunate duty to notify you that each and every pregnancy in the United States must be terminated, effective immediately."

Cameras snapped like strobe lights. The crowd murmured

amongst themselves. Several people called out, "Mr. President! Mr. President!"

"Please, calm down." He put his hands in the air and waved the crowd quiet. "This is our only option until we can ascertain the root cause of these mutations. Martial law will go into effect immediately. All hospital and clinic databases have been searched by the CIA and all pregnancies have been logged. We implore you. Please. Comply with our wishes. Lethal force will be taken if need be. Remember . . . these are not *your* children anymore. They are vicious killers with a voracious appetite for human flesh."

"Mr. President! Mr. President!"

The questions started and Teagan decided she'd had enough of that nonsense. She did feel sorry for all of the excited, expecting mothers who would have to abort their children. What did he mean by lethal force? Would they actually kill women and girls that refused to have an abortion? Again her stomach swirled and she darted to the bathroom. As she knelt next to the toilet she had a startling revelation. On the wall sat a calendar full of art from some of the greatest artists that ever lived. October had the famous picture of the alien looking woman with her mouth open, hands to her face. They called it "The Scream" for a reason. And at that moment, Teagan wanted to scream at a terrible and startling realization. According to the calendar, her period was now two weeks late.

14.

ALEXA'S MOUTH WENT slack at the president's announcement. She slumped into the couch.

Ross shook his head, stony-faced and wrapped his arm around her. "That's the most horrific news I've ever heard in my life and I had friends killed on 09/11."

"I can understand the logic behind this decision. But it is horrifying." She cuddled into him. In a way, she did agree. The pregnancies must cease, lest the human race be consumed by cannibal children.

"I'm pro-life all the way and this is going to spin a lot of heads. One thing's for certain . . . " Ross let go of her and stood, adjusting the firearm under his jacket. "They better be ready for a war."

"Why's that." This time she took his outstretched hand. He nearly hoisted her off her feet.

"You've heard the saying 'Hell hath no fury like a woman scorned?" His eyes held her in a trance.

"Never mind 'Hell hath no fury . . .'" She glowered, breaking his pseudo hold on her.

The dim glow of the monitor accentuated his chiseled jaw and made his eyes sparkle as he looked back at her. "All I'm saying is that this is going to get bad, very quickly."

"There are three pregnant women who work in this office that I know of. I've received emails from several more that are now on maternity leave. This is just one office. How many are there just like it in the world at this moment?"

"Thousands, I gather." He rubbed his nose with two fingers.

"Headache?"

"Just concerned."

His empathy was commendable.

Commotion came from outside the room. People barreled and shoved, headed for the east side of the building.

"This can't be good." Alexa stood and went to the doorway.

"What's over there?" Ross closed the gap behind her, his massive body towered over her tiny frame.

"The balcony."

"Why would they be gathering around the balcony? Holy shit." He pushed by her., seeing something she couldn't.

He dashed into a room full of cubicles, Alexa close behind. A crowd had gathered in front of a large storm window and double glass doors. They stared and whispered amongst themselves, jostling to stare at something she couldn't see.

Her assistant, Ray stood in the doorway; his robust frame blocked the crowd from entering the balcony. He was talking to someone outside, his words drowned out by the melee.

"F.B.I.. Let me through." Ross held his badge high above his head as if warding off a seven-foot vampire.

The metro sexual Red Sea parted.

Alexa kept steady pace with Ross as he sifted through the group of onlookers. She fell a tad behind. He reached back and she took his hand, not wanting to lose him again.

"What's going on?" Ross asked Ray, who ignored him, his attention focused on something beyond Alexa's line of sight.

Ray spoke slow and steady. "Charlotte. Please don't do this. Think about the baby."

That's when Alexa saw her. One of the many congratulatory emails she'd skimmed over a couple of weeks ago. The newly-pregnant lab assistant had crawled over the rail; her hands barely grasped the metal bar behind as she leaned over the edge. Tears dropped hundreds of feet below, and she gasped huge amounts of air between sobs.

"You have to let me talk to her." Ross turned Ray around. "Ray. Let me through."

Ray stood his ground. "If she's gonna listen to anyone, it's going to be her boss."

"Taking orders from someone who can discipline her isn't wise," Alexa said.

Ross smiled at Ray. "Let me out there, I've dealt with jumpers before. I'll bring her back."

His cool confidence sent a chill to places within her mind and body that hadn't been tapped in more than a year. But smug still came to mind.

"Okay." Ray agreed and moved out of the way.

Ross turned to Alexa. "Stay here, too many people out there might spook her."

"I have no problem with that." In her mind, she didn't have an issue with staying put, she would only talk the girl into jumping. Her people skills weren't the best in sensitive situations and at times like this she'd rather get it over with in the most efficient way possible. Somewhere deep inside, she did feel sorry for the woman. She remembered a time when she too had been four months pregnant. The smell of tuna fish and ham sandwiches came to mind, making her stomach rumble. Not the worst cravings to have. What if she'd been forced to terminate her pregnancy? A lump welled in her throat and a deep-seated pressure deep in her belly threatened to explode up her esophagus.

The thought of having to abort Teagan spoiled her insides. Now, every pregnant woman in the US would be forced into aborting their unborn children. Hopefully Ross could talk this woman off the ledge, but who would talk the others off their respective ledges?

15.

ROSS HADN'T LIED. He'd had firsthand experience with plenty of jumpers. Only . . . his jumpers usually showed up on America's most wanted federal fugitive's lists. Not wanting to alarm the woman, he started talking very softly. "Hello there. My name's Ross. I just thought I'd come over and see how you're doing." He sat down at a round table.

She had two hands on the bars behind her and leaned forward. Tear-streaked makeup smudged below her eyes like a pro football player after a game.

He needed to establish some sort of rapport with the woman. Niceties are a must.

She closed her eyes, yet her lips moved as if she were saying something to herself. When he got closer, he recognized her recitation of The Lord's Prayer. It quickened his pulse and urgency. *Sphincter pucker factor, DEFCON four.*

"Our Father, which art in heaven, hallowed be thy name, for thine is the kingdom, the power and the glory . . . "

She whispered the prayer over and over, but never ended with 'Amen'.

"My name's Ross." He repeated. You're Charlotte? What's yours?"

Charlotte ignored him and kept on with her contemplative reverie.

"Can we talk?" If he could get her to open up to him, his chances of keeping her from jumping would raise considerably.

She fumbled with her words but continued with the prayer.

This told Ross he had gotten through to her.

"I know this is a lot to take in right now and you're not the only woman in this situation right now." He kept his voice steady and confident.

She stuttered and turned towards him. Despondent eyes ate into his soul.

"Please. All I want to do is talk." He motioned down with his hands, a technique he'd learned at the F.B.I. academy, a calming device. Sometimes it worked, others, well, he didn't want to think about the times it hadn't.

She opened her mouth and quickly shut it.

"It's okay. We're just two people chit-chatting. Would you care to join me? I heard the dining here is out of this world."

The joke brought her thin red lips into a half-smile.

That's it. Stay with me.

Any minute she'd burst into tears and climb back over the rail. With her safe in his arms, he'd escort her back to Alexa's office for a nice cup of tea, and he'd convince her everything would end up okay, though he knew it to be far from the truth.

Charlotte glanced away from Ross, down at the pathway below but said nothing. She turned, and for a long moment he thought she'd crawl over the rail and into his arms. Her eyes went blank and he lunged for her as she let go of the rail. His hips rammed into the metal but he grasped a handful of sweater to stay her. The light-knit stretched and tore. Ross lunged, wrapped both arms around her, and pulled. She winced as he cinched his grip across her swollen belly. A wave in her stomach rippled across his forearms. The two fell backwards onto the concrete patio with a thud.

Cheers rang out from behind them.

Charlotte sobbed in his arms. "What am I gonna do? I can't . . . I can't lose my baby."

"It's will be okay." He wrapped his jacket over her shoulders, hugged her close and led her towards the office. "They'll figure this out. Dr. Mason's working on a cure. You trust her, don't you?"

Charlotte clung to the lapels of his jacket. She nodded.

"She's gonna make everything better. Okay, Charlotte, let's get you inside."

16.

SAVANNA REVELED IN her third new skin, and her emergent ability to stand upright. The tunnel's cold walls closed in as she scampered toward a faint light which laid lines down the tunnel toward her. She burst through the metal grate at full speed, landing on Salem Hospital's flat roof. Now on two legs, she stretched her clawed hands high. Lights flickered and flashed and the food bustled below.

Though the growing rumble in her stomach needed to be satiated, some of the prey had fought back with the loud snap and sharp sting; an uncomfortable feeling she'd rather not deal with again. Holes in her flesh healed fast and the fluid seeping from them dried quickly. An unseen force drew her to the roof and kept pulling. She shot forward in a dead sprint. A crevice appeared between the roof and another structure. She leapt and landed on all fours, sliding to a halt on the pavement of the parking garage.

A large creature with glowing eyes barreled toward her. With a loud yelp it swerved, missing her by inches. The beast screamed as it came to a halt. Savannah's stomach bounced in unmitigated glee as two delicious meals burst forth from its innards. But instead of the screams which came from the food below, these sounds calmed and soothed.

Savannah listened intently to the noises coming from them. Then, as if a switch clicked inside her head, the jumbles of sounds began to fit together.

The one with long strands of hair similar to her own said, "Come here, sweetie." But the words meant nothing to Savannah.

The woman beckoned her to come. Savannah's intrigue wore off; it was time to eat. She leapt and landed on the woman claws first.

She jammed both fists into the woman's chest, sprayed by bubbles of blood and spittle from the woman's gurgling mouth.

"What the hell?" The other one backed away, not taking its eyes off Savannah, until it bumped into the snarling beast.

More. Savannah leapfrogged the woman's body.

After she had licked the males sweet fluid from her fingers, she approached the beast with caution, unsure. A low rumble came from it, not unlike the sound her belly made when the hunger hit. Maybe the creature was hungry?

Open flaps on either side of the beast beckoned for food. Savannah dragged the woman's carcass by her tussled brown hair and tossed her in, hoping to satisfy its hunger. The carcass slumped into the beast's mouth. The beast cried out in anger. She figured she'd feed the other open mouth and hope to calm the monster before it lunged again.

She sank her nails into the wrist of the second dead body and yanked it over to the creature's open mouth. As she heaved it in, she heard a click and leapt back. The creature screamed again and burst forward into the stone wall with a crunch. A loud continuous noise blared. She covered her ears, her head rent with the pain of the noise.

With the smoking, yelping creature in ruins, Savannah noticed similar beasts lined against the walls of the room she'd entered. They slept. She fled the den for fear the creatures would wake and attack her.

Outside she felt the pull again and knew where she had to go.

17.

From the crowd's expressions and quick disbursal, the harrowing experience had come to a positive conclusion.

This is only the beginning. Alexa had an idea how bad it could get. The government had linked the satellite imagery via her Smartphone. The screen grew redder by the moment and good deeds such as stopping for every damsel in distress would not get her the specimen she needed to complete her work.

Sweat poured from Ray's brow. His hands went into the air. "I need a drink. See you back in the office."

"No drinking until we . . . "

She threw her hands up as he waltzed back to the office.

Agent Harris scooted next to her with people still patting him on the back and congratulating him. "It's so hard to find good help these days." The patting on the back continued.

"Good work." Her commendation is all she could give. High five, knuckle bump, hug, kiss . . . no way.

"As cliché and dumb as this sound." He straightened his tie and slipped back into his jacket. "This is only the tip of the iceberg."

"I'm afraid she's not going to be the only suicide attempt we see in the next few months. But agent Harris, could we please focus on the task at hand? If you stop for every person who needs your help during this crisis, you're not going to . . . "

"I got it."

"No. I don't think you do." She wanted to stand on her tiptoes and look at him in the eye, but even that wouldn't get her there. "Please. Let's get back to work. Look." She held her phone in front of his face."

She didn't mean for him to take it, but he swiped it from her.

"Yeah. They're popping up everywhere, that's for sure. But we can beat this."

Cocky. "It may be possible. If you would get out there and procure my specimen."

He handed her the phone. "And if I can't?"

She didn't think the word existed in his vocabulary. Maybe she'd found a chink in his armor. "The world as we know it will change."

"No shit. We're fucked."

"Maybe." She stuffed her hands into her lab jacket. "Man will prevail. The human race is very good at adapting to change. This too shall pass and mankind will go on, business as usual. But let's not sit on our hands. I have a lab to tend to and you have a lot of work to do." She folded her arms, hoping to put a little stamp on her logic.

"Darlin', that's the best idea I've heard all morning."

Darlin'? Did he really just call me Darlin'?

"Lab. Now." She directed him forward. "You need to learn a few things before heading out on your task."

"Yes, ma'am."

A bit facetious, but she'd take it.

Ray had kicked his feet onto his desk and thumbed his cell phone furiously. "More deadly child births in every . . . "

"Break's over kid." Ross flicked his head toward the door.

"You're not the boss of me." Ray scowled and took a sip from a steel flask he had in his drawer.

Alexa put her hands on his desk. "No he isn't, but I am."

Ray nodded and stood. "What can I do for you?"

"Grab the centrifuge report off the printer, would you?"

"Sure thing." He tipped an invisible hat and disappeared into the stock room, where they kept the printers.

"Looks like you can handle yourself around here." Agent Harris sat in Ray's chair and opened the bottom drawer of his desk.

"I beg your pardon." *What does he think he's doing? This is not getting back to work.*

"I've always said you can tell what kind of person you're dealing with by scanning the items in their bottom desk drawer."

She failed to see the logic in this statement. "How's that?"

He reached into the drawer and pulled out a box of half eaten powdered donuts. "Unsure of himself. Eats for comfort."

Donuts did frequent his desk.

"Manicure set. Mama's boy." Harris raised the kit above his head.

That one made more sense. "Okay. You made your point. Put it back before he catches us sifting through his stuff."

Harris stood and looked around. "Which desk is yours? Oh yeah, it's in your office."

Ray walked back into the room and Harris stuffed the contents of the drawer back. But before he did, he pulled out a little tube of eye liner and whispered, "Closet cross dresser."

She knew Ray had a girlfriend and on the weekends did superhero cosplay at different conventions. "Wrong."

"What are you two doing?" Ray didn't see Harris push the bottom drawer closed with his foot. "Something smells a foul." His eyes darted from Harris to Alexa.

Quite amusing.

Agent Harris put his hands behind his head. "Nothin' man, just shootin the shit."

"Yeah right."

She took the report from Ray.

Her heart caught in her throat. She squinted at the paper, hoping she'd read what she thought she had. "This is fantastic, though quite puzzling."

"Why's that?" Ross peered over her shoulder.

The smell of his mint gum wafted around her like the herbs her Grandmother used to grow in front of her house. It almost made it bearable to be around him.

"Well?" His foot tapped.

"First I need to give you a short lesson in genetics."

"Here we go. You'll need this." Ray gave Harris his chair.

"Thanks."

"If I had a pillow, it would be yours too."

"You think so?"

Ray chuckled. "You have no idea."

"Let's hear it." Harris flipped his chair around and sat in it backwards. His comfort position for sure. A bit macho, but she'd let it slide.

She scowled at Ray. "Thanks a lot."

"Don't mention it, *Boss* lady." His thumb went to his nose, fingers twinkled and he stuck his tongue out.

"Very mature. And you know I don't like being called boss." She threatened to throw her clipboard at him, but he ducked around a corner. "Go ahead and run. You can't hide forever!"

"Oh yes I can." His voice came muffled from the other room.

Harris seemed to be enjoying the show.

"Sorry about that." She pulled up her white board.

"Again, it's not a problem. I like seeing you interact with your coworkers. It's . . . *entertaining*." He swiveled his chair in a circle.

Boys . . . always playing.

"According to varied criteria, there are several classifications of mutations." She started her tutorial, scribbling little notes on the board as she went. "An allele is an alternative form of a gene—one member of a pair—that is located at a specific position on a specific chromosome. These DNA codes determine distinct traits that can be passed on from parents to offspring. The process by which allele's are transmitted was discovered by Gregor Mendel and formulated in what is known as Mendel's law of segregation."

"Hold it." Harris held up a hand. "Can you tell me in English?" He looked as if he'd had an anvil dropped on his head, perplexed and somewhat in pain.

"Would you like me to stop?"

"No way, this is fascinating. Just put it in somewhat layman's terms."

He seemed sincere about learning.

From the hall Ray slid his finger across his throat. She pointed at him and shook her head. He raised his hands in mock disgust and crawled back into his testing hole.

At least she had the attention of the agent. This time she put it into layman's terms. Or near enough. When she finished the abridged version of her three hour lecture on gene mutation, she waited for a confused response.

"Have there been any cases to prove this?"

Alexa found it fascinating he'd kept up with her. Maybe a closet genius existed in this man; *another genetic anomaly.* She smiled.

"Recently a southwestern Indiana farmer found a sick bald eagle, Subsequent tests showed the bird positive for mercury poisoning.

State wildlife officials say it's unclear if the bird's poisoning resulted from the consumption of contaminated fish caught in an Indiana waterway. One environmental watchdog organization stated the state ranks fourth nationally in mercury emissions from coal-fired power plants, and the contamination ultimately ends up in the food chain."

"And . . . how does this affect our babies?"

"The bald eagle they sent to me for testing because it had been genetically altered. It wasn't only sick, it was mutated. The Eagle had a third allele. The tri-allele eventually killed the bird." She handed Ross the calculations; to prove a point more than anything else.

He took it and gave her a perplexed look, as expected.

"I found the same genetic mutation in our baby Staten's husk of skin. And even better; or worse, depending on how you look at it, an unidentified gene. This new gene, coupled with the Mercury genetic deformity, created the tri-allele attached to all embryo's on earth. I'll need to do more testing and see if we can't isolate this gene."

"But?"

"But I need a fully grown tri-allele to isolate the gene and see if we can't reverse it. The good news is that my team and I have already isolated the gene mutated by the Mercury poisoning. However, in the DNA strand we have, a chromosome has fused with the Mercury mutated gene." She studied his features.

"I think I see where you're coming from. So, what you're saying is . . . we need to get you a fully grown tri-allele. Is that what you're calling them?"

"Would you prefer genetically-altered man-eating babies?"

"No, but Trill works. Tell me one thing ..." He crossed his arms.

"Yes."

"Can this be reversed?" A concerned look shadowed over him like a storm cloud.

How am I supposed to know? Men always seem to want yes or no answers.

"At this moment in time, Agent Harris. I really don't know."

"I sense this is new ground for you."

"What's that?" She didn't like the direction the conversation had taken.

"Not having a clue. You seem to always have the answers. How does it feel being on the other side of things? Like us common folk?"

She gave him a derisive glare. "It's not so wonderful, that's for sure."

"Welcome to my world."

She wanted to smack the smug grin off his face. "And what a wonderful world you live in."

"Hey. That's my favorite song. Nothing better than Dizzy singing and playing that trumpet."

A modicum of culture. This chauvinistic brute of a man might have a bit of depth to him after all. And she had to be honest; he wasn't awful to look at. She figured Teagan and her friends would say 'doable'. But that wasn't in her vernacular.

Ross pulled out his cell phone, probably to message his boss of the findings. Langley would probably want the child's skin.

"I can see your mind's elsewhere," he said, stuffing his cell phone into his shirt pocket. "And rightfully so, guess I'll leave you to it. If you need me, I'll be hunting down one of your babies."

Alexa cleared her throat.

"I mean toddlers." He put his suit coat back on and batted at some dust on his sleeves. "The Trills. Do the tests show they are growing?"

"Yes. From the regenerative properties these tests are showing, I believe you may be looking for a young teen by now; thirteen, maybe fourteen years old."

"Okay. We'll keep our eyes out for a heart-eating teenage girl. Are you joking?"

"No, I'm not kidding. The tissue is regenerating at an alarming rate. I predict by this time tomorrow, our subject number one, will appear to be in her late teens."

"Okay. Looking for a creature of some sort in its late teens, is that possible?"

"Not a creature, Agent Harris. You're looking for a girl. This being has all the human genome. She will look like us and probably sound like us."

"Are you sure?" He scratched his head.

"Logic dictates she should have all the physical traits of a homosapien, but we won't know for sure until you get me my specimen." Though she didn't believe in a God per se, she figured she'd humor him. "If you have a deity you put your faith in, now would be the time to do what you do."

"What's that?" His perplexed look gave him another edge of wonder.

"Pray. Sacrifice small animals. I don't know, but if you do worship. Now would be the time. "Then you do what you do best."

His eyes narrowed. "Kill every last one of those bastards."

18.

TOO TIRED TO crawl under the covers, Teagan curled into a fetal position on the floor next to her bed. "Oh my God, oh my God, oh my God." *This shit ain't happening. No way.* Her hand shook as she tapped the call button on the cell. She wasn't excited to hear the response waiting for her on the other end.

The cell rang. *If you don't answer, Ellie, I'll hunt you down and kill you myself.*

Her silent threat worked. Ellie answered after the fourth ring.

"What's up, babe?"

Relieved to hear her best friend's voice, Teagan lost it and sobbed. The kind of sobs you get as a child and can't stop no matter what you do.

"What's wrong?" Teagan knew Ellie's counseling voice better than anyone.

The words wouldn't come out, only blubbers and gibberish.

"Simmer down. Take a deep breath and talk to me girl. What the fuck's wrong?"

Teagan still couldn't catch her breath. "I . . . I . . . "

"C'mon, you can tell me anything. Ya know?"

"I might . . . " Sob. " . . . be . . . preg . . . preg . . . "

"PREGNANT!" So much for the counselor, the mother hen in her had shown up and kicked the counselor's ass out the door.

Teagan pulled the phone away from her ear. "I think so. I'm late. And I'm never late."

"Fuck! Really? Didn't you guys use a . . . "

"NO, dip shit. I told you we didn't."

"Well, duh. Shoulda kept your dick in your pants."

"I know, right?" Teagan felt better already. "Now what?" Ellie seemed to always have the answers

"You have to tell your mom."

Wrong answer. "No way."

"You have to. She's supposed to fix this shit, isn't she? Isn't that what she does for a living?"

"I don't give a rat's ass, there's no way I'm telling her."

"Teag? At least she's trying. She'll take care of you. By the time the baby comes, everything will be better. You'll see. I can't believe I just said that. You're gonna have a baby. A little, shit-dealing Tea Bags rolling around the house. Or eating everyone in sight."

"No! No! I'm not having this . . . this fucking thing. They already said all pregnancies are being terminated by law. So there you have it. No baby. Not ever."

"First. Let's figure out if you're preggo. Then we'll deal with it. How late are you?"

"Couple weeks."

"Shit. Strike one. You need to get tested."

"Quit, El. They're monitoring the stores. We can't go buy a pregnancy test and we sure as hell can't go to a doctor."

"Never fear. Your El is here."

"What's that supposed to mean?"

"You're lucky my mom's a whore."

"She's married."

"Well. She's a whore with my dad. Why do you think I have six siblings? Those two are like bunnies."

"Gross."

"And they keep a healthy supply of pregnancy tests in the garage. I can swipe a couple and get them up to my room."

"No shit?"

"No shit! Now get your preggo ass over here now, bitch."

"Okay. I'm out the door." Teagan tossed her phone across the room where it landed with a soft bounce in her laundry basket. After she finished buttoning her jeans and before she pulled her gray hoodie over her head, she checked her tummy in the mirror, patting the tiny lump several times.

Un-fucking believable.

She retrieved her phone and jogged down the stairs. In the

kitchen she found her keys hanging on the rack mounted by the front door, swiped them and locked the door on her way out.

It's all in my head. It's all in my head. You're not pregnant. You're not pregnant. She clicked the car door's unlock button and auto started it from her key-chain. The tires left little black streaks as she tore out of the driveway. *Mom's gonna to kill me for that one. Doesn't matter, I'm fucked anyway.*

19.

SINCE SHE LEFT the lair of the sleeping beasts, Savannah had grown quite a bit. The transformations had tingled and annoyed her. This last time her figure changed, and with it, the pull increased. The ethereal tether had led her into the wilderness.

Another curiosity occurred when she transformed. Sounds from the prey came into her head. They took shape and she knew words. The beasts they rode, they called cars. The material they covered their bodies with, clothes. The world around her made more sense. Trees, roads, people, places, objects and even the small insects flitting about the lights had meaning; purpose. One thing remained a constant; her need to feed. This necessity sizzled through her body.

A car skid through the dirt next to the road behind her, a vicious cloud of dust blew through its brilliant lights. Two men emerged from the vehicle. They waved their weapons in the air.

One called to her, "This is the police. We mean you no harm."

She knew that wasn't true, turned and headed down the embankment toward a rushing body of water.

Bullets pinged off rocks and lodged into the dirt as she darted down the hill. The guns shot fast and she couldn't avoid the entire barrage. Several hit her in the right leg and one pierced her side causing some minor skin damage, but a viscous fluid seeped from the wound.

More vehicles sirens whelped in the distance.

Somewhere behind her she heard a man say, "We found her, she's cornered between us and the river."

Other men pursued. She hit the edge of the river and didn't stop. With a flex and lunge, she soared over the river, landing on her hands and legs in a patch of grass on the other side. Over her shoulder, several lights bounced up and down as the men made their way down to the water's edge. She listened hard and their voices became clearer.

"Did she just do what I thought she did?" one of them asked.

"Yeah. Better call the F.B.I. guy and tell him we lost her again."

"He's gonna be pissed. Hell no. You call him."

"Let's have the sheriff call him."

"Good idea."

Savannah disappeared into the waiting arms of the forest. The moon bathed her as she maneuvered through dense shrubs and thickets of trees. Dark thoughts from one of the men clouded her mind. The things he wanted made her heart race and the terrible realization of her nakedness overcame her. She knew what she needed but had no idea how she would go about obtaining them. She needed clothes.

20.

ROSS PARKED BEHIND two sheriff deputies' cars and a bundle of state troopers' vehicles. Flashlights bounced as the men hauled ass down the embankment. Tracer rounds zipped across the river from the automatic AR-15's being fired from this side.

The officer had spoken in broken jargon, most likely into a handheld radio while running. He'd said, "Little . . . g . . . jump . . . river . . . lost her." Ross thought he'd said a little girl jumped into the river and they lost her. From what he'd heard on the news and his debriefing, the creatures could take a licking and keep on ticking, like a damn Timex Watch.

He pulled the riot shotgun from its unopened box on his back seat. A little something he'd snaked from headquarters in Portland. He'd be damned if he was going up against one of these things with his government issued Glock 9mm. That would be like whipping out his dick in a knife fight. No way in hell. With resolve he snapped the flashlight into position under the barrel. When he stepped out from the vehicle, he checked his sidearm and ammunition.

On his way down the hill, not twenty feet from the car, his right shoe stuck in the mud and came off.

"Shit."

He wobbled on his left leg. *Probably could have used a change of shoes.* Then he reached his foot back into the murk behind him, slipped it into his shoe and yanked.

After he tied his shoe he pulled his handheld radio from its belt clip. "This is Harris. I'm on my way down. Where are you guys?"

"Down the hill," the same deputy crackled.

"No shit, Sherlock. Where are you in relation to the cars?"

"That would be southwest. I'm staying put, the rest are tracking the girl from this side of the river."

Why had he said this side of the river? Maybe she swam across? Damn. He'd hoped she couldn't swim.

After working his way through another thicket, he saw the bobbing flashlight of the officer.

"I'm right here." Ross clicked his flashlight on and off.

"Hey, secret agent man." The deputy, who looked no wider than a bus stop pole, was startled, but he laughed as Ross busted through the last set of bushes. "Uh . . . the trail's right there." He pointed his flashlight about seven feet to the left of where Ross stood.

"Son of a . . . " He grimaced at the kid. "Tell me everything."

"Not much to tell other than we saw a suspicious person hiding in the bushes and stopped to check it out. That's when we noticed the little girl."

"How little?"

"Maybe eleven, twelve at the most, but she was stark raving necked."

"Did she look deformed?"

"Other than a set of halogen-like glowing eyes, she looked like any other girl her age, rose buds and everything."

Ross ignored the remark. "Then what happened?"

"She took off. Faster than I ever seen anyone move in my life; a blur of flesh. When I came around the corner . . . " He shined his flashlight on the trail again. "... she'd already jumped."

"Into the water." Ross mused.

"No, Sir. Across goddamn river."

Ross's whipped his light over the swift water of the Willamette River and shook his head. "No way, that's at least fifty yards, if not more." He scratched his chin as if it would help him judge the distance between the shore he stood on and the embankment where the deputy said the girl landed.

"I ain't shittin' you, Agent. She jumped the entire thing. Where do you think she's heading?"

Ross put his hand on the deputy's shoulder. "Not sure. Looks like she's headed toward Independence or Monmouth."

"I don't know man, but these fuckin' things are startin' to give me the heebie-jeebies. If she has the power in her legs to clear the river, how strong are her arms? And from what I've seen of the carnage they leave behind, they have wolverine sharp claws. Like Wolverine's claws in the X-men."

"No." Ross outlined a chunk of tree she'd taken out. "Like in wildlife, claws sharp enough to tear through a bear. A real wolverine can tear through a bear like butter that's sat out all night in a warm house."

"Shit." The deputy kneeled and examined a footprint in the mud. "Look how small."

"I know." Ross pulled out his cell phone and dialed his boss. This news had to become public.

"Ya gonna call them wolverines?"

"Nope. They have a name. They're called, tri-alleles."

"Well that's a stupid name."

"Tell that to my scientist. She might tear your heart out herself. I've shortened the name to Trills. That easier for you?"

"Yup, much easier than the ter-allie name. The two men shared a laugh as the phone rang at the other end.

21.

WHEN ELLIE OPENED the door, the flood of tears came again. Teagan stepped into the two-story home and fell into Ellie's arms.

"Shhhhh." Ellie hugged Teagan tight. "If my mom hears you crying she's gonna know something's up. And you know my mom, she won't stop badgering us until we give it up."

Teagan sniffed, holding in the remaining sob. "That's the whole issue. I already gave it up."

Ellie smiled.

Teagan swallowed down some mucus and wiped her eyes. "Let's get this over with. I need to know . . . like . . . now."

"Chill. I swiped the tests and put a couple of 'em in my bathroom. Praying Mom doesn't figure it out. I hid the rest to make her think she lost them. Though she's been stock piling shit all day. She said Winco had lines that went from the tellers all the way back to the pharmacy. "

"That blows." Seemed like pretty long lines to her. But she had more important things to deal with right now. "Let's get this shit over with."

"Come with me." Ellie started to lead Teagan up the stairs.

Teagan felt like Marie Antoinette as she traveled to the gallows. The result at the end of the stairs meant life or death for her.

Ellie's mom bustled by with two cases of Evian water in her arms. "What are you girls up to?"

"Watching porn, smoking dope. You know . . . " Ellie answered, " . . . girl stuff."

"Very funny. Oh, by the way, thanks for the help. Your dad and I got it all. Most fit in the garage, this is going in the pantry freezer."

"No worries, Ma." Ellie ushered Teagan up the steps.

Teagan liked everyone in Ellie's family. Her father, Ed, who liked to be called 'Uncle Ed' worked at Firestone in downtown Tigard; office manager of some sort. Her mom taught the local kids piano and claimed to be queen of the domestic goddesses. Ellie had six siblings. Her two older sisters went to college. A thirteen- year-old sister, eleven-year-old sister and two younger brothers still lived at home. The boys weren't twins, but Teagan still had a problem telling them apart. She realized the house was extremely quiet. She didn't see any of the other kids.

"Where're your brothers and sisters?"

"They're staying with my Aunt Marjorie in Olympia Washington. She has a ranch on the outskirts of town. They'll be safe there." Ellie's voice seemed confident, but her eyes told Teagan a different story.

"I'm sure they'll be fine. Why didn't you go?"

"You called. I had to stay and take care of your sorry ass." She giggled.

Teagan smiled and went into Ellie's room. She plopped onto the bed and said, "How do we do this."

Ellie tossed the box toward the bathroom.

Alyssa stepped out and caught the small pink box. "Sup whores? Or should I say slut?" She nodded at Teagan. "And virgo?" She smiled at Ellie.

"Shit." Teagan glared at Ellie. What's one more added to the mix? Jesus. By morning, everyone will know. The thought had her tummy churning again like a Lazy Susan clomping cookie dough.

"What?" Ellie gave Teagan her stank eye; the one where one eyebrow is raised and the other eye is squinky like Popey. "You think I'd leave Lyssa out of this?"

"Guess the fuck not. Fine. Let's get this shit over with." Teagan hopped up from the bed and took a deep breath. *You can do this. All you have to do is pee.* Jumping beans took the place of her heart. The fact that Alyssa's eyes held compassionate sorrow didn't help. Teagan took the box and the girls shut the bathroom door.

22.

SAVANNAH STALKED AROUND the house for an easy way in. She stuck to the shadows in an attempt to hide her nakedness and herself. Of course she could have burst through the front door and devoured the humans inside, but instinct told her different. Instinct said to stay hidden, feed on them one at a time. This would be her best chance of getting away without them alerting others. They worked best when in groups and their weapons seemed to be getting stronger. The bullets that hit her leg had left bruises, the one in her side still bled, though she was sure it went straight through.

The voices inside didn't come from the occupants, but from the television set they sat in front of. A beam of light shot across the lawn from the cracked open back door, Savannah slipped inside.

A young male stood several feet in front of her, his mouth agape. "Mmmom!"

Savannah didn't want him alerting the others. Instinct and natural reflexes took over, and like a wild beast threatened, she attacked. She whizzed by the boy with her claws extended. The tissue in his neck tore as her nails slashed his throat.

Silenced, the boy slumped to the floor.

Blood from her fingertips tasted sweet as she lapped at them. Blood spurt from the boy and sprinkled the flower patterned wallpaper; a spring shower of death.

"Danny! Danny!" A woman ran past Savannah as if she didn't exist.

Crouched in a corner of the small entrance to the kitchen, like a discarded appliance, Savannah reached out and wrapped a clawed hand around the woman's ankle. Time stood still as the woman tried to stop from falling. She fell forward. Her head smashed against a small table. The right side of her face caved in. She coughed. Blood, sputum and several teeth spewed from her mouth as she gurgled and tried to scream.

Not wanting to risk others in the house hearing the woman's cries, Savannah stood and stomped on the woman's skull. It crumpled under the extreme pressure. A gasp turned her attention to the doorway where two more people stood. One, her same sex and height, the other, a large man, neither of them moved.

The girl grasped the man around the waist. "Daddy, it's one of them isn't it?"

"I . . . I think so, honey. Let's back up, very slowly. No sudden moves. I heard they attack if you run, just like what we told you about big dogs."

"But it's only a girl. Is . . . is mommy—dead?" She cried.

The man sniffled. "I'm afraid so honey."

Savannah understood their words and looked at the two family members she'd killed. For a brief moment she felt their loss and tears welled in her ebony eyes.

Hand-in-hand the father and daughter backed out. They didn't break eye contact with Savannah, who for the first time, felt sorrow for what she'd done.

The two exited the house through another door. Savannah wasn't there to eat. She came for one thing only, clothes to cover her nakedness. She searched through the rooms until she found a pair of shorts and a t-shirt that fit her tiny frame. But just as she started to pull the t-shirt over her head, the itch began again.

Not again.

Tiny prickles jittered under the skin of her big toes and worked its way up her feet, into her ankles, legs, buttocks, back, head and face. A tear in her forehead skin started the process. She inched her fingers into the crevice parting her scalp and face. The skin peeled back, revealing a new epidermis. Her old hair and skin sloughed to her back like a morbid hoodie. She followed the tear down her chest and when she peeled the skin back, two large mounds of flesh peaked out of the new skin.

When the transformation completed, she stepped away from the dead skin and found a mirror in a nearby bathroom. The young girl's clothes would no longer fit. But the mother wasn't much larger. In a room adjacent to the kitchen she found four baskets full of clothing. She pulled on a black t-shirt and skirt.

Platinum-blonde hair slicked across her shoulders with the same clear salve as before and crinkled down to her waist. Full rose-red lips contrasted her ebony eyes. The look startled her; so different from the warm colors of the human's eyes. She'd also seen her reflection in windows when her eyes glowed making the night into day.

More objects in the house took shapes and names. The television in the living room had a woman standing in front of a familiar area to Savannah, the river's edge where she had gotten away from the policemen.

" . . . *and that's when the officers stopped following. Again, this is Sakina Merchant from News Channel 12 coming to you live from a sighting of one of the infected children. We're attempting to get a statement from a Federal officer who pursued the child.*"

The camera panned to a man in a suit. Words at the top of the screen took form and Savannah understood them. Then she tried something she hadn't before. She opened her mouth and tried to mimic the humans. At first a quick chirp escaped. When she focused, the chirps turned into a long screech, which rang throughout the home. Once more she focused until the screech deepened into a low growl. Then the sounds came out. "Breaking news." She said and smiled at her cleverness. She didn't know how she knew how to read and speak. Maybe she had absorbed some of the meal's (now humans) thoughts.

A deep grumble came from her belly. She pulled up her shirt and looked at her flat, defined, abdomen. Again her tummy growled letting her know it needed sustenance. The urge had to be satiated or the pain would start. She didn't want to feel her insides seared again.

She scanned the house for a meal, wondering where the two she let go ran off to.

23.

Ross ANSWERED THE reporter's questions and dodged any regarding Dr. Mason. He thought she'd been kept a secret, but obviously not. After he trudged back up the hill he whacked his mud packed shoes against the front tire, crawled back into the SUV and found his phone.

Duty urged him to call his boss, but others needed checked on first. The thought of losing his daughters scared him to death. His heart ached for them. But he had a job to do and they should be safe enough out at his ex wife's sister's farm. It seemed like the Trills only attacked densely populated areas.

Then he had to call . . . her. For some reason she'd drilled her way to the front of his mind. Now he wanted to give her the news himself, to make her proud. Maybe show off a little. Never hurt before when he'd tried to hook up with a hot chick at one of the local bars. One acronym usually sealed the deal . . . F.B.I. But this woman, she would see right through his bullshit. She wasn't out for a good time or a one night stand. This woman, she was . . . *No way in hell. Not this obnoxious, plain Jane, know it all. Not now. Not her.* "Shit. That's all I need." . . . special.

By the time he'd texted and received a smiley face from his oldest, he knew what had gripped him about the insufferable woman. One small attribute sucked at him like a magnet to a steel mill. They weren't the hypnotic, gorgeous, bedroom eyes which usually made his heart thump in the southern region of his body. Her eyes were stoic—pretty much all the time—but when she looked at him, they twinkled. That's what got him. Now he felt responsible for her safety as well. Once he'd confirmed that, then he'd badger her for answers. Hopefully she had some because the shit had hit the fan hard. Not just any fan, one of those huge ones they use for wind in the movies, covering the entire world with little piles of crap.

His thumb fumbled across the screen of his phone before, as it often did when using the damn contraption, landed on the wrong number. He ended the call to some girl named Amber and clicked on Alexa's name.

"This is Dr. Mason."

Her quick answer startled him. "Ms. Mason, er . . . Dr. . . . this is Ross."

"I know who you are. How may I help you, Agent Harris?"

She sounded upset, if you could call it that? He'd have to spend more time with her before the subtle tones meant anything to him. He figured he'd keep it all business.

"Sorry to call and interrupt you, Dr. Mason." *Crap. Too formal.*

"That's quite all right. Have you procured me a specimen?"

"No, but we've got a line on the Staten Trill. Are there any results from your tests yet?"

"The tests haven't revealed anything conclusive at this time but I may be on the right track here."

"Well, that's a start. You wouldn't happen to know any way of killing one of these things, um . . . Trills?"

"There's nothing I can do at this point to put a proverbial chink in their armor. Give me some time and a *live* specimen and we may find a way. However, there's some good news that comes from this." She paused.

"Which is?"

"If I can break the foreign gene down, I may be able to stop the transformation in a fetus, but it's going to take some time."

"Do whatever you can." The entire world knew she was their only chance. Every couple of seconds the world became more deadly for humans just from the babies alone. Now it seemed as though the adolescent Trills would ravage and kill anyone in their paths. A shiver ran down his spine.

"Have you had contact with one of the tri-alleles yet?"

"No. But, you know what this one did?"

"Um . . . I'm at the lab, remember? So, no."

"Right." He chuckled under his breath. She'd actually made a joke. He imagined her smile.

"So? What did it do?"

Or a scowl, he sighed. "She jumped clear over the Willamette River."

"How far?"

"We think somewhere near fifty yards."

Alexa swallowed hard. "Muscle density, strength, speed, enhanced senses. All of these could be traits of the third allele."

"How's that possible?" He tightened his grip on the steering wheel. "Do they have some super leaping ability?"

"Usually proteins are the major functional end-points of the DNA template and account for the majority of the dry weight of a cell. From that we can . . . "

"Time out." Even though she couldn't see him, he made the timeout signal with his hands. "Gonna have to slow down just a bit."

"Short answer?"

"Yes please."

"I don't know what their molecular structure is like or how their internal anatomy works. We do know that they thrive on human flesh, mainly the heart."

"Why would their eating habits have anything to do with their molecular structure?"

She sighed and he could imagine her pinching the bridge of her nose. "Well . . . cardiac tissue *is* the densest muscle in the human body. There could be a correlation between their eating habits and their molecular structure."

He laughed.

"What's so funny?"

"Gives a whole new meaning to the saying, 'eat your heart out'."

She humphed. "Very funny."

"Agent Harris? Come in. You there?" the sheriff's deep voice boomed over the receiver, causing radio static.

"Dr. Mason, the sheriff's on the line. I need to go."

"I should be able to form a better hypothesis before you return. Do you know when you'll be arriving?"

"Depends on what the sheriff wants."

"I'll probably be here all night. I need to call Teagan and see how she's doing. I'll talk to you later."

"See you when I get there." He picked up the hand-held radio. "This is Agent Harris . . . over."

"'Bout damn time!" The sheriff panted, which couldn't be anything new for him. With his size, he probably got winded from eating a donut.

"What's going on, Sheriff?"

"We just . . . got a call from a family in Independence. Most of 'em were . . . wiped out by what the survivors are calling, 'one of *those* things'. They described the creature as an eleven year old girl . . . with black eyeballs."

Black eyeballs? Ross didn't know the significance of those, but he did know one thing . . . "That's our patient zero. Baby Staten." *Good.* Maybe they could bag her and the nightmare would be over.

"Not a fuckin' baby no more. She killed a boy and his mother."

"Ross knew what he had to do. "How'd the others get away?"

"That's the pickle of the whole damn thing, now. The dad and little girl say she slaughtered the mom and boy and then just watched them walk out of the house. They're trying to say if you stare one in the eye and back away, they'll leave you alone. Like a goddamn grizzly."

Ross didn't believe it for a second. "I'll get a chopper out there and whoever else I can get headquarters to send.

The sheriff cleared his throat. "I'm headed to the Independence police station to talk with the family. I sent several deputies, the state police and a SWAT team out to the house. 771 First Street Independence."

"Got it." Ross keyed the address into his dashboard GPS.

"Get your ass out there, but be careful."

Maybe this sheriff does have a heart? Hopefully, he'll get to keep it. "Aww, Sheriff . . . you do care."

"Now don't go buying me flowers or a ring. Just get your ass out here."

Ross laughed. "You got it. Be there in ten minutes."

"And where the hell is the goddamn National Guard?" Sheriff Lawson looked at a couple of his deputies.

"President's got them rounding up pregnant women. I'll check out the house. Let me know if you learn anything else from the witnesses." The sound of tires hitting pavement blared over the radio.

"Summbitch . . . there's a . . . holy mother of God."

Ross flinched and pulled the radio away from his ear as the blast from the sheriff's hip cannon crackled over the line.

"Sheriff? Sheriff?" Ross clicked the mic over and over as if something mechanical had gone wrong. With his emergency lights flipped on, he tore the SUV into the mud on the roadside and jumped it back onto Highway 22, toward Independence and whatever waited for him at the police station.

24.

"WHAT'S A BLUE X mean?" Alyssa held the little white stick out from the bathroom door.

Teagan slumped from the bed to Ellie's shag carpet floor, well aware of what the blue X meant. Her erratic breathing invited the walls closer, the ceiling to cave in. Instinct took over and as the room blackened around her, she curled into a fetal ball on the floor, gasping for breath. Even though she'd read the directions on the box four times before she peed on the stick, she didn't want to believe. How could she, at seventeen, be pregnant?

Ellie scowled at Alyssa. "It's a plus, not an x dumb ass!"

"OMG." Alyssa turned the pink stick this way and that. "You're right. It's a plus. What's the plus mean?"

Ellie dropped to the floor and put her hand on Teagan's shoulder.

Teagan scooted until her head rested in Ellie's lap. She sobbed.

"Shhh . . . It'll be okay." Ellie stroked Teagan's hair.

Alyssa flopped across the bed, above the other two. "Yeah, we'll get through this like we have all the other shit we've been through. Remember when Brady told everyone he went down on Ells and her cooch smelt like fish bait?" She giggled.

Teagan turned her head and through tear-blurred vision saw the girls next to her. Her girls. Her best friends. And she knew they always would be. She smiled. "Yeah, we turned the tables on that shit-dick. Didn't we?"

"Ughh." Ellie frowned. "Yeah. I told everyone he had a tiny prick and his pee hole was in the wrong place, upside down or some shit like that. Weirdest dick I ever saw, but the sex was actually pretty good. I'd have to say above normal."

"It's called hypospadia." Alyssa sniggered.

Teagan suspected Alyssa might be some sort of genius. She got honor roll every year, knew huge words neither her nor Ellie had any idea about, but acted like the biggest knob head in the world. She knew it had to be some sort of front.

Teagan still had no idea what to do. "I'm so screwed."

Alyssa landed on the floor next to the other girls with a thump. "I heard abortions are cheap this time of year."

Ellie smacked Alyssa across the forehead. "You insensitive bitch."

Alyssa rubbed her red forehead. "Sorry. Just trying to lighten up the conversation a little, Jesus."

"Do you see either of us laughing? Seriously, Lyss, if you don't start thinking before you talk, you're gonna wind up pissing off the wrong person."

Alyssa popped out her full bottom lip. "Sorry for being eclectically sound."

Teagan had absolutely no idea what she meant. "Quit it. Both of you. The president ordered all pregnant women to get abortions and the government's paying for it. So Lyssa is right."

Ellie brushed the hair out of Teagan's eyes. "But you're anti-abortion. You hate the word."

"Well, I don't have much of a choice, do I? It's the law now."

Alyssa started to open her mouth, but Ellie held her hand up and opened and closed it fast, as if she were doing a shadow puppet of a snake.

"But . . ."

"Shhh," Ellie snapped her hand python's mouth open and closed again.

Alyssa sat on the bed with a *humph.* "Fine." She crossed her arms.

Teagan appreciated the silence. An abortion? What in the hell would she tell her mother? They'd never been open about sex. While her mother praised her for her staunch celibacy, she had secretly started seeing the older boy. Now she'd have to let her mom know she wasn't a virgin anymore. *Ugh.* She'd never hear the end of it. Maybe they could secretly go to one of the government clinics and have it done there? She'd seen the videos of how they cram a rod up inside of you and blend the baby up before pulling it out. Her insides crumbled at the thought of spaghetti baby on a stick.

She sprinted for the bathroom.

Alyssa slapped her hands on her cheeks. "She's gonna blow!"

Teagan didn't have time to put up the toilet seat. When she finished heaving, she wrapped her arms around the bowl. Someone behind her flushed the toilet. She'd recognize the scrawny arms of Alyssa anywhere.

"Sorry about before. Ya know me. Always sticking my foot in my mouth." She'd pulled Teagan's hair up, away from her face and the toilet; a human scrunchee.

"It's okay Lyss. I'm just overwhelmed." Teagan pulled away and propped against the counter across from the toilet.

"I know, right?" Alyssa gave a crooked smile.

Ellie rummaged through a shelf. "Here. Brush your teeth." She put a brand new toothbrush on the counter.

"Yeah. You smell like Ells did after Ryan puked on her at Erica's party last year." Alyssa laughed.

Ellie punched Alyssa in the arm.

Alyssa stumbled and fell into the tub. "Bitch"

Teagan couldn't help but smile.

After brushing her teeth several times, she went back into the bedroom where Ellie and Alyssa lay on the bed, staring at the ceiling.

Ellie sat up. "What's the verdict, Tea Bags?"

When someone mentioned pro-choice she'd gotten a knot in her stomach and wanted to punch the idiot in the throat. Even though it scared the holy shit out of her, she'd made up her mind. "There's no way in hell I'm letting anyone rip this baby out of me."

Alyssa's eyes widened. "Ya wanna keep it? Are you out of your mind? Uh uh. No way in hell! Fuck that! It's not a baby. It's a genetically mutated monster that eats people. Didn't you watch the news? Those things are chewing their way out of their mothers." She poked Teagan in the stomach. Tears welled in her eyes and streamed down her cheeks. "I can't lose you Teag. You gotta get that thing outta you." Her arms draped around Teagan and she cried.

Teagan squeezed Alyssa close. "I can't kill it," she whispered. "No matter what it is, it's still my baby . . . my choice."

Ellie hugged and looked Teagan in the eyes. "Then you'd better pray your mom fixes this before that thing comes out." She patted Teagan's stomach.

Alyssa held up her cell phone. "Check out what I found."

Teagan wiped the tears out of her eyes and focused on the small screen. "What?"

"It's a safe-house in Corvallis. Someone just posted it on Facebook. They'll harbor you and help deliver the baby. There's a number, want me to call it?"

"Okay." Teagan sniffled.

Alyssa walked into the bathroom, dialing. Teagan couldn't hear her and didn't really care at that point. Her eyes were bloodshot, her stomach hurt and all she wanted to do was curl up next to Ellie and sleep.

Alyssa stepped back into the room.

"Well?" Ellie asked.

"They gave me another phone number to call when we get to Corvallis. Teag, you wanna go?"

"What about my mom?" Teagan still didn't know what to tell her mom. She'd probably bring her to the hospital and perform the abortion herself.

Alyssa stuffed her phone in the front pocket of her jeans. "You don't tell her nothin'. If ya wanna try and have the baby, then you can't tell anyone except us and whoever the hell we run into at the shelter thing."

Ellie pulled on her brown leather jacket. "It's settled. We tell no-one, even our moms. So, let's get to steppin'. "

"Now?" Teagan's heart raced.

Ellie and Alyssa both helped her up.

"Yeah. Right fucking now. Get your prego ass off the floor and let's bounce." Ellie pulled on Teagan's arm.

"I'm driving, bitches." Alyssa dangled Teagan's keys.

"As if!" Ellie snatched them from Alyssa's hands.

"You little bitch, give 'em back." Alyssa swiped for them, but Ellie moved her hand too quick and she missed them by an inch.

"Both of you shut the fuck up. I'm fine to drive. It's not like I'm drunk." She held out her hand and Ellie dropped the keys into her palm.

"Shotgun!" Ellie called out.

"Dammit, Elle, I never get to sit in front." Alyssa folded her arms.

Teagan smiled. "Whose lap do you think I'm going to hurl on?"

"On second thought." Ellie waved her arms forward. "It's all yours Lyss.

The two girls giggled, but not Teagan. She couldn't laugh. Her mind chastised her. It screamed at her stupidity. First for not making the jerk wear a condom, then for not having the guts to tell her mother, and most of all, for saying she would have whatever thing she had growing inside of her.

25.

On Ross's GPS, Independence Oregon fit between Salem and Monmouth like a chewed up puzzle piece split in half by the Willamette River. From Highway 22, the GPS took him on some winding back road. Things seemed normal until he hit the twenty-five mile-per hour sign and rolled into downtown Independence. Businesses were shut down, windows boarded up, and lights turned off. Other than street lamps the only lights he saw came from flashing lights behind several building.

When he turned the corner onto Monmouth Street, lights from emergency vehicles ricocheted off the rigs windshield. A fire truck sat in the road sideways, blocking any oncoming traffic from the west. Two patrol cars did the same on the east side. Between the vehicles sat an ambulance, a Jeep with emergency markings all over it; probably the fire chief's, the sheriff's cruiser and The Independence police station.

He clicked the button on the CB radio. "Salem dispatch. This is Agent Harris. Do you copy?"

"Dispatch, what can I do for you agent?" A young man's voice came over the radio.

"Can you try and call the Independence Police station for me? I need to know what's going on inside. Also, get SWAT over here as soon as possible."

"Yes, sir. I'll see what I can do. Over." Muffled gun shots cracked through the silence and a flicker of light flashed in the window of the police station.

"I'm gonna need all the help I can get. Over."

"Dispatch copies, Agent Harris. Good luck."

"Thanks. I'm gonna need it." He pulled over and retrieved the riot shotgun from the back seat. "C'mon, baby." He kissed the handle of the gun and started for the police station, staying low and out of the light. He had no idea what he might encounter and prayed the shotgun could bring down one of them.

"Agent Harris, this is Dispatch." The voice over the radio startled him.

He pulled the hand held from his belt. "Go ahead, Dispatch."

"No-one's answering at the station. The line goes to the voice-mail. Usually at this time of night, I can get someone there. What's going on?"

"I'll let you know when I find out. What about SWAT?"

"They're at the other scene, surrounding the house. I've been told that they have one of those things trapped inside."

Ross didn't think it possible. No-one could trap one of these creatures. Unless . . . it wanted to be trapped. She'd set up a reverse trap.

"Can you patch me through to the SWAT team leader right now?" Ross asked, the realization they may be dead sat heavy in his chest.

"Sure. Give me one second."

After a few agonizing seconds and another gunshot from within the building the SWAT guy came on the line. "Sergeant George here." His voice had a rasp to it. Either he'd been smoking his entire life, or yelling.

"Sergeant, it's good to hear your voice. This is Agent Ross Harris. I'm at the Independence Police Station. There's no-one to be seen inside or out and I heard shots fired from inside. No telling what we're up against in there. Think you can spare me a couple of your team members for some backup? I know you're not too far from here. I think Sheriff Lawson's in the building, over."

"Roger that. I've got a few men I can spare and still keep the house surrounded until you get here. This one isn't going anywhere. We've got her pinned down."

"I wouldn't be too sure of that. They witnessed one of them jump across the river today. It's probably the one you have surrounded."

"With the fire power I've got out here, there's no way she's getting through us, or, over us." He chuckled. "I'll get some men out your way after I shuffle things around a bit out here. Don't do anything stupid. They'll be there in ten."

"Thanks." Ross put the handheld back on his belt.

Ten minutes? What the hell are they thinking? With lives at stake, ten minutes might as well be two hours.

Again the report of gunfire came from somewhere within the police station. From the distinct bang the gun made, it had to be from Sheriff Lawson's cannon. Ross snuck from car to car. He kept to the shadows and any line of sight the creature inside might have on him. At each vehicle he crept by, praying there wouldn't be any bodies in them and checking for weaponry.

A megaphone lay on the ground below the open door of the sheriff's cruiser. He thought to use it to contact whoever might still be alive in the building, but his gut told him it would be a bad move. His best bet would be to catch the Trill off guard, maybe get a lucky shot.

Basic instincts screamed at him not to go into the building as he came to the front door. Blood spatter covered the insides of the glass. A glow from the light within lit the murk revealing several clear spots he could see through. Inside the building, there was no movement, no sound.

Ross's heart pounded. Sweat poured from his brow. He pushed open the door with his right foot and shone his flashlight inside. His gut wrenched and he swallowed to keep from vomiting.

Inside to the right, and parallel to the wall, stood a long wooden desk. Blood smeared the floor leading to the desk as if a mountain lion had killed a small deer and dragged it back to its den.

His eyes went wide.

Across the crimson soaked desk lay the body of what used to be a female police officer. The woman's legs had been spread apart. Blood dripped down the insides of her bared thighs. Multiple gashes in her upper back ended where her skirt and panties dangled in bloody strands. The horrific damage to the woman's backside made him erupt from within. Vomit splattered and mingled with the puddle of blood which oozed across the floor.

He looked away from the carnage, wiped his mouth on his shirt and continued through the station. Light glistened off the pale walls, revealing several smeared hand prints. The morbid path, which looked as if a child had gotten carried away with the red finger paint, led to a room on the right. His hope of finding survivors dwindled as he slowly opened the door.

26.

ALEXA READ THE results again. "Are you sure?"

Ray nodded. "Yeah."

Her trust in Ray's work had never faltered, however, millions of lives hung in the balance of these results. "Do it again."

"I've already done the test four times."

"Again, Ray. We have to be sure. If not, we could kill the mother and child."

"Okay. I'll run it again." He scurried out the door.

She searched through her pocket until she found her phone. On the fourth ring Teagan's voice-mail message came on.

"You've reached Teagan. ("Tea Bags" chimed Ellie. "I'm with my girls, probably getting some fro yo, so leave a message and I'll call or text; if you deserve it. Peace out."

The line beeped.

"Young lady, I've asked you time and again to please keep your phone on. Especially with everything going on right now, I need to know you're safe. Call me immediately." Then she said something she rarely ever said, "I love you. Call me back. Please."

She'd never been one to easily say those words to anyone, not even her own daughter and had only told her husband a handful of times. He'd say, "Why don't you ever say that you love me?" She'd answer, "Because if you say it too much, one day it will no longer be true. The words jumble back into letters and cease to be emotions. They become a scratched record that gets stuck on a line over and over until someone lifts the needle." He'd answered, "But if it never got to that line in the first place, we wouldn't have what we have." He'd flipped a picture of Teagan out of his wallet, effectively ending the conversation.

When he passed, she thought those words died with him, that her record had been smashed against the wall. She realized this was the first time she'd said those words since his passing and hated herself for it. To blame her non-emotional father or verbally abusive mother on her intimacy issues would be ridiculous. If she knew one thing, she knew that she had control of her emotions. She owned herself and could give herself to whoever she wanted.

She texted Teagan: *Please call ASAP. 911—MOM.*

She had to get back to work. If the test came out positive again, she'd know her idea had worked. Something no-one had ever accomplished . . . extract a gene from a live fetus, using DNA from the stem cell to cease or destroy a mutation. What could this possibly mean? The end of genetic disorders as we know them, no more cystic fibrosis, sickle cell anemia, trisomy 13, and any other physical or mental disorders known to man. She sat back, studying the calculations on her computer as she waited for the final results and a call back from Teagan.

27.

Ross GASPED AND nearly pissed himself. Tucked in the corner of the dispatch room, amongst kiosks with telephones and computer monitors, were bodies—at least six. Each person had met a horrific end. Several had their hearts ripped out. A male officer's head rested at the center of his spine. His eyes wide open, staring at Ross as if to say 'why weren't you here to save me.' Streams of blood flowed from the corpses in the room.

Ross checked the bodies, making sure Sheriff Lawson wasn't amongst the dead. One of the bodies he found wore civilian clothes. He figured the man might be the little girl's father. The one he came to question, but no child. A cringe shot through him as he imagined what might have happened.

One of the officers had a chain thick with keys hanging from his belt. Ross leaned over and unlatched them, then secured them inside his front pocket, hoping they wouldn't make any noise as he searched the rest of the station.

"Agent Harris?"

Ross grabbed thee radio and clicked off the receiver. If the Trill didn't already know he was there, it did now. He wiped his sweat-laden palms on his pants and tightened his grip on the shotgun. Then he waited for what seemed like an eternity. His ears tuned in to every sound in the station: the click of the wall clock every second, a hum from one of the lights above him and something else; a patter of feet, down the hall.

From the outside the building had looked small. He didn't think there could be much more to it; maybe a small court room, an interrogation room, lunch room, and holding cells.

If I were being chased by an indestructible creature, where would I go?

The jail cells.

He backed out of the room into the hallway.

Still empty.

The lunch room door wobbled on one hinge, blocking entrance into the small room. Through a crack in the door he saw a pool of blood in the center of the room. *Poor bastards. Several bodies would have to be drained to make a pool that big.* He backed away and continued down the hall. Past the empty interrogation room on his right he came to a large metal door with a small slit in the center.

Locked. He tugged the handle again to make sure. With a light hand he extracted the keys from his front pocket. They clinked and he grabbed them, listening close to make sure he hadn't alerted anyone, or thing, to his presence.

Ross tried two of the keys to no avail, but the third spun 180 degrees. The door clicked and swung open. Jail cells with wrought iron bars lined the long concrete hallway. They faced a wall with a single red fire alarm in the center.

"Anyone here," he whispered.

A faint whimper came from one of the cells.

"Shhh . . . I'll be there in a second. Where did it go?"

A dainty hand came from the last cell on the right and pointed down a second hallway directly in front of the cell.

Shit. Didn't even see it. The situation couldn't be worse. At least he knew the creature wasn't behind him. But it would be tricky to get to that cell without being seen.

The door clicked shut as he slipped into the dank hallway.

Again the hand appeared, this time it motioned him to stop.

Ross froze. A faint scraping noise came from down the hall.

A moment later the hand motioned him to come.

Man. This is a brave little girl. He hated the idea of telling her that her dad had died. For now he crouched with the shotgun pointed toward the hallway opposite and crept forward. After a few steps he'd pause and listen. The closer he got to the occupied cell, the more he could hear the girl as she tried to stifle her sniffles.

Dribbles of blood disappeared into a room to the left down the other hallway. More blood led to an open door with the words 'Emergency Exit' above in neon lights. Ross turned around.

Inside the locked cell a little blonde girl huddled in a corner. On the cot next to her lay what looked like the lifeless body of the sheriff. From the description of the girl over the radio, Ross knew this girl had to be one of the survivors from the Independence attack down the road.

"Are you okay sweetie."

She nodded.

"Ok. I'm gonna get you out of there. Is it still in the building?"

She nodded again and pointed down the hall.

Now what? Any second he could be face—to-face with one of the creatures. If he could get inside the cell and wait for SWAT, maybe he'd have a chance.

The mangled bars bent in, some out and some stretched wide, but no gap big enough for a person to squeeze through.

"Has it come back?"

She shook her head.

"Is it the same one you saw at your house?"

Her eyes went wide and she shook her head; an emphatic *no.*

"I'm going to try and open this lock." He looked behind him. The hall remained empty and he couldn't hear anything coming from the room to the left. *What the hell is that thing doing in there?* "If you see *it* behind me, let me know, okay?"

She nodded.

He tried each key, inching them in one at a time until the cell door clicked. His knuckles blanched as he gripped the bars and pushed. The door wouldn't budge. He'd made enough noise to alert the creature. With his shoulder into it, he watched the girl for any signs of the creature behind him, and shoved. The bars ground hard as they opened.

The girl squeezed further into the corner, nearly crawling under the cot.

Puffs of agonized air whistled through the unconscious sheriff's bush of a mustache. When he inhaled, his barrel chest rose up and down. Blood seeped through a pillowcase she'd wrapped around his head. *Smart girl.*

On the ground in front of her lay the sheriff's revolver and a rifle. Ejected casings from the rifle and pistol littered the floor.

"Did you use those?"

The timid girl shook her head and pointed at the sheriff.

Traumatized. She'd watched her father and who knows how many others slaughtered by the beast. Such horrors would stay with her the rest of her life.

No way in hell I'm gonna get him out of here and still keep this one safe. "I think we have to leave him for now, sweetie."

The girl latched onto Sheriff Lawson's arm and held tight.

"He'll be safe in here. I promise." Ross held his hand out to her.

Her hands trembles as she reached for him.

"Okay. Let's get you out of here." He took her outstretched hand and helped her stand.

She slouched, her head down. Beautiful straight-blonde hair tussled from the night's activities hid her face and eyes. The girl swayed to his right and peeked behind him. Hair whipped from her face as she snapped her head back. Both eyes flew wide open. Her entire body shook as she held her arm up and pointed behind him.

28.

TEAGAN COULDN'T BELIEVE how many emergency vehicles zipped past. They still had an hour drive to get to Corvallis and having to pull over every few minutes sure pissed her off. According to Alyssa's constant internet updates, they'd closed the OSU campus and locked down the dorms. Even the calmest of their friends had gone ape shit online. Still, they should be able to find the people running the shelter.

Alyssa pushed between the seats. "We need to stop somewhere. I gotta pee like a race horse."

"Nice Lyssa." Ellie glared at her. "You'd think you're the preggo. I swear she has the bladder of a ninety-year-old spinster." She looked at Teagan, but cocked her thumb toward Alyssa.

"No. I have to pee too. There's a 7-11 up here. We stopped there on a beer run a couple of times." Teagan pointed forward.

"Good. Hurry the fuck up." Alyssa bounced in her seat.

They pulled into the gas station. The bell dinged twice. No-one came out.

"Full service my ass." Ellie got out and slammed her door. "Good thing you don't need any gas."

Alyssa hopped out of the back seat. "Where's the pisser?" She began tapping away on her phone.

Teagan grabbed her arm. "Inside, c'mon, my eyes are floating." She pulled harder on her arm. Sometimes Alyssa needed to be gently coaxed into doing what she set out to do in the first place.

The girls entered the store. The cold quiet sent waves of needles up Teagan's spine. None of it seemed right. No-one stood behind the counter and no customers wondering about. The restroom sign directly in front of her beckoned and she dragged Alyssa away from a magazine rack, where the latest copy of *Seventeen* had caught her attention.

She yanked her arm from Teagan's grip. "Wait. Taylor broke up with another boyfriend. I've gotta see who she's porking now."

"I'll be in the bathroom." Teagan felt as if her bladder would burst any moment. Still, a nagging feeling overcame her as she pushed the bathroom door open and locked it behind her. Were they completely alone?

After she washed her hands, she splashed cold water across her face. Hot flashes come with the whole being 'pregnant' thing and she figured that's why she couldn't stop sweating and her mouth felt like someone stuffed it full of cotton. Through the wheeze of the jet dryer she heard a scream.

The scream continued as she fumbled with the lock, her hands still not completely dry.

"What the fuck Lyss," she heard Ellie say before she got the door open.

The gut wrench returned as the door slammed against the wall and she saw Ellie with her arms wrapped around Alyssa, who sobbed into her shoulder. Teagan searched the room for whatever had spooked her.

"Look behind the counter." Ellie flicked her head toward the cash register counter.

Blood spatter across the linoleum floor behind the counter looked like a macabre psych evaluation card the school counselor made her look at once. Bat or Elephant ears? A choice she hated more than anything. What the hell did it mean if you picked one or the other? Teagan already knew she was a psycho. Crazy for wanting to have this child.

Teagan inched around the counter. Not super excited to see where the blood came from, she closed her eyes for a moment. When she reached the edge of the counter she opened them. Her terror meter hit *tilt*. Sprawled on the floor lay a young man and luckily she'd vomited up everything in her stomach earlier. A rancid smell of death wafted from the body and she dry-heaved.

The guy couldn't have been more than nineteen. He lay face up with his eyes wide and mouth agape. Blood had encrusted on his cheeks and neck. A hole torn through his work apron, blue-collared shirt and chest, where his heart should have been, had dried and flies flitted in and out.

"You think it's still here?" Ellie propped her elbows on the counter.

Teagan turned. "Fuck if I know. Maybe, but the blood on his chest is dry, so I bet it left. The guy on the radio said they eat and eat and won't stop. You see any more people for it to eat here?"

Ellie looked at Teagan, Alyssa, and herself. "Duh!"

"We need to get the fuck out. Now!" Alyssa bolted for the door.

"Shit, Lyssa. Ellie! Stop her!" Teagan nearly leapt the counter.

Ellie caught Alyssa at the door where she collapsed into Ellie's arms and both slumped against the glass. Tears poured down Alyssa's face.

Teagan went to her friends. "We have to be smart about this." She knelt next to them. "Survey the area before making a run for the car."

Alyssa looked up from Ellie's bosom. "You . . . you said it was gone. Is it? Or isn't it?"

"I don't know. Not for sure. That's why we need to be smart." Teagan put her hand on Alyssa's shoulder.

Ellie stood with Alyssa and handed her off to Teagan. "I'm gonna check behind the counter for a gun. Most of these places have guns."

"Good idea." Teagan's eyes roamed the shelves for some sort of weapon. They settled on a pair of scissors. *I'd have to get too close to use those.* In the corner of the same shelf, she found a can of WD-40. "This is flammable right." She held the can above her head.

"Yup," Ellie called out from behind the counter.

Good. Now if I could just find . . . "Sweet." She pulled a foot-long lighter from its package and tested it out. With the WD-40 in one hand she pulled out the slim plastic tube and connected it to the nozzle. She'd seen her daddy do this many times for squeaky cupboard doors. Her mother hated the sound of a cupboard creaking more than just about anything, except for mud on her plush carpet. Desecration of the Berber could mean the gallows for the perpetrator.

Once she'd connected the nozzle she tried out her makeshift flame thrower. The foot-long lighter and nozzle worked perfect. The flame shot out five feet in front of her and she couldn't even feel the heat on her hands. "Check this . . . " she started to say.

Ellie popped up from behind the counter. "Got it." She held a pistol in her hand.

"No shit, really? Can't believe you actually found one." Teagan put her weapon in a duffel bag she found.

Ellie slid back over the counter. "Yeah bitches, I'm packin' now."

Teagan didn't know how to use a gun. Point and shoot. Didn't seem like rocket science to her. "Where the hell did you find that?"

"Under the dead guy."

"Gross," Alyssa said from the glass door.

"He emptied a full clip into one of those things."

"Are there any extra bullets?" Teagan figured if they had a gun, they'd need something to shoot out of it.

"It's empty. But I found a box under the counter." She clicked a lever and the magazine popped out from the bottom of the gun. Then she started putting shells into the clip she held in her hand.

"Where'd you learn that?" Teagan crinkled her nose.

"My dad used to be a cop."

"I didn't know that."

"Not many people do. He quit cuz he had to shoot a guy. But he used to take us to the firing range. This is a Glock 9 millimeter. I've shot one before."

Teagan sighed. "Thank God one of us knows how to use the gun; might need it if we run into one of those . . . things." With someone in the room able to fire a gun, and actually hit something, Teagan breathed easier as she looked down at her belly.

"Okay. Let's get the hell out of here. Teag, should we go home?" Ellie stuffed the gun into the front of her jeans.

The thought of going home, telling her mom and maybe getting some sort of intense lecture about responsibilities didn't sound fun. She also knew her mom wouldn't let her keep the baby. She'd made up her mind. "The college is closer. I say we get to the safe house."

Alyssa had both hands and her nose to the glass of the front door. "I wanna go home!"

Ellie crouched next to her. "Don't worry, Lyssa. We'll go to the safe house, get Teagan set up and stay the night there. It'll be safer than driving home. Right now, we need to get to safety. This place obviously isn't safe and one of those things is out there – somewhere."

"Ya think?" Alyssa's eyes widened.

"No worries baby, I got this." Ellie pulled the weapon from her pants. She yanked on the top and a metal piece came out which snapped back when she let go. "Locked and loaded."

The girls gathered by the door. Ellie crept out first, the gun waving side to side in front of her. Though she seemed brave, her hand shook.

"Is it clear?" Teagan held Alyssa's hand, ready to run if they had to.

"Yeah. Not even a car on the road."

The blank look on Alyssa's face worried Teagan. "It'll be okay, Lyssa. Just stick by me and Ells."

Teagan took a few cautious steps and glanced about the area to make sure no creatures lurked. The clouds parted, revealing an infant evening. Stars twinkled. They reminded her of the nursery story her daddy used to tell her before bed. But she didn't have to worry about the location of these stars. Still their twinkle made her miss her daddy. *Damn. More tears. Gotta be tough, for Lyss.*

"Looks clear to me," Ellie half whispered.

Teagan scanned the area one last time.

Ellie dashed to the car and opened the passenger's front and back doors. Then she motioned for Teagan.

Lyssa sat with her arms wrapped around her knees. Teagan reached down and pulled her up. "A little fucking help would be nice, Lyss." With Alyssa's arm wrapped around her neck like a wounded soldier, Teagan dragged her to the car. She stuffed her in the back seat and buckled her in.

Ellie kept guard. "Hurry up!"

"I am." Teagan ran around to the driver's side. For a moment she searched her pockets for the keys.

"They're in the ignition." Ellie flicked the keys against the console.

With a sigh, Teagan started the car. She sped out of the convenience store parking lot and bottomed out in a large pothole.

"OMG, Teag." Ellie grabbed the ceiling.

"Sorry."

Ellie rubbed her head.

"Might wanna put your seatbelt on?" Teagan smirked.

"No shit." Ellie rolled her eyes.

Teagan stopped talking. Her mind raced as they headed into the vast farm country between Tigard and Corvallis. Cows on one side of the street, rows and rows of corn on the other and every so often a small boarded up house.

Several miles down the road Teagan broke the silence. "Let's listen to some music." She turned on the satellite radio and switched it to current hits.

Ellie sang along.

The soft melody calmed Teagan. She noticed in the rear-view mirror that Alyssa had closed her eyes. Her head drifted to the left. She looked at peace.

"She asleep?"

"Let's hope."

Teagan let out a few long, slow breaths.

"You okay?"

Ellie's despondent eyes freaked Teagan out. "I'm good. Really, Ellie. We should be more worried abou . . . "

A loud crunch of metal jostled the car. Teagan bit her lip. "Fuck!"

The steering wheel spun out of her hands as the car slid across lanes. Teagan stared out the window, wide-eyed. The side of the car thumped into dirt. Airbags exploded as the car toppled. Teagan clenched her eyes. Her world twisted, turned, and went black.

29.

THE LITTLE GIRL'S high-pitched shriek sent a tremor of fear through Ross. Somewhere behind them lurked a predator. Ross had seen the carnage the creature left behind. Sweat trickled off his nose as he prepped for the attack. But he wouldn't go without raising hell. Moments crept like slugs up a slide. He took one arm off of the girl and gripped the hand cannon he'd stuffed in his belt. *I hope you reloaded this thing.* The sheriff laid on the cot as if he'd taken a catnap on a slow day.

Its shadow blazed across the wall in front of him, unnerving, motionless. Over his shoulder Ross could make out the silhouette in the exit doorway. The warm glow of the street lights shone off his bald head. Not thick like a body builder, the man had tight defined muscles, like those found in men's fitness magazines. One apparent anatomical issue stood out. It had no genitals; a Ken doll with glowing eyes, rows of jagged razor sharp teeth, and claws that could skewer a man. Its eyes had a soft red glow; heavy with intent as they dipped, resting on the girl.

She hugged Ross tighter and hid her face in his stomach.

With his left arm he pulled her close. Her body trembled against his. He'd set his shotgun down, but still had the sheriff's pistol.

The girl whispered into his chest, "Daddy said don't make sudden moves, just back up slow."

"Shhhh." Ross patted her on the back.

The Trill seemed to stay in the doorway as long as they didn't move. An appendage peaked out from between two flaps of vertical skin between its legs. The snake-like form slipped until it dangled back and forth like a sick pendulum. Its eyes burned dark amber as they settled on the girl.

What now?

The limp appendage thickened.

Ross cringed.

While it appeared to be a man's normal, large erection, a three hundred sixty degree hood flared around the head. Barbs flexed in and out towards the creature's torso like the hood of a horned lizard. Ross understood where the damage to the women had come from.

"It's going to kill us, isn't it?" The girl pressed her face further into Ross's chest as if she wanted to crawl inside and hide.

"No, sweetie. I'm not going to let it."

The creature lunged at them.

Ross shoved the girl back into the cell. She stumbled and landed on her rump. Ross dove to close the cell door as the creature blasted down the hall. One of the bent bars caught on a straight one and the door wouldn't slide shut.

Heavy machine gun fire snapped through the hall. The force of the bullets forced the Trill against the wall, a few feet from the cell door.

Ross covered the girl so she wouldn't get hit by any stray bullets. The Trill retreated further down the hall. A small trickle of blood followed.

"Cease fire! We're humans."

The SWAT unit down the hall stopped firing.

Obviously a few of the bullets had hit soft tissue on the creature. But where? How long before it recovered?

Several heavily-armed, fully-armored SWAT team members hurtled down the hall. Two of them went after the Trill; two entered the cell.

"Agent Harris?" The smaller of the two put his gloved hand on Ross's shoulder.

"Yeah. Take the girl." Ross handed the girl to the man. She lunged back into him and wrapped her arms tight around his waist.

Ross hugged her and nodded toward the SWAT member. "It'll be okay, sweetie. Go with officer . . . er . . . "

"Franklin, Sir."

"Go with Officer Franklin. He'll keep you safe."

Franklin knelt next to the girl. "Come on, Sweets. Let's get you out of here. You ever seen the inside of an armored truck?"

She shook her head. Her eyes wide, her skin wet with fear.

"Well, boy have I got a treat for you. There's lots of fun stuff inside."

She took the man's hand, cautious fingers limp inside his. Franklin scooped her up and whisked her down the hall.

"Help me get the sheriff." Ross looked at the other SWAT member.

Two SWAT members stood in the hall firing their automatic weapons into the room on the left. The creature appeared as if out of nowhere and slammed his hands through their chests. Blood sloshed against the wall behind them.

"Take him." Ross helped hoist the sheriff onto the officer's shoulder.

The officer waddled down the hall, with his burden in a modified fireman's carry, knees buckling under the weight.

Blood gushed from the hunks of human flesh in the Trill's hands. Strands of other organs still attached dangled from the hearts like tentacles. The Trill held the hunk of flesh to his nose and sniffed long and hard. He took a large bite of the heart one in his right hand. He chewed, swallowed, and bit into the next one. Blood covered almost all of the creature's body.

With his foot against the opposite wall, Ross heaved at the door. The bars scraped and screeched as it loosened in the frame.

The Trill turned its attention on Ross. It dropped the half-eaten hearts and raced toward him. Ross dove forward and to the right. His shoulder slammed against the wall as the Trill sailed over him and crashed into the back of the jail cell.

"Gotcha, sucker!" He kicked the cell closed.

It turned and slammed into the tough metal. An inhuman high-pitched wail came from him as he rammed into it over and over again. Ross slapped both hands over his ears and waited for the fit to end.

30.

AN AGONIZED CRY woke Teagan. The seatbelt dug into her shoulder and pinched her right boob. Blood dripped from a gash above her left eye. To her right, Ellie looked much the same, swaying in her seatbelt upside down.

"El . . . El . . . " Teagan pushed her hand against Ellie's arm.

Ellie stirred, but didn't wake.

Teagan continued pushing on Ellie's shoulder. "El . . . wake up, El."

Ellie moaned and wriggled around each time Teagan poked her. Even though her airbag had deployed, a spider web crack in the front windshield and the smears of blood on Ellie's forehead and face told Teagan the device hadn't worked that well.

Teagan stretched her head around. A lump welled in her throat and her heart flip-flopped in her chest. The passenger-side door and Alyssa weren't there. Teagan figured she'd probably been ejected from the vehicle when it flipped.

Another gut wrenching screech echoed through the night.

"That's Lyssa." *She probably woke up in the middle of the field, broken, bruised—lost.*

Teagan reached around and swiped at the seat belt latch. Her bloody fingers slipped and slid over the mechanism. She screamed in frustration and wiped the blood on her pants. The gash in her brow throbbed. Blood poured down her forehead, into her hair and pooled on the ceiling of the car.

Again she tried to release herself. "Fucking piece of shit! Let me out!" After taking a couple of deep breaths, she calmed down. There had to be another way out of the seatbelt. Then she remembered an item she kept in the console between the seats which could help her.

When she pulled open the lid the contents fell out. Several tampons, three different colors of lipstick, her cell phone, and her manicure kit crashed to the roof. While she wanted to grab the phone and call for help first, she needed to get free and find Alyssa. She grabbed the kit and pulled out the manicure scissors. Surprised at how well the scissors worked, Teagan cut at the belt just under her breasts.

"Wha . . . what happened?" Ellie pushed on the crushed ceiling below her.

"We crashed, I'm stuck. Cutting myself loose. Lyssa's missing. Can you get free?'

Ellie checked back seat. "Is she okay? Did she go for help?"

"I don't know, but I heard her scream a little while ago." Teagan continued cutting at the strap.

"Why didn't you just . . . " Ellie pushed Teagan's seat belt button.

Teagan dropped and landed on her head. Her body flopped into the seat. Her foot hit something.

"Ow!" Ellie pushed Teagan's foot away from her face.

"Are you hurt?" Teagan asked.

"My head feels like shit. I think I busted out my window."

Ellie wiped at the blood on her forehead. "Me too. My forehead's killing me. Can you get out?"

"Yeah. I think I can get through. I'll come get you." The crushed door didn't leave much room, but she might fit.

"Okay." Ellie released herself.

Teagan clutched tufts of ragweed and pulled herself free from the wreckage. The cool, moist grass stunk of sewer water. Someone told her once sewage was used to water some of the farm land. Her nose crinkled at the stench.

She flipped onto her back.

Dark gray clouds crept below a crescent moon. She took a deep breath and got to her knees. All of her parts worked as they should. The blood on her forehead had slowed to a trickle and she wiped some from her left eye with her un-tucked t-shirt.

"You okay out there?" Ellie's voice came muffled.

"I'm so far from fucking okay it's pitiful. But I'm not hurt, other than my head."

"Wish I could say the same."

"What's wrong?"

"I think I broke my foot."

"Shit." Now she had a lame friend and one missing.

Teagan wobbled. She held onto her demolished car for balance and walked around the back side.

A scream of sheer terror permeated the air. Spindles of red-hot gooseflesh squiggled up and down her spine. To Teagan, the sound reminded her of someone being tortured, not a plea for help. On the other side of the car she saw the path through throws of tall grass the car made when they crashed. "Gonna be hard to find her in the dark."

Another shriek, followed by violent grunts one after another, brought a lump to Teagan's throat. "Ell?"

"What? Get your ass over here and help me out."

"I think one of those things is attacking Lyss." She crept to the passenger side door.

Ellie crawled through the passenger side where her window had also been broken. "What the hell's going on out there?"

Teagan knelt next to Ellie. "Lyssa's out there. Can you stand?"

"I think so." Ellie held onto Teagan as she lifted her to her feet. "Ow! Ow!" She hopped on her left foot.

Teagan looked into Ellie's eyes. "We need help. I'm gonna try and find my cell."

"I saw it fall out of that middle thing when you opened it." Ellie sat next to the car, her back leaned against the upside down wheel well below the front tire.

"I saw it too." Teagan crawled back inside the car. The grunts from the field continued. Alyssa's cries had died down. Teagan thought she heard her whimper, but it could have been the wind.

"Found it." Teagan pulled the phone from between the fractured passenger seat and the center console. She frantically hit the buttons, praying she'd get someone.

"9-1-1 what's your emergency," a soft, inviting female voice said.

"We're on Highway ninety nine, between highway twenty two and Monmouth. We crashed in a field."

"Are you hurt?"

"No. I mean . . . yes. Well, I'm not, but my friend broke her foot and I think our other friend is being attacked by one of those things."

"Did you see the creature?" The question seemed more personal than business.

"No, but I can hear it . . . um . . . attacking her."

"I'll get police and an ambulance there right away. You need to get as far away from that thing as possible. Don't try to be heroes, just go the opposite direction until you can't hear it anymore. I beg you. "

"Okay. Thanks."

Teagan clicked end as the dispatcher cried out, "Don't hang . . . "

"Well?" Ellie tried to get to her feet.

Teagan turned to Ellie. "They're sending someone and she said we need to get far away."

"Damn straight." Ellie hobbled over to Teagan.

"We have to help her." Teagan squeezed the phone.

"What? I think you hit your head harder than I hit mine."

Teagan handed the phone to Ellie. "Take this."

"What do you want me to do?"

"Stay in contact with someone. Anyone."

"What are you doing?" Her blood crusted eyebrow lifted.

"It's Lyssa, El. I gotta try." Teagan rummaged around the inside of the car. "Where's the fucking gun?"

"What?"

"Where's the gun?"

"How should I know?"

"Fuck." *Now what?* Maybe she could find something in the trunk. She crawled into the back seat and felt around until she found the secret latch. "Damn fat ass." Her hips barely fit through the hole into the trunk. Inside she pulled the carpet down. The jack and tire iron fell and almost hit her in the head. Her makeshift flamethrower was sitting on the ceiling, but the tire iron had a sharp end to it and she figured it would do better than if she just flashed some flames at the monster.

"What do you think you're gonna do with that?" Ellie hobbled scooted toward Teagan when she exited the car.

"I really don't know. But I'm going out there."

"Teag, you're gonna get yourself killed."

"Pray I don't." Teagan crouched and followed the sounds coming from somewhere in the dark.

31.

THE TRILL'S CLAWS scraped wrought iron like a rake against chalkboard. Ross's heart pounded as he suspected the bars to give out at any second. He aimed the long, fat barrel of the Sheriff's .44 between its eyes. "Give me a reason you piece of shit, c'mon!"

It strained and pulled against the metal, even until its pallid face turned blue. The bars only moved a fraction of an inch. In a flurry, it slammed its fists and shoulders into the three-foot wall behind it. Chips and small chunks of brick sprinkled to the floor. After a few minutes, and a hearty chuckle from Ross, it gave up. Tiny shards of bone poked through the skin on its hands and shoulders. Blood trickled from the wounds. Each shoulder also looked dislocated and several cracks of skin and lumps covered its scalp.

Cuts stitched together. Bones snapped into place. Joints realigned and the bruises disappeared as if the injuries had been erased from a drawing. Other than the Ken doll-ish genital area the creature in the cell had the physiology of a hairless young adult male. Not one hair on its head, no eyebrows, no chest hair and no pubes. The plastic look freaked Ross out, but most of all; its eyes send chills through Ross. The glossed-over shards of wet coal filled the entire area around an almost Neolithic raised brow bone.

"Where the hell did you come from?" Ross slammed his hand against the bars.

The Trill stopped pacing, turned and glared at Ross. Those eyes, ebony pools of carnal thought, burned into him. It stared at his chest and licked thick, calloused lips that curled into a snarl with two rows of razor-sharp teeth.

"You want it? Come and get it? Not so tough trapped in there are you, Guy?" He kicked the side of the cage. "That's your name from now on, you goddamn murdering bastard."

Guy sniffed the air as if taking a whiff of a fresh baked pie. Froth oozed from the corners of his mouth. He opened his mouth and let out a high-pitched screech, like several wolves howling.

A call came over the radio. "Independence Fire and Rescue, Monmouth Fire Department, Medic Three, respond with local police to an MVA Highway ninety-nine between Highway twenty-two and Monmouth. This is a single car accident. The caller thinks one of the creatures may be involved."

Ross heard all of the units copy.

"Dispatch, this is Sergeant George. All units hold off until SWAT gets there. We're sending a rig now, over."

"Copy, Sergeant George."

The rest of the units copied.

A moment later sirens blared from outside. Where the hell did the fire department come from? Ross wanted to go, but knew he needed to stay and babysit Guy. He pulled out his cell phone and clicked on Alexa's name.

"Just a minute she's playing with her toys." Ray laughed.

Alexa took the phone from Ray. "Give me that. Sorry. I was working with the centrifuge and left my cell on my desk."

Ray did a drive-by whisper. "Her toy."

"Very funny," she said. "What can I do for you, Agent Harris?"

"We have a Trill in custody." He beamed. "And you can call me Ross."

"You captured one?"

"Sure did."

"Is it still alive?"

"Yeah, he is . . . and looking at me like I'm a raw steak."

"Where, um how did you . . . "

"In Independence. He attacked the police station and we trapped him in one of the cells."

"Why do you keep calling it a him?"

"Because he's purely male, I named him 'Guy'. Don't worry; he can't get through the bars."

"Makes sense. They said in Europe they're delivering them early and keeping them in cages."

"I'm sorry, but that's insane. I think the President got it right. Those pregnancies need to be terminated. You should see the carnage here. Everyone's dead, except the sheriff and a little girl. Sonnofabitch was smart, hid in the jail cell and kept it at bay."

"That's awful. It really can't bend the bars?"

"Just a little bit, can't smash through the cement at all. The bars are too thick and he's just staring at me, standing, smelling the air."

"From what we've seen on TV, the males have an innate lust for the human heart and our females, unfortunately."

"But why such an intense sexual desire?" That's one thing he couldn't understand. Why the vicious sexual attacks?

"Any organism introduced into an environment works as hard as possible to take over. These aren't any different. How are you going to get it here?"

Ross said nothing.

"You have no idea do you."

He imagined her shaking her head. "Nope. But there's a backup plan."

"What's that?"

"They have the Staten Trill trapped inside of a house not too far from here."

"Oh. No."

The response startled him. "What?"

"If I'm right about this, the females are attracted to the males or vice versa. It seems she's been making her way to the male in your area."

"If that's the case, why hasn't she left the house yet?"

"Perhaps she knows she's in danger. I'm thinking the tri-alleles are gaining brain power as fast as they're gaining strength and age." Alexa coughed. "Excuse me."

She continued. "It will be interesting to study one up close. You have to find a way to restrain it and get it here."

"I'm thinking tranquilizer darts. See if we can knock him out. These suckers are strong."

"Don't underestimate it. See if someone can bring you a horse tranquilizer and then give it ten times the dose." She suggested.

"I'll see if I can get someone at the Oregon Zoo. They knock out elephants for god's sake."

"That would be a wise choice."

Ross gave himself a mental pat on the back. The zoo had to have a drug strong enough to knock this one out. Then, maybe an armored truck or . . .

She cut off his thoughts. "I could come to you."

"No way. It's too dangerous."

"But maybe it's the only . . . "

"No buts about it. You stay put. I'll get him to you." In that moment he knew he didn't want anything to happen to this woman. Was it because of her work? Another reason stood between them. "There's another one in the area?" he blurted.

"Really?"

"One smashed up a car not far from here."

"Male or female?"

"What?"

"The other tri-allele, is it male or female."

"I have no idea. What the hell does its sex have to do with anything?"

"I'll place a wager it's a male."

"Why's that?" The thought of another male in the area did bring up a question or two.

"To my knowledge, the Staten tri-allele is the only female anyone has encountered. Like I said before, their attraction to each other is uncanny. My tests detected a distinct pheromone emanating from the skin of the female tri-allele. Musk like a doe would send out to a buck during the rut."

"That makes sense. Is there any

"The pattern is very close to the natural pheromone a human female gives off. It's why we're attracted to some people more than others."

He laughed. "I thought you have to think someone's good looking to be sexually attracted to them."

"Not sexually . . . innately. And it's not always about looks, Agent Harris!"

Crap. Now she's mad. How to fix this? Maybe say something smart, she seems mildly amused when he says something intelligent. "So, it might be like some sort of homing beacon causing the male Trills to search out the female?"

"Exactly. I'm curious which way. If the one that attacked the car is male, then I guess we have our answer."

That made sense to him. "I'll see what I can find out."

"Ross?"

"Yeah."

"Can you hold on a minute? I'm getting a text."

"Sure."

Guy stood in the corner, his eyes fixed on a spot in the cement wall. The splendid perfection of the man-like body overwhelmed Ross. He'd never had any kind of feeling when he saw a man naked before, but the sheer perfection standing before him sent chills up his spine.

Alexa still hadn't come back. Ross could only wait and watch his captive. He mimicked Arnold Schwarzenegger's famous line in *Predator*. "What the hell are you?"

Of course, Guy had nothing to say, he didn't even turn, only stared at the wall.

"Ross! Ross!" Alexa yelled through the receiver, startling him.

The urgency and terror he felt from her made his pulse pound. "What is it?"

"The text was from Ellie. She's using Teagan's phone. I'm sending you the exact GPS coordinates now."

"Why?"

"The car accident in Monmouth . . . it's them. I mean, Teagan was in the accident." She sniffed as if she were crying. This stoic woman with the personality of quicksand actually showed some emotion. But the emotion didn't come from the doctor. No. This emotion came from a terrified mother.

"What the hell? Why are they out here?" His ears felt on fire. Why would those girls venture away from their homes. He immediately thought of his daughters, he'd be livid. But like Alexa, scared piss straight.

"She just wrote, crashed, Lys hurt, me n Ellie okay, HELP! MONSTER!"

"Holy shit. I know Police, Fire, ambulance and SWAT are on their way out there."

"Ross." Her voice trembled.

"Yeah."

"Please. Make sure they're safe? I know its breaking protocol, but we need that Trill. But it's my daughter." The plead in her voice got him

"I'll get someone to babysit Guy. He's not going anywhere. I'll bring her back. I promise."

"Thank you, Ross. Thank you . . . " She closed the connection.

Guy came out of his corner. A sinister smile crept across his face. Then Ross noticed blood flowing down Guy's chin. The stupid ass creature had completely chewed off his bottom lip. Maybe he'd bleed to death. But Ross didn't care, his priorities had changed. Guy wasn't the priority. He had to get to the girls and make sure of their safety. When he made a promise, he kept it.

32.

ON A KNEE-HIGH table in the center of a large room, a small box caught Savanna's eye. She picked it up and shook it. Her thumb grazed a button and the television set on the wall in front of her switched on.

A woman spoke and a picture of one of the infant males appeared behind her. The young one sat on the body of his host. Flesh dangled from his mouth. The woman said, "One of the creatures has been spotted roaming the streets of Hillsboro. Authorities ask that you find a safe place to hide. Lock all of your doors, get to a basement or closet as soon as possible. Do not try and engage these creatures. They are nearly impervious to conventional weapons and . . . "

Humans could try to hide. But their beacons of life drew her kind to them like fish to water.

Why hadn't the men surrounding the house attacked? If they did she'd destroy them without a moment's hesitation. The thought reminded her of something else gnawing at her inards; she hadn't eaten in some time. The food really wasn't the matter at hand. Each second more of the *chosen* entered this world. Their numbers doubled by the minute. She felt them; not only the two males in the vicinity, but twelve others heading her way. The gathering had commenced. She didn't know why finding the others had become so important, only that it needed to be done.

A powerful, agonized cry ripped through her mind. One of her males needed help. She dashed up the stairs, through the master bedroom and slipped out the window. After crawling onto the roof, she assessed the situation. Fifteen fully armed men surrounded the home. Most stood in pairs, except for one. He leaned against a fence, his weapon on the ground in front of him. A lit cigarette dangled from his lips as he flicked his fingers against his phone.

Her trajectory would put her on her side of the four foot fence. Then she could leap over him and head straight for the distressed male, but one thing began gnawing at her insides, the hunger.

The glowing hunk of meat pulsed within his chest. With each throb of the man's heart a vibrant glow of electric light coursed through the vessel in his body, calling to her. She ran barefooted, across the edge of the roof and leapt. No longer did she care about stealth. No longer did she care about the clothes on her back. No longer did she care about the feelings of the humans as she had with the father and daughter earlier. The hunger won. The hunger always won.

Splinters of wood scattered across the lawn as she burst through the fence, landing on the officer. Several jagged stakes of wood protruded through his flak vest. He struggled beneath her. The nails on her hands extended into razor sharp spikes. This time she wanted to see the torture on his face. She scraped her nails down his sides, just deep enough to scratch through his clothes and reveal his hair-covered barreled chest. His eyes went wide with fear under the clear visor of the helmet he wore.

Feeling her own power Savannah inserted the nails of her right hand into his chest. Blood seeped around the five spikes as she tore through skin, cartilage and bone. The man gritted his teeth and grunted, but didn't give her the scream of satisfaction she wanted. With her left hand she tore the visor from his helmet. His glaring eyes held nothing but contempt. She tapped his wide-open right eye. The blue-green orb exploded like a popped water balloon. Fluid Gushed down his cheek and the scream he'd withheld before came out loud and clear. His mouth quivered as she leaned down and lapped up the blood tinted fluid which seeped from his lips as she tore his heart out.

The machine-gun fire drowned out his screams. Lights from tracer rounds beamed through the night and bullets riddled her back. They sent her flying off the man with the force. The heart still clutched in her hand, she crouched and leapt into the air. The rattle from the guns behind continued while she sailed over the nearest house and landed in the driveway. She crept behind a car and bit into the heart. Warm fluid exploded into her mouth. She tore off a hunk of cardiac muscle, and let it slide down the back of her throat. The meal re-energized her. Small holes in her skin healed and bruises from the bullets disappeared.

Footsteps pounded the pavement behind her. Satiated for the moment, she let the half-eaten heart slap to the ground, sprang to her feet and sprinted down the sidewalk, hurdling trash cans, children's toys and a couple of parked cars. The men became a distant memory as the call of the male turned her northwest.

33.

TEAGAN CINCHED HER grip on the tire iron. Her knuckles blanched. In a cat-like stance she slinked through the grass and shrubs toward the grotesque sounds. In a clearing, a distant street lamp outlined the vague silhouette of an intimate couple.

Alyssa's chest rested in the damp grass, her head cocked into the air as if she smelled roses dangling from above. Whimpers came from her as if she couldn't scream anymore. A blond guy knelt behind her. He couldn't have been more than eighteen or nineteen. One hand clawed deep into her raised hips, the other tugged her hair like a horse being reigned in. Blood poured down the outside of her bare left leg.

What the hell? Is he one of those . . . ? But he looks like a teenage boy. Teagan shook her head and looked again.

Muscles rippled and bulged with each thrust of his hips.

Under constant assault from the creature, Alyssa only let out a slight whimper when Teagan expected her to scream. He answered with a pleasure-filled moan. Teagan couldn't help but feel a snip of pain as she remembered her own virginity being taken.

The best chance she had of saving Alyssa would be when the thing finished. Travis had always rolled off, basking in his after-orgasm bliss or whatever it was that guys do. Most of the time, they just fall asleep. Travis wasn't any different; he'd sleep while she cleaned his shit up. The moment after the creature's orgasm would be the perfect time for her to strike. She crouched, ready to pounce as soon as his complete attention focused on one thing—release.

Rhythm changed, grunts slowed, thrusts became harder, more vigorous. Instead of chirps Alyssa began to screech from the pain.

Teagan couldn't breathe. Mud, sweat, blood and hate permeated every pore of her body.

He lunged one last time, raised his hands and let out a high pitched wail like four different people screamed at the same time.

Teagan dropped her weapon and covered her ears. When the deafening shriek ended, his body shuddered.

Fucking boys.

Alyssa screamed.

The guy finished. When he pulled out, a spurt of blood and throws of flesh slapped against his bare stomach. Teagan vomited into her hands and then dove into a patch of tall grass. She prayed he hadn't heard her.

Clouds merged, stars disintegrated, and Alyssa's screams dwindled to nothing. Her silence horrified Teagan. It signified that one of her best friends could be dead. She wiped tears on her sleeve, her hands on a bushel of weeds, and picked up the weapon with new conviction. The piece of shit just killed her best friend.

It must die!

She stood.

His eyes glowed like lit candles and snapped to her position. The long, jagged fingernails doubled in length when his hands flexed. Though fear trickled down her body she stood her ground. She glanced at Lyssa's limp, slaughtered body and didn't see him pounce.

His weight smashed her into the grass and mud. A thistle of pain pricked every nerve in her body. All air escaped. She struggled to catch her breath. Its intentions became apparent, *was its mother fucking dinosaur prick writhing around on her stomach?* If she could've breathed, she'd have gagged again.

Drips of slobber dangled from his lips. He grasped her throat. She coughed and kicked. Her screams came in muffled rasps. Pain seared her hips and abdomen as he tore at her clothing.

Sirens sounded in the distance.

Off its guard, Teagan brought her knee up hard. The blow startled the creature and he dropped to his knees. Her right hand still had the tire iron clenched in it. When her arm came free, she swung. The claw end of the tire iron struck its mark between his legs and the creature fell to the side of her.

Like a wounded coyote, he howled and writhed in the grass as blood sprayed from his groin. A hunk of flesh resembling some sort of dead snake hung from the tire iron. Barbed spikes flexed in and out as if they had no idea what to do next. Teagan tossed the tire iron with the rank appendage attached to it and ran to Alyssa.

34.

Ross listened to the prattle over the police radio as he sped toward the scene of the accident.

"Dispatch, this is Engine Seven."

"Go ahead, Engine Seven."

"We're on scene. Looks like a one-car MVA. How far out is the ambulance?"

"The closest ambulance we have is coming from Salem. It'll be about 20 minutes."

"Forget the ambulance. We need Life Flight. We've got an approximately seventeen-year-old girl with severe trauma."

"I'm afraid Life Flight is down."

"What do you mean it's down?"

"We lost Life Flight on Halloween night. They were transporting a pregnant woman."

"Sorry. I hadn't heard."

"Do the best you can until the Ambulance gets there or transport the girl to Dallas Hospital yourself. They're also pretty understaffed since the incident."

"Thanks, but she needs a level one trauma center. We'll get some I.V.'s started, but she's lost a lot of blood."

"I'll let the Paramedics know."

"Thanks Dispatch. Seven, out."

"Dispatch copies, Seven. Good luck."

Ross hoped the injured girl wasn't Alexa's daughter. The thought of making that call tightened his stomach. What would he say? "I'm sorry Dr. Mason, but your daughter was killed after a Trill had his way with her." He shook his head, remembering the horror he'd witnessed at the police station. Those images would stay with him the rest of his life.

"Dispatch! Dispatch!" a panicked voice came over the radio.

"Go ahead, Seven."

"Are there any officers in route?"

"That's affirmative, Seven, SWAT and the F.B.I. should be there any minute."

She said it as if Ross had the entire agency with him. *Anything to get the freaked out firefighter to calm down, I guess.*

"Thank the lord," the firefighter said. "I think we got one of those things here. It ain't movin', looks hurt pretty bad. Little girl ripped off its balls . . . with a goddamn tire iron."

"Copy, Seven. And thanks for the details. Dispatch out."

"Seven copies."

At near ninety miles per hour, the lights from Engine Seven came into Ross's view. Rain clouds rolled through the sky, threatening a downpour. Not a good sign. The Trills weren't just ruthless, downright vicious, with primal desires; they also began to show signs of cunning. Finding one in the dark would be much harder. How in the hell did a little girl take one out with a tire iron? If she had taken it down by hitting it in the gonads, they may have found the Trill's Achilles heel. A fact he'd need to get to Alexa as soon as he proved it.

Ross pulled behind two Sheriff's Deputy's cars. A cloud of dust blew over the rig. Before he could get out someone slammed their hand on his window. Ross jumped and promptly flipped the firefighter standing next to his car the bird.

He rolled down the window. "Thanks a lot. You trying to give me a fucking heart attack?"

"Sorry. Didn't mean to scare ya." A firefighter with broad shoulders, flat face and mustache, which looked as if it could crawl off his lip and attack, stuck his head into the car.

"No worries buddy." Ross leaned away so the killer insect on the man's face couldn't get him.

"You gotta see this. Where's the SWAT team?" The firefighter looked around. "And the other F.B.I. guys? Thought you guys were bringin' an army."

Ross looked down the empty road behind him. "No clue. SWAT should be behind me. What you see is what you get from the F.B.I.."

"Lot of that goin' round right now." He opened the door for Ross. "A couple of days ago Life Flight took off from the Rogue Valley Hospital helipad up and disappeared. Guess it crashed in Gold Hill, near the Oregon vortex. Place is like the Bermuda Triangle. Some things go in and never come out. If ya know what I mean?"

Ross ignored the witless conversation. "What's your name, buddy?"

"The guys call me Beef."

Ross smiled. "As in . . . beefcake?" An easy assumption given the man's burly physique.

"Nope. As in 'Where's the beef?'." A large grimace scrawled across his face.

Ross climbed out of the driver's seat, motioned Beef out of his way and opened the back passenger door.

"Those guys nickamed me in the shower . . . if ya catch my drift?"

"Don't let those guys get you down. They're just a bunch of ass hats in uniform."

"Firefighter ass helmets." Beef slapped his knee and howled as if he'd just told the funniest joke on earth.

Ross had never heard a worse joke, but chuckled anyway. Then his serious face as he'd retrieved the necessities to go into the field. "Are the girls safe?"

"Two are. The other died a few minutes ago. You shoulda seen her, privates all torn up like someone turned her inside out and ran her through a wood chipper." Beef ran his hand along the barrel of the riot shotgun. "Wow. You gonna use that thing? I heard one of them monsters can take a shot point blank with a shotgun and live. That true? Guess we're gonna find out, huh? "

A steady panic festered inside Ross. *One of the girls died. My God, what am I gonna tell Alexa?* "Did you get an ID off the girl?" He swung the riot shotgun over his shoulder and closed the back door.

"Yeah. Name's Ali Roth."

"You mean Alyssa Roth?"

"Yeah. That's her. Guys were wondering if she's related to Old Man Roth in Salem. The customer's always right, why?"

" . . . because there are more of them than us." He remembered reading an article or something where Old Man Roth made his town famous quote.

"Where's the Trill now?" Ross paced back and forth.

"The what?" Beef looked perplexed.

"Oh . . . sorry. You don't know what they're called."

"You talkin' 'bout that creature what looks like a kid?"

"Did you see another male?"

"Yeah. He's big. Ever seen the movie *Blue Lagoon*?

"I think I saw it when I was a teenager." This guy's train of thought had to be the most insane Ross had ever come across. "Why?"

"Well. That thing's the spittin' image of that kid on there; the one with the curly blonde hair. The guys are callin' the monster *Curly* on that account."

Ross figured if he could call one *Guy*, they could name one *Curly*. "Beef. Focus. Where is he?"

"Who?" Beef asked.

"Curly, where's Curly right now?" *Slow and steady wins the race, Ross.*

"We strapped him to a backboard. Nothing can get out of them straps."

"Show me." Ross motioned for Beef to lead on.

Beef stuck his thumb out like a hippie trying to hitch-hike to California. "This way." He waddled off

They walked down a steady slope of dirt into a small grass field. The fire engine's high-beams illuminated the scene. Skid marks from Teagan's car flipping and sliding mapped out a perfect path to the crash site. Ross imagined the girls being thrown back and forth and injured as the car skid and flipped. He cringed.

They worked their way through a patch of tall grass the car had bunny-hopped when it flipped, and came to where Curly lay face up on the backboard. Ross could see the tires of the upside down car poking above some shrubs and grass in the distance.

Curly and Guy looked nothing alike. Curly had a full tuft of blond, twisting hair with strands of grass making serpentine loops through some of the swirls. Beef was right. He did look kind of like the kid from that movie.

Blood between the Trill's legs oozed off the backboard. Firefighters had attempted to pack the groin with large gauze pads, but the pad had turned a dark crimson. It didn't seem as if the bleeding would stop anytime soon.

"We've got to get this thing to the hospital." Ross knelt next to Curly and studied him closely. From the blank look on his face, to the ashen color of his skin, Ross knew he could die any minute. Or the sonnofabitch had some sort of healing going on inside.

"What the hell are you talking about?" A tall, slim firefighter turned Ross around by the shoulder. "After what this thing did to the girl, we should string it up or dismember it. Do whatever we can to kill it."

"Curly here could hold the keys to our salvation. We have to save his life. We need him alive."

"For what?" Beef cinched up his trousers.

Ross glanced up at Beef. "To study, find out what we can, see how it ticks and whirls."

Beef hawked a string of spit at the backboard, missing the Trill's feet by inches. "So we can kill 'em all?" He beamed and replaced the wad of chew in his cheek.

"Shut the fuck up Beefy, no-one's talking to you." The slim firefighter glared at the bigger man.

Beef bowed his head."S . . . sorry."

In Ross's mind he reeled around and cracked Slim in the nose with the butt of his gun, sending shards of sinew into the man's brain. Instead, he whipped around and grabbed him by the lapels of his firefighter jacket and curled the smaller man to him. "I'll let it slide this time." He placed his nose between Slim's eyes. "But if you talk to Beef again like that . . . I'll find a reason to throw your ass in jail. Or I'll just kick it from here until next week. You understand?"

Slim nodded and Ross let him go. Slim traipsed over to the medic kit next to the backboard. He knelt and rummaged through the equipment, pulled out another large gauze bandage and packed it on top of the other one. Curly stared into space. If it wasn't for his chest moving up and down, Ross would have thought he'd been killed.

"What the fuck did you do that for?" A girl's voice drew Ross's attention to the back of the fire engine where two teenage girls sat with firefighter's coats draped over their shoulders.

One of them, a tall redhead, had an air splint wrapped around her right leg. She had her arm around another girl, who sobbed into the redhead's shoulder. The second girl bore a striking resemblance to her mother, except she had a bit more curves and black hair.

"Let the fucker bleed to death. It killed Alyssa." The redhead glared at him.

Ross walked up to the girls. "You Teagan?" He touched the crying one on the shoulder.

"Yeah. Who the hell are you?" She pulled the hair covering her eyes behind her ears.

"I'm Agent Harris."

"Is that supposed to mean something to us?" the other girl asked.

"You must be, Ellie." Ross gave the girls a warm smile. He had to put on the friendliest face he could. Win the girls over to his side. "I'm a friend of your mother's." He looked at Teagan. "She's worried about you."

Teagan cocked an eyebrow. "Friend? How did . . . "

Ellie interrupted, "I might have texted your mom while you de-balled that bastard."

Teagan shook her head. "Great, now my mom's going to go psycho and never let me out of her sight."

Ross waved his hand around the area. "It's not a bad idea, given the situation."

"What?" Teagan snapped him a quick, volatile look.

"Your mom wants me to bring you back. And, we need to take Curly over there with us." He thumbed over his shoulder at the Trill.

"No way. I'm not traveling with that murderous rapist piece of horseshit." Teagan humphed and folded her arms.

"None of us are." Ross held up his keys. "We'll take my car. SWAT can transport Curly. I just hope he doesn't die before your mom has a chance to dissect him." He smiled.

Teagan responded with a sinister grin. "Okay. I'll go. But I want to watch."

"Me too," Ellie said.

Teagan groaned. "Who's gonna to tell Lyssa's mom and dad?"

"Don't worry about that. I'll let them know." Ross escorted the girls to the SUV and called Alexa.

35.

ALEXA EXAMINED THE calculation again. "This can't be right."

Ray had his face in a computer screen, tapping away at the keyboard below. "I ran it twice, boss. It's right."

"This is amazing. If we can test this against a live tri-allele, we could end this right now."

"Hell yes we can." Ray kicked himself away from his desk. His computer chair slid across the lab's linoleum floor and skid to a halt next to Alexa's desk. "Up high." He raised his hand, poised for the high-five.

This little ritual of Ray's didn't appeal to her. Neither did the knuckle bump Teagan's friend Ellie kept trying to give her. Not only did she not enjoy touching other people's hands, she didn't get the concept. Yes, recognition for a job well done or a suburban pat on the back. Why not say, 'wonderful work' and leave it at that? She halfheartedly brushed her palm against his.

The cell phone in her upper right lab coat pocket buzzed against her breast. She whipped out the phone and sighed with relief. It was Agent Harris. "This is Dr. Mason."

"Alexa . . . err . . . Dr. Mason, this is Ross."

A bit of pain, guilt, hurt clumped in her belly. "Did . . . did you find her?"

"Yeah."

"How is she?" The clump surfaced in her throat.

"She's safe, unharmed. We think Ellie's leg is fractured."

She relaxed a bit, but sensed something amiss. "What is it? What's wrong?"

"It's Alyssa."

"Oh, no. Is she . . . " The word wouldn't come.

"I'm sorry. We're lucky any of them walked away from that wreck. There wasn't anything anyone could do for Alyssa. A Trill attacked her. But from the looks of it, with the injuries from the accident, she probably wouldn't have survived the night."

Alexa sensed a vain attempt to make her feel better. There's no way he could tell if the car accident did enough internal damage to cause her death, but she did appreciate the effort. "This is awful. How are Ellie and Teagan?"

"They're pretty shaken up. But they're tough girls, they'll pull through."

"I know they are and will." Teagan had to be the most bullheaded person she knew, other than herself.

"But one thing positive came of it," Ross said.

"What's that?" She couldn't think of one thing that could cheer her up at this moment. One of Teagan's best friends had died an horrific death, a memory Teagan would carry for life.

"We caught another Trill. Well, actually, Teagan caught him."

"She did what?" If the tri-allele had killed Alyssa, there's no doubt in her mind Teagan would go after it with fists, teeth, and claws if she had to; stubborn girl.

"She disabled one of the male Trills, damnedest thing I've ever seen. In the process she discovered there."

"How's that?" What vulnerability could a seventeen-year-old girl find on a seemingly invulnerable species? Alexa thought.

"The male Trills have a fierce sex drive, right?"

"Correct. That appears to be their M.O. if I'm using your F.B.I. lingo correctly?"

"Exactly. It's in their M.O. where Teagan found the vulnerability; in the process of her being attacked."

The shock of hearing the words 'attack' and 'daughter' together sent a chill through Alexa's body. "what's this weakness?"

He continued, " . . . she struck back with a tire iron and ripped off his ball. He's nearly bled to death."

That made perfect sense to her. "I've heard that the male genitals tuck into the groin area and are very much protected. Much like a dog or cat's. "Genitalia? Really?" The cleverness of her daughter never ceased to amaze Alexa. "I guess she listened to what I had to say about boys."

"What was that?"

"Nothing. Just glad you all are safe." Except for poor Alyssa, what torture she must have endured.

"Well, Teagan did that and more. The damage caused the Trill to bleed – a lot. We think he might die, but he's alive for the moment. I hope he stays alive long enough for you to do an exam and get what you need."

"I need him alive so I can test this new formula on him."

"New formula? What's it do?"

"If my calculations are correct, it will isolate the mutated gene and hopefully reverse the mutation."

"That's great news. If it works on this one, we can test it on the one sitting in the Independence Jail cell."

"Ross. May I talk to my daughter?" She hoped Teagan would take the phone.

"Of course, give me a second."

The line went quiet.

"M . . . Mom." Teagan sobbed, sniffed and composed herself. Alexa had taught her well.

"I'm glad you're safe. Ross is bringing you up here. You'll be safer here than anywhere else right now."

"Can you fix it, Mom? Can you kill the fuckers?"

Alexa let the bad language go. "Let's get you and Ellie to safety."

"It killed Alyssa. Alyssa! Mom!" Teagan's eyes narrowed.

"Agent Harris informed me already. I'm sorry. I'll call Alyssa's parents. We'll have a doctor take a look at Ellie when you arrive."

"Yes, mother." Teagan sniffled.

"Put Ross . . . I mean, Agent Harris back on the phone, please."

Ross came back on the line. "We'll be there in about an hour."

"Drive safe. Make sure the tri-allele is secure. I don't know how fast they heal."

"Will do." The phone call ended.

"Teag okay?" Ray put his hand on her shoulder. Another thing she normally despised. The kid had no boundaries and loved to make her uncomfortable. His touch this time soothed her a bit.

She reached up and placed her hand over his, which he quickly withdrew wide-eyed. She'd surprised him and herself by making the physical connection. She needed to be comforted. Because that's what normal people do in these kinds of situations. They also confide and console one another. To her knowledge, she and Ray had a kind of friendship. No-one else ever sat with her during lunch or made any sort of effort to talk to her about anything other than work. She decided to tell him.

"Yes. But one of her friends was killed by a Trill."

"That sucks. Sounds like they're bringing us a live one, eh?"

"They are." Alexa stared at the computer screen. If the serum failed to destroy the third-allele, she'd have to start at ground zero. She needed to know the trigger. Biochemical weapon would be her first guess. But no-one had the technology to do such a thing or she would know about it. How could anyone add a third allele and alter the genetic code of every fetus on the planet? No scientist she knew of and she knew the best in the world.

At best her serum would be an in-vitro vaccination for every woman currently carrying an infected fetus. But she'd have to do some extensive and very painful testing on a live specimen to get true results. She crossed her fingers, hoping, wishing, and maybe even a little praying, they would get the male to her alive.

36.

ACROSS FROM THE Independence City Hall and Police Station, Savannah stood atop a rickety home with boarded up windows and a porch swing which dangled from one chain. It creaked in the breeze. A man in a black suit and tie burst through the double front doors. He hopped into a large vehicle and slammed the door. The car tore down the street. Inside the building she detected two life forms besides the male of her own species.

The warmth of the male's lust caressed her senses. His need permeated her every pore. Sensations deep within her stirred. She dropped from the roof, indenting the overgrown lawn beneath her. She leapt, bounced on a car in front of the station and blasted through the police stations front doors. Shattered glass stuck to the thick pools of blood on the floor.

A man knelt at the end of the hallway leading to the jail cells, his weapon at the ready. Before he could fire she slammed his head against the cement wall. The bones in his neck snapped. With a flick of the wrist she tossed him aside. His body slid down the hall.

Another human guarded the cell which held *her* male. When she pulled the door open and entered, his weapon went off. Shells ejected into the air. The metal clanked and bounced against the cement. A few caught her by surprise and penetrated the softer skin under her arms. She weaved her way through the hall, dodging bullets as they ricocheted off the concrete all around her. Momentum shot her up the side of the wall, running parallel to her prey. The sudden feat startled the man, who let his finger off the trigger for a moment giving her an opening. She slammed her claws into the man's helmet. They tore into his skull which imploded under the extreme pressure. A wash of blood and brain matter splattered to the concrete. The officer slumped to the floor.

Inside the cell, a male of her species stood tall. Other than the child she'd seen on the television, this is the first time she'd been in the presence of one of her own. His looks didn't allure her, yet she longed to hold him, and feel his flesh pressed against hers.

The bars bent out a few inches but wouldn't budge. She screamed in frustration, sending the male to his knees, holding his ears. Savannah hadn't realized how powerful her voice had become.

She examined the metal bars and found a keyhole. In a room down the hall she found a dead human with a set of keys in his hands. The male looked puzzled as she fumbled with the keys, jamming one after another into the hole, twisting and pulling. A loud click startled her but the door jammed on itself. Impatient, the male yanked the door open. Metal ground on metal and sparks flew. The two slammed into each other in a jumbled mix of pallid skin, torn clothes and ripped flesh. The hood between his legs pulsed. The skin attached spread out and hardened. He extended his claws and tore the skirt off her hips.

The male threw her to the ground and landed on top of her. Confused, she tried to push him away, but the smooth, untainted flesh between her legs reached out and drew him in. At first his relentless thrusting annoyed and disgusted her. It also hurt a bit, but after a while it began to feel good, unexplainably good.

37.

THE RIDE BACK to the hospital was silent for some time. With Ellie's intermittent sobbing and her own sniffling, Teagan decided she needed to lighten up the situation with a little conversation. Agent Harris hadn't said much since he gave her cell phone back except to ask if they had their seat belts on and if they needed anything. One thing had been weighing on her a bit and she decided to get it off her chest.

"So, what's up with you and my mom?" She watched the cool F.B.I. guy to see if he'd unravel. *Different when you're the one being interrogated.*

His fingers did a drum roll on the steering wheel. "Nothing. There's nothing up with your mom and me. Right now, we're colleagues working on a project. Besides, she hates me." He shot her an awkward smile.

"I think she might be into you." She sniffed and smirked.

The SUV swerved.

"Didn't mean to get your panties in a bunch."

Ellie giggled and winced in pain. "Ouch."

Teagan whipped around. Ellie had hold of her side under her left breast.

"Shit, Ell's. You break a rib?"

"I don't know. Hurts like hell when I laugh."

"Probably a fractured rib." Agent Harris looked at Ellie through the rearview mirror.

"No shit." Teagan scoffed. "Can we do anything for it?" The man must have answers. *He's an F.B.I. guy.*

Agent Harris adjusted the review mirror; probably trying to get a better look at Ells. "Try not to make any sudden movements or laugh," he said.

"Nut up, Ells." Teagan glared at her. She wasn't the one who got attacked and almost defiled by a monster.

Ellie smacked the back of Teagan's seat. "Kiss my ass biatch. You didn't even get hurt."

"Bullshit. Got my skull cracked pretty good. Plus, I almost got mauled by that thing. Then I lopped his dick off. So, quit whining."

"OMG, Tea Bags. Are you fucking . . . ?"

"Hey!" Agent Harris interrupted. "Let's try and keep the language PG-13"

Ellie humphed. "That means we can say fuck every thirty minutes."

Teagan tried not to giggle and snorted instead. She caught Agent Harris smiling into his hand.

"I'm sorry Ells, this shit is starting to get to me. I'm pissed off, sad and confused."

"What's new? You're like that ninety percent of the time." Ellie's hand cupped over the top of Teagan's.

Teagan thought about pulling her hand away, but left it and let a tear trickle down her cheek when Ellie squeezed her hand softly.

"We'll get through this. You did good, girl. Fucked that thing up good. That's the best revenge you could get for us, and for poor Lyssa."

Agent Harris looked at his watch. "Umm . . . your thirty minutes isn't up yet."

Ellie shot him her 'shut the fuck up' glare. Teagan knew it well. "Relax Mr. Agent Man." Teagan reached over and patted him on the shoulder.

"Ross."

"What?" Ellie lifted an eyebrow.

"Call me, Ross. It's my name. As in Ich bin, Ross. Or, Je suis, Ross."

Ellie's crinkled. "Got it. Man of a thousand languages. You also a man of a thousand faces? Got any cool F.B.I. disguises in here?"

"If I told you, I'd have to kill you." He smiled.

The sincerity behind his smile showed Teagan that she could trust this guy. She checked him out a little closer. *Kinda hot for an old guy. Seems nice too and family-oriented for sure.*

"So, Ross." Teagan turned so she could look at him without twisting her head. Her neck had stiffened.

"Yep."

"Where are you from?"

"I grew up in Southern Oregon, small town called Phoenix, it's near Medford. You heard of it?"

"City just before Ashland?" Teagan looked back at Ells, who looked drifted in and out of sleep.

"One of 'em."

Ellie opened her eyes. "My mom took us to Ashland once. There's a cool theater down there."

Ross looked at her through the mirror again. "It's an outdoor Shakespearean theater."

"Yeah, it was pretty cool when I went." Ellie laid her head against the window and closed her eyes again.

"You married?" Teagan asked.

"Married and divorced." Ross shifted in his seat.

That one had got to him. Teagan smiled. "Kids?"

"Yep. Two daughters."

"How old?"

"Fourteen."

"Both?" Ellie asked.

"Twins?" Teagan mused.

"Correct. Twin girls. Madison and Mellisa."

"Cool." Ellie laughed. "The M&M twins."

Teagan smiled.

"We get that one a lot," Ross laughed. "You two need to get some rest. We'll be at OHSU in about forty-five minutes."

Teagan curled up next to the window. In a lot of ways he reminded her of her dad. Solid dependability emanated from him, yet a quiet arrogance lingered, something her father didn't have. She closed her eyes.

38.

THE MALE'S EYEs turned from dark charcoal to a burnt red. He convulsed. A warm burst of fluid filled her stomach. She pushed him off and he rolled onto the concrete next to her. His erection slithered back into its pouch. Her belly tingled. She writhed on the ground with each subsequent orgasm. A sudden realization came to her. When he had pulled out of her, she had used muscles in her groin to close the barbs on his penis. The human female's reproductive organs must not have this feature. This very apparent by the torn apart human females she happened upon.

Inside a room full of lockers Savannah found a short black leather skirt hanging from a hook. A black t-shirt neatly folded beneath with red pumps and some sort of undergarment she'd never seen before. She put on the shirt and skirt but didn't want the shoes. The claws on her toes made it easier for her to scale walls and climb trees.

The male's head cocked sideways in a fixed question.

She scrabbled through the men's lockers and found a shirt and jeans that she shoved in the male's face. He tore the shirt in half. Savannah extended her right hand claws and slapped him across the face. He hissed and bared his teeth. She raised her hand again and he cowered. She forced the jeans onto him.

A pain gouged her as if someone had twisted a knife into her chest. Another male wasn't far away. She sensed his cry for help. Once she'd gathered him to her, she would mate with him as well. The more males she had, the better chance she had to create a child. This perfect creature would be the new race, she felt certain. She didn't know why, but the need to find more males burned deep within her.

They left the police station. The empty streets showed no humans in the vicinity. This had the male worried. His stomach rumbled. In her mind, she said, *we will find food.* He dropped behind her more content than before.

A wave of pain hit her, knocking her to the ground as if she'd been slammed between two large boulders. The male came to her aid. He knelt next to her and whimpered. She touched his hand to let him know all would be okay.

This energy that had plowed into her left a wake she could follow. Not a visible thing, but an ethereal connection drawing her to the injured male. His pain enveloped her.

The two raced down the street and leapt over a building. They landed in a large field. With a glance over her shoulder, to make sure the first male followed, she continued through the endless fields of grass and other plant life toward the gathering of vehicles several miles away.

Then, as if she'd been hoisted from her own body, she looked through the eyes of the injured male. Again she fell to the ground and squirmed when spikes of pain hit her chest. But this wasn't her pain. This agony belonged to the other male. She saw the human males surrounding him, smelled their stench, and tasted the blood on her lips. All of his senses belonged to her. From the confines of his mind, she felt her own body and willed herself to get up and move toward him. Inside him, she attempted to help him move. Straps and large chains held him down. Humans stood about, talking amongst themselves.

"Get this piece of shit out of here." Someone kicked the right foot of her trapped male.

Savannah lost the feeling in her right foot and stumbled.

Firefighters crouched and took hold of the large piece of plastic they'd strapped him to. "On three. One . . . two . . . three." The men lifted.

Savannah realized she could wiggle his big toe. Her mind fused to his and she had use of all his senses, muscles, and mind. She flexed all of his muscles, but weakness had set in from the damage done. She stayed with him until they loaded him into the back of a large truck where several other men covered his body with a net made of steel and attached it to several hooks embedded into the floor.

"That oughta hold till the doc can get her hands on ya. You bet. She's gonna slice and dice you until there ain't nothin' left." A man spat in his face.

"We'll take it from here guys," a fully-armored man said. He carried one of the large guns which caused damage if the bullets hit their soft areas. Though, if injured, they all healed very fast.

Savannah telepathically told the male with her to *ram the truck*. They would both hit it on one side and flip it to rescue one of their own.

39.

ALEXA COULDN'T BELIEVE the results came out positive every time. "Run it again." She directed Ray back to his desk.

He rolled his eyes, threw his hands up and stomped back to the lab. "It's gonna be right."

"I'll believe it when I see it. We're going to run this test again and again until I have a specimen to test it on."

"You're the boss." He ugged and disappeared into his hole.

She had to be sure the formula worked to perfection. She'd isolated the third allele and created an agent that could stop the effects of the mutagen. An injection into a new fetus would be a great risk at this point. Once she cleared the anti-mutagen with top military scientists, she'd put it into production. This frightened her. Human trials in genetics almost always ended with less than desirable results; however, she had isolated the third allele and could probably say with about a 98% certainty, it would work.

Ray strolled back into her office. "Dr. Mason."

"Yes."

"We have another positive result. You think that'll be enough to start trials?"

"Run it again."

"Jesus."

"We'll continue to run the test until the specimen arrives. Then we'll see what it does against their blood cells."

"Thought it was for a viable fetus only?"

"We need to see what it does against a fully grown tri-allele first. I've developed a marker to isolate the gene. That way we'll be absolutely sure we have the correct one."

"I know what isolate means."

"Good. Kindly run the test again."

"Fine." He turned and left the room.

The office phone rang. She didn't know who could be calling the office this late at night and almost ignored it. Against her better judgment, or worse depending how you looked at it, she answered.

"Dr. Mason here."

"Hulo," a foreign voice said.

"This is Dr. Mason. Can I help you?"

"Yes. Dr. Mason. My name is Yahira Madeed. I am a Geophysicist from India."

Alexa had no idea what a geophysicist would be calling about.

"Dr. Mason?"

"Yes, Dr. Madeed. How may I assist you this evening?"

"You are working on the anomaly, yes?"

"I am in charge of the tri-allele project. We've had great progress so far and have even procured a live one for testing."

"Tri-allele is a good name for them. I think I may have stumbled across their origin."

What could he possibly have found? "Tell me your theory doctor."

"Are you familiar with Earth's magnetic field?"

"Yes. I'm very familiar. The Earth's magnetic field protects us from the effects of the deadly solar winds originating in the fluid motion of the Earth's outer core. Due to geomagnetic secular variation, the field changes over time."

"Ahh . . . splendid. I have been tracking the comet for the past year. We named it "Madeed". It's a 'sungrazer' comet. Are you knowing the terminology?

"I do Dr. Madeed. Please continue."

"As Madeed passed by our sun it broke into tiny particles. By the time it hit Earth's magnetic field, it disintegrated into billions of ions that should have dissipated. I tracked the ionization from this cloud which enveloped the entire planet. They did not dissipate as expected; instead, they discharged into the ozone layer."

She jotted notes into her computer as he spoke. "What does this have to do with the Trills?"

"The ions entered our atmosphere on Wednesday October thirty-first. Now you understand."

"Halloween. You're saying there is a direct correlation with these ions and the appearance of the tri-alleles in the current human fetus?"

"Yes doctor. That is what I believe happened. It could be coincidence, but highly unlikely. And I do not believe these were random ions. I believe they came from another galaxy and were designed to do exactly what they are doing."

Alexa gasped. "Where did the comet originate from?" The proverbial puzzle pieces began to snap together in her mind.

"This particular comet came from Epsilon Eridani."

"That's 10.5 light years from us." She grimaced.

"Yes, the nearest known planetary system. The strangest part is that Madeed stayed the same size for the entire year. This is very irregular comet activity."

"What are you saying, doctor?"

"I believe the comet wasn't an accident. It may have been caused by other worldly beings."

"An attack?" A million probabilities as well as magazine clippings, stories, scientific proof all barraged her thoughts.

"It's possible, or another race sending their DNA through time and space, to repopulate on a planet compatible with their own. Doing anything they can to keep their species alive."

Aliens? She shook her head. Logic dictated her life and statistics show the possibility of extra-terrestrial life. "It is plausible."

"Only in theory, doctor. I'm working on tracing the exact origin of the comet."

"Keep me apprised of your findings. If you identify the chemical makeup, maybe we can come up with a way of killing the ones that have already come to term."

"This is good. I will keep in touch. Goodbye."

"Thank you for the call." Alexa hung up the phone.

She took a deep breath and relaxed into her chair, laid her head back, closed her eyes and found herself dreaming about creatures exploding from her daughter's abdomen and the tri-allele population dominating Earth. She woke

40.

A FRENZIED PANIC of conversation blared from Ross's hand held radio.

"Dispatch! Help! Them things knocked over our rig. We need help?"

"Engine Seven, could you give us more specifics?"

"Two of 'em attacked. We flipped. They yanked Gabe and Dean out through the front window. I . . . I think those creatures ate them. One looked like a girl."

Ross picked up the radio. "Dispatch, this is Agent Harris. I'm not far from the accident. I'll head back, see if I can help. That you Beef?"

"Yeah, Agent. It's me."

"Hold tight buddy. Stay out of sight. I'll be there soon." The engine had been bringing up the rear of the caravan and couldn't be more than a few miles behind them.

Dispatch chimed in, "Negative, Agent Harris. SWAT is trailing the transport truck. They can double back and . . . "

"Dispatch," Beef interrupted.

"Yes Seven."

"SWAT and the truck carrying Curly also got hit. I seen an explosion and heard gunfire for a couple of seconds"

"Dispatch. This is Agent Harris."

"Go ahead, Agent."

"Have you heard from either of them?"

"I've attempted to hail them on the other line. But, I'm getting nothing but static. Seven, this is dispatch."

"I'm here," Beef whispered and Ross heard fear in his breathy words.

"Are you injured?" Dispatch asked.

Beef whimpered, "Not yet."

"Sorry dispatch, I'm going back," Ross said.

The dispatcher said, "Good luck Agent Harris."

"Thanks dispatch. I'm going to need it. Agent Harris out." Yeah he needed luck all right and a whole lot more.

"Dispatch copies and is going to get a stiff drink."

"Bring me one." Beef cleared his throat.

"You got it sweetie, just be safe."

Ross pulled into a rundown gas station. If he didn't get to Beef soon, the man would die. But to do so he'd be putting the girls in harm's way and he couldn't do that. They might as well be his own daughters and there was no way in hell he'd take them back.

41.

TEAGAN WOKE. Ross shook her—again. "Ow! What?" She rubbed her arm. Every muscle in her body ached and her head felt like someone drove over it with a tractor. She'd do anything to slip into a nice hot bath with some Epsom salts and her favorite pink loofah.

"Sorry. But I need to drop you and Ellie off here for a bit. Something went wrong with the transport. It's only a few minutes behind us, shouldn't take long."

Teagan noticed they'd stopped at a rundown gas station near the four-way split in highway 99 which took you to Salem, Tigard, Corvallis or the Coast.

The deserted, dark, maleficent gas station reminded her of a cabin in the woods you might find in a horror movie. *No way in hell.* "Are you out of your mind? Ellie's leg is broken. She could even have internal bleeding and you want to drop our assess off in the middle of bum-fucked-Egypt so you can go play hero? Fuck that. What if there's one of those things here. We're staying with you."

Ellie sat up and rubbed her eyes. "Are we there?"

"No Ell's. This jerk wants to drop us off here and go save that thing."

Ross put his hands up. "I surrender. You two can come, but if the shit hits the fan, you need to take the car and get to your mother's office. Understood?"

Teagan smiled and sat back, arms folded. *This guy caves easily. He'd be a good step dad.* She sniggered.

"I still don't know what's going on." Ellie yawned and rubbed her leg. "My leg's throbbing."

Ross turned and looked at her, then at Ellie. "We'll get your leg taken care of soon. But we have to go back. The rest of our caravan fell behind."

Teagan frowned; she knew it was a lie. "Fell behind?"

"Okay. They were attacked and a firefighter's in trouble. We have to see if he's okay."

"Fuck the firefighter. My leg's killing me."

"I know, Ellie. But you have to understand a man's life is in danger and we're the closest. Here." He unbuckled and scooted toward Teagan. It kinda weirded her out. *What the hell is he doing?*

From the glove box he pulled out a bottle of what looked like Ibuprofen. "Here, take three of these and call me in the morning." He smiled.

An award winning smile if Teagan had ever seen one.

Ellie took the bottle from him and popped a couple into her mouth. She re-situated. "Fine. Let's go."

Ross slammed his foot to the pedal. Teagan sure hopped he knew what the hell he was doing. *If mom finds out about this she's gonna shit bricks.*

When they reached the first accident, Ross pulled over several hundred feet before the wreckage.

He pulled out his radio. "Beef, you still with us?"

"I'm here."

The whispered words freaked Teagan out even more.

Ellie leaned forward. "This doesn't feel right."

In the distance, lights from the toppled fire truck swirled. The tipped over semi's headlights and Ross's SUV gave the only light in the vicinity.

"Hold tight buddy. I'm gonna check the situation here. See if anyone survived the crash."

"M . . . kay, but hurry. I think I hear them . . . out there."

"I've got you covered, bud. We'll have you out in no time." Ross clipped the radio to his belt. "You two stay put. There's no telling where the creatures are."

"No way." Teagan opened her door. "You don't give a shit about the firefighter. You just wanna see if that thing's still alive. We're coming with you."

"Fine. You can come, but you need to stay as close as possible."

After he hopped out, he went to the back of the SUV and retrieved a large gun.

"Will that kill it?" Teagan folded her arms to shield the nights chill. She'd left the firefighter jacket in the front seat. *Stupid me.*

The passenger side window rolled down and Ellie stuck her head out. "If you both don't mind, I'll take my chances here."

"You're a gimp anyway. You'll just slow down our roll." Teagan giggled.

"I'll save a special place for you in hell." The tinted window whizzed shut.

Ross swung the big gun over his shoulder and pulled a flashlight from a black bag. "Keep it down. We do this quick and quiet. We'll check on the one in the back of the truck, then go help Beef."

"I was right. You do only care about that fucking monster. What about the cops?" *Sonofabitch political bullshit.* She walked cautiously toward the downed semi. The engine still hummed. From the looks of it, the truck had been hit from the right side, tipped over and slid across the road until it stopped. The back door of the trailer hung halfway open.

"I'm gonna check the driver first. Don't go anywhere near that trailer." He pointed the flashlight at the back of the truck.

"Okay." She moved her legs back and forth and rubbed her arms as she watched Ross climb up the bottom side of the cab and shine the light into the window.

"You okay in there?"

She heard a slight tap on the window and quickly scanned to make sure he hadn't alerted any creatures.

"Oh my God." He jumped down and jogged back over to where she stood, freezing to death.

"What . . . what did you see?"

"The driver and passenger are both dead." He panted.

"Oh . . . shit. You think the Trills are still here?"

"You're a quick study." He cocked the big gun. "Let's pray they're gone. Stay here. I'm gonna check the back. See if Guy is still in there."

Hell yes she was staying there. You couldn't pay her enough to go inside the back of that truck. The lump in her throat pulsed with every beat of her racing heart as he disappeared into the dark.

42.

Ross's WIPED HIS sweat covered palms on his slacks one at a time and tightened his grip on the shotgun. What he hoped to find in the back of the trailer was a living specimen in chains. He feared the other Trills had freed Guy and remained in the area, lurking about. Crouched, he crept under the closed door and scanned the bed of the truck.

The backboard hung empty from snapped, dangling chains. The straps torn to shreds lay on the ground at his feet. A set of bloody footprints led toward the front of the truck. His light illuminated them one at a time until they reached their horrific end. Two tactical team members lay crumpled in bloody heaps against the inside wall of the trailer. Their chests splayed open like a bomb went off inside.

"Where do you think they went?"

Ross jumped and whipped around, his light illuminating Teagan's face. "Fuck. You scared the shit out of me."

"Sorry," she whispered.

"Just stay behind me." The footprints led out the door and into a field beyond the wreckage. They disappeared into tall tufts of grass.

"Damn. We lost him. Let's get Beef and get the hell out of here." He took her arm and started to lead her back to the SUV. A scream sent a chisel of fear up his spine.

"That's Ellie!" Teagan screamed and lunged forward.

Ross wrapped his arms around her waist.

She struggled against him. "Let me go asshole!" Her fingernails clawed into his arm.

He swung the shotgun over his shoulder and covered her mouth. "Shhhh."

She shook her head, mumbling under his hand.

"We need to be quiet and out of the Trill's line of sight."

Snot and tears dribble onto the back of his hand. She continued to struggle and let out muffled cries.

The black SUV rocked side to side. He could make out the backside of the naked Trill attacking Ellie. *Poor girl. Shouldn't have let them come. Should've left them at the Goddamn gas station.* This death was on him.

Together, they backed under the door and to the back of the semi. "We'll hide in here." Their only chance of survival meant staying out of sight. The old cliché 'Out of sight, out of mind' came to him.

"Teagan, there are three of them outside. We don't know where the other two are. We need to stay quiet and out of sight until the coast is clear. You understand?"

She nodded.

"Are you going to be quiet?"

With a faint whimper, she nodded again.

"Okay." Ross took his hand from her mouth and wiped it off on his shirt. Then he remembered a piece of equipment he'd left in the car, his cell phone. Hopefully Teagan had hers.

"Where's your phone?"

Teagan fished in the back pocket of her jeans and pulled out the iPhone with pink sparkles. He took it and led her into the furthest corner of the truck where the backboard also blocked them from view. With his thumb he surfed through the contacts list for the one person he thought might be able to help them, or at least send help: Mom.

43.

ONCE AGAIN THE generic chime and buzz startled Alexa. Without looking she clicked 'talk' on the cell.

"Teagan?" The voice of her daughter was the only sound she wanted to hear.

"Alexa, it's Ross," he whispered.

Wrong voice. Why wasn't Teagan calling from her phone? This question sank deep into her gut like a boar struggling in quicksand. They should have been back by now. She couldn't help but think something must have gone terribly wrong.

"Where are you? Why are you whispering?"

"We're in the back of the semi truck. The Trills attacked our caravan. They crashed the fire truck. Semi's tipped over, the driver and guards are dead and our specimen is missing."

Alexa took a deep breath. She didn't want to ask the next question. But he did say 'we', so the spark of hope settled her nerves a bit. "Is she alive?"

"She's with me. We're safe, but not out of danger."

Reprieved for the moment from the insanity which followed the Trills' every move, she sighed. "You said Trills, plural?"

"Yeah."

"How many?"

"Three for sure. Two of them rescued the one we captured."

"Interesting." She meant to think it. Had the Trills somehow organized? Did they have a hierarchy? Their current actions certainly gave the perception of coordination, planning, and possibly plotting. Much higher brain function activity than she had anticipated. This could be a good thing. It meant they could be taught.

"*Interesting*?" Ross growled. "They killed everyone and rescued their own. This is so far from fucking interesting it's pitiful."

Stressful situations did breed acrimony. "You and Teagan are safe. What about Ellie?" She couldn't keep the tremble out of her voice. Although Ellie had the foulest mouth of just about anyone she knew, her fondness for the girl had grown over the years. So if she had to choose, Ellie could be considered her favorite of Teagan's friends.

"I'm not sure. Her attack is the reason we're hiding."

"There's nothing you can do?" Teagan sniffled in the background.

"You don't understand. There are at least three of them out there. If I give away our position, they'll kill all of us."

"Understandable under the circumstances, but I believe if you are talking, you're position is already compromised." Alexa cringed at the thought of Teagan and Ross facing three of the vicious creatures.

"I'm coming to get you."

"No way! The world needs you where you are. Call the national guard."

"This is not negotiable." She'd made up her mind. This would be a good opportunity to test out one of her theories.

"For a genius, you're out of your damn mind? You can't come down here."

"I can bring something to you that will help, possibly save your lives."

"What?"

"Tell her to bring the army," Teagan said in the background.

Ross shushed her.

"One of the side effects of the agent I'm developing should suppress the mutated gene, to an extent."

"Should? You're not convincing me. What if it doesn't work?"

"We die, dumbass," Teagan interjected.

Alexa knew, the formula would work. "It's a chance we have to take. It's been tested over and over."

"But you haven't tested it on a live Trill. What's it supposed to do?"

The equations spun in her mind. But in layman's terms they

meant a breakdown in the molecular structure of the Trill's thick skin. "It should make them more vulnerable to our weapons."

"How?"

"We don't have time to get into that right now. I'm on my way."

"Don't do it . . . "

She'd made up her mind and hung up on him.

"Ray!"

Ray speed-walked into the room. "What? The test is done. Another positive."

"Good. Make four vials of the serum. Get one of the guns we use to inject animal test subjects and load them into the darts."

"What the hell, Boss?"

"I'm going to get them."

He hesitated.

"Do it now!" Sometimes his lackluster raked her like nails across sandpaper.

"Fine. But you're going to get yourself killed." He stomped out of the room.

"I don't care. I have to do something." She sat back in her chair trying to think of another way. Police, fire, SWAT? They seemed to be the ones in trouble. "It's the only way."

Five minutes later Ray jogged back in. "Here." He slapped the gun onto the table and set a small case with several darts on the table next to it.

"Loaded?"

"Yes." He covered the gun with his hand. "You can't do this."

"That's not your decision." Alexa pulled on her trench coat and put the gun and cartridges in opposite pockets.

With the weapon secure, she stormed out of the building and ran to her car. Another ambulance sped by with lights flashing and siren blaring. *No doubt another attack victim.* This madness had to stop. No more attacks. No more killings. She didn't even think of an alternative if the agent didn't work. It had to.

44.

A HIGH-PITCHED SCREAM bounced through the cargo bay. This one didn't sound like Ellie at all. Teagan recognized the yelp.

"What was that?" Ross turned to her.

The familiar sound rousted her innards.

Ross looked as if he were concentrating, listening.

Another scream.

"Doesn't sound like Ellie."

"Because it's not her. That's the same sound the *thing* made when I whacked his dick off."

Ross ran his hand through his hair. The sweat matted it down. "Do you think?"

"Yeah. I think Ellie's fighting back."

"We need to get out there. If it's injured, maybe I can finish the job."

"What about the other ones?" One, they could probably handle, two or three, not a chance in hell.

For the first time during their time together, Ross looked like he had no clue. "His screaming will probably bring the other two."

"Agent Ross, its Ellie. We have to try."

He grabbed her by the hand and they slunk out of the trailer.

Teagan's eyes swarmed the area looking for the other two Trills. "Maybe they eat their dead."

"What?" Ross let go of her and pulled the big gun from his shoulder.

The light from the shotgun didn't find any glowing eyes, but she felt them. They lurked somewhere in the dark.

"Is that a bazooka?" she asked as they crept toward the SUV.

"No. It's a riot shotgun. A bazooka is much, much bigger. Look." He pointed the gun toward the car.

A Trill stumbled from behind the SUV's open passenger door, his hands gripped between his legs.

"Guy?" Ross shone the light on the Trill. He wobbled like a linebacker at a kegger. Blood spurt between his fingers and ran down the insides of his legs.

"Guy?"

"He's the one I caught in Independence. I had him locked up. One of the others must have freed him as well."

Teagan rolled her eyes in disbelief. "You named them?"

"Two of em. If the other one's from Salem, then we already know her name."

Guy looked at his hands and dropped to his knees. Blood flowed from his groin onto the street. His eyes rolled back and he gave another mind numbing screech.

"He's calling for help. You have to try and kill him now." Teagan demanded. She knew if the others came before they got to the SUV, her, Agent Handsome, and Ellie would all be dead meat.

"Exactly. First we have to make sure there aren't any others around."

"There's nothing coming. Kill him. Fuck. If you won't, I will. Give me a gun." Teagan held her hand out.

"Funny girl." Ross looked at her with a raised eyebrow. "I don't think so. But you're right. He dies . . . now." With the caution of one walking across thin ice, Ross made his way to the creature in the road and put the shotgun to its head. "Dodge this motherfucker."

Teagan turned and plugged her ears. Even though she anticipated it, the blast of the gun startled her. "Is it dead?" she called out without looking.

The gun went off again. If it wasn't dead with the first blast, the second one probably did the trick. She opened her eyes and turned around. Guy had fallen back with his legs under him. Blood and brains scattered across the street. A dry heave rushed to her throat.

Ross spit on the carcass. "I think it's fair to say he's dead."

"Check Ells. See if she's okay." Tears dripped down Teagan's face. If she lost Ellie and Alyssa in the same day, well, she didn't want to even think about it. She turned away, standing just off the street beside the semi. There's no way she could watch him pull Ellie's limp, dead, mutilated body from the car. Maybe the pain inside would go away if she punched the cement. After dropping to her knees, she did just that. Hit after hit until the only feeling left in her body was pain.

A shuffling from behind froze her. One of them must have caught her off guard. Any second it would strike the killing blow. With her eyes clenched shut and her knuckles bleeding, she waited for the guillotine to drop.

45.

THE HIGH BEAMS lit up the naked man standing in the road behind Teagan. Alexa veered across lanes, aiming the Volvo straight at him. This would at least stun the Trill or knock him out. Maybe even give her time to shoot it with the formula.

Teagan dove out of the way as the front end of the Volvo plowed into the side of the creature. Alexa heard a crunch as if she'd hit a deer. That's when the airbags exploded in all directions. She couldn't see, but slammed her foot on the brake. The car came to screeching halt. At least she'd stayed on the road.

The engine rumbled and steam whistled from the front of the car. Though muffled, she thought she heard someone calling her name. She reached up to her keys and unlocked the doors.

Both passenger and drivers side doors opened.

"Alexa!" Ross waved his hands in the air.

"Mom!" Teagan called out.

Before she could catch her breath, Teagan and Ross both pushed and pulled on airbags until their faces popped up on both sides of her. After taking several deep breaths, she blew the hair out of her eyes. "I'm glad you're both safe. Where'd the one go that I hit?"

"Ran off. Are you hurt?" Ross looked at her eyes.

"No. Could you please assist me?"

One thick hand held back the airbag; the other took her left arm and helped her out of the car. Then he leaned in and turned the car off.

"Little wobbly. Did you hit your head?" He examined her top to bottom.

"No. I'm fine." She searched her trench coat pocket, relieved to find the weapon she brought for him intact. "Here." She handed him the pistol.

He took the gun and examined it. "This is a dart gun. What's it for?"

Still dazed and a bit woozy she pulled the box of darts out of her other pocket. "It's the gene blocking agent, modified into a serum."

"For what, Mom?" She hadn't noticed Teagan kneeling next to her.

Alexa looked at Teagan and then at Ross. "In theory, it will reverse the effects of the mutated gene, suppressing their altered DNA, basically making them human and should render them vulnerable to our weapons." Her eyes fixed to Ross's. "Are you going to stare at me all day or go get that creature, Trill, or whatever you want to call it." She was getting more and more used to Ross's nickname for the creatures.

Ross shook his head. "Not before I know you girls are safe. Ellie got a little banged up. She's unconscious in the back seat of the rig. Wait for me in the car."

"We'll be fine." Alexa tried to blow the confounded bangs out of her eyes again.

Teagan pulled a clip from her hair and haphazardly clipped her mom's hair out of the way.

Alexa thought it a nice gesture. "Thank you Teagan."

Teagan pointed to the field. "We're good. Go get those murdering bastards.

"Okay. But if you hear anything other than me, duck down. Understand?" With the dart gun in one hand and the riot shotgun in the other, he headed into the sea of grass behind the wrecked semi tractor trailer.

"You really think you can reverse the mutated gene?" Teagan asked.

"The facts point to that conclusion, they will become vulnerable once the mutated gene is blocked."

Teagan smiled. "Awesome, Mom. You created Kryptonite." Then her face went blank.

Alexa knew the look well. "What is it? You have something to tell me, I know that look. So, spit it out."

"This is big though, Mom. Huge." She sobbed as they walked toward the SUV.

"You know you can tell me anything, Teagan? We look at it objectively, come to a conclusion, then . . . "

" . . . rationalize the outcome. I know the drill. Ughh. You're so infuriating."

Alexa didn't understand where the animosity had come from.

"You remember the talk you and Dad gave me a few years ago?" Teagan stopped and looked into Alexa's eyes. Her makeup had smudged her cheeks and the whites had striations of red throughout.

"We gave you many talks."

Teagan's teeth ground together. "The one about—boys."

"The birds and the bees." Alexa mused. The tone of the conversation had taken a wrong turn somewhere.

"After that."

"What?" Then it came to her. "Protection?"

A tension built in the pit of her stomach like a thousand cockroaches in a box. It couldn't be? Not my daughter. Well she had started her period several years earlier. But they had always talked about her first time, how she would inform her parents first and use protection no matter what. Teagan's eyes told it all.

"Are you pregnant?" Alexa hadn't cried in a long time. Only a few forced tears when her husband died so people wouldn't think her heartless at the funeral. Nothing could have prepared her for this. And she certainly didn't think it would affect her this much. The Trills' births had been horrific. What these babies do to the mothers, she couldn't bear the thought of her daughter being eaten from the inside out.

"M . . . M . . . Mom!" Teagan's eyes widened.

Alexa prepared for the worse news of her life. "Please answer the question."

Teagan pointed. "There's one behind you."

46.

Ross had followed the droplets of blood for some time. The pattern zigzagged through the tall grass as if the Trill had stumbled back and forth, trying to stop his self from falling.

He's gotta be close.

Blood spatter in the grass dwindled. If he didn't hurry, Guy would heal completely and he'd lose his opportunity to see if Alexa's formula worked.

A tuft of grass rustled ahead. He flicked the safety off on the dart gun and took off in a dead sprint, scanning the field in front of him as he followed the crimson trail. He stopped where the path in the grass split. One track doubled back toward the truck. The blood path continued forward.

The girls.

Ross knew if he didn't get back fast, he'd probably lose all three of them.

He turned.

A wolf like shriek pierced his ears from behind. It happened fast and deliberate. He switched the shotgun from his right hand to his left and pulled the dart gun from the back of his pants where he'd tucked it into his belt. In a fluid motion he dropped to his back. He steadied the pistol, took aim and fired. The dart whooshed, unlike the blast of the shotgun that followed. Guy sailed over him and rolled on the grass. He flipped back to his feet and took an attack stance.

Ross rolled onto his belly. The dart dangled from Guy's neck. Not knowing if the dart had injected the formula, he again pulled the pistol's trigger and shot Guy in the chest, twice in the already-healing shotgun wound.

Guy stood, stumbled forward and fell face first into the grass with a thump. For some strange reason Ross felt bad for shooting him. Since he named him and all, it seemed like they had a connection. Hopefully he'd survived and they still had one live specimen for Dr. Mason.

Tufts of breath laid a dismal path as Ross crawled through the mist toward Guy. No clouds of air wafted in the cool evening breeze from Guy. When he reached him, Ross felt for a pulse. He didn't even know if it had a heart, let alone veins and arteries.

Ross's skin crawled as he placed his two fingers on the Trill's throat. The plasticity of its skin unnerved him. He crawled to his knees and rolled Guy toward him, onto his back. His eyes were closed. No muscles twitched. The wound in his chest hadn't healed. She'd done it. Alexa had either reversed the process or found some sort of miracle poison to weaken them. Now he needed to get back to the girls; the other Trill had definitely doubled back.

47.

ALEXA DIDN'T KNOW if movement antagonized the tri-alleles. Still as a statue, she whispered to Teagan, "What's it doing?"

"This is a trip. It's a girl, about my age and really pretty."

"You did not answer my question."

"She's standing above the dead one. Now she's on her knees. I think she's crying."

The Trill seemed to be stifling a sob.

"Mom." Teagan's eyes doubled in size. "She's coming this way."

Alexa inched her head around and glanced over her left shoulder. What looked like an attractive teenage girl strolled towards them like one might approach a neighbor for a chat. One thing Teagan hadn't counted on, the tri-allele had clothes on. This one act filled Alexa's head with new and important information. They obviously had the capacity to learn, to feel, and if so, it also meant they might listen to reason.

Alexa turned back to Teagan. "I couldn't see her facial expression, does she look angry?"

"From here she looks kinda . . . well . . . sad."

That's odd. If they have the same gambit of emotions as humans, then the Trills will be going through Kubler-Ross's five stages of grief.

"Mom! She just went to all fours and is crawling toward us."

Guess she hit the anger stage. But Alexa had to see for herself. Her heart raced as she turned around. Should she stand and confront the creature stalking them. This lioness, ready to pounce, which she may or may not be able to reason with? Maybe they didn't know the concept of revenge. She still felt sorry for the creature. A new species tossed into an unknown world. This female's only connection to her kind had been killed in front of her.

A tear dripped from the Trill's nose onto the street. Her eyes blackened like charcoal left in the rain. The corner of her lip curled, revealing an elongated, jagged, incisor. The creature's focus went beyond Alexa, and fell upon Teagan.

"Don't you dare touch her!" Alexa scowled. *Confrontation it is.*

The female Tri-Allele snarled. One moment she crawled toward them from thirty feet away, the next, a hand crushed Alexa's shoulder and launched her into the air. Pavement ground her back and cracked against her skull as she hit and slid. A cloud of darkness and flickers of light obscured her vision. When she came to a halt, she reached back and felt her blood-matted hair.

Teagan screamed.

Alexa rolled over, dreading the thought of having to watch her daughter's heart being ripped from her chest. Teagan curled into a fetal position. The female Trill loomed over her.

Please don't kill her.

Alexa's head throbbed from the base of her neck forward. The vision of Teagan and the Trill swam in a dismal haze. She struggled to keep her eyes open. *Have to stay awake. Save Teagan.* The thoughts faded as she lost consciousness.

48.

HEAT FROM THE girl's breath danced across Teagan's neck sending a chill of fear through her. Lucky she had peed earlier or there would be a puddle below her. She didn't want to look at the one who would end her life any closer than she already had. Something sharp, perhaps teeth scraped across her skin. One pricked the flesh and she felt dribbles of blood as they slid down her neck and chest. Quick breaths in and out slipped from her as she tried not to panic and run. *I don't want to die.*

"Don't kill me," she pleaded.

The girl put her face against Teagan's. Warmth covered her own cheek, but it didn't feel real. Almost as if she wore a Halloween mask. She took a whiff of Teagan's hair and whispered into her ear. "Why not kill you? Your people killed two of mine."

"Holy fuck! You can talk?" Teagan opened her eyes.

The girl's head snapped away until her black eyes met Teagan's. She then tilted her head to the side as if curious as to why Teagan had asked such a silly question.

"I didn't do anything to you. We didn't do anything to you."

She touched Teagan's leg, trailing dagger like nails up her thigh.

Teagan whimpered as her jeans tore and lines of blood blossomed. The girl's hand slipped under Teagan's shirt. Her touch sent a shudder through Teagan's body. "Step the fuck off, bitch!"

Her warm, damp palm rested on Teagan's belly. She closed her eyes and swayed as if in a trance. "You carry one of us with you. You will die soon enough." The girl's teeth ground as she said it. She turned and looked at Teagan's mom. "But she doesn't have one within."

"Don't you dare touch her."

The girl stood.

"I swear to God I'll rip your fucking head off." Teagan focused on her mom, who seemed to be struggling to sit up.

In a blur of speed the girl turned and snapped her jaws in Teagan's face.

Teagan flinched.

"We don't want to hurt you." She stood. "But, we have to eat."

"Eat a fucking cow."

"They won't sustain us."

Teagan rolled her eyes. "How do you know? Have you tried?"

"I can smell their stench from here. But she's so much sweeter." Again she turned and sniffed the air between them and her Mom.

"Fuck you. You piece of shit."

"Relax." The blackness in her eyes disintegrated to a deep brown. *Normal human eyes?*

"I'm not going to touch her." The eyes became night again. "I'm going to rip her heart out and eat it in front of you."

"Please . . . don't." Teagan sobbed.

The girl ignored Teagan's pleas and started for her Mom.

Teagan caught her by the shirt and pulled. "Leave her alone!"

With a flick of the wrist, claws swiped across Teagan's left cheek. Her head snapped to the right. Blood flung from her face. Teagan slapped her hand against the lacerations. Out of the corner of her eye, she saw the girl appear next to her mom. "Mommy!"

49.

Ross CRINGED AS he watched Savannah toss Alexa like a rag doll. The truck's headlights lit up Teagan as the Trill approached her. Even at a dead sprint, he'd be too late to save her. But if he stopped and attempted a shot with the pistol, he might make the save. He anticipated Savannah stuffing her claws into Teagan any second. But he needed to get closer to be accurate. Darts lose their velocity much faster than bullets and at this range he didn't know if the dart would hit its mark.

Even while running through the tall grass he heard Savannah snap her teeth at Teagan.

The fear in Teagan's posture bore deep into Ross's heart.

On the road, Alexa attempted to sit up. He figured at the distance she'd been tossed she had to have at least a concussion. Definitely scrapes bruises and maybe a laceration or two.

Ross only had two darts left. He had to make sure to hit the creature in the jugular vein, ensuring quick absorption of the agent.

Sweat dripped from his forehead and drenched his underarms and back as he moved through the tall grass. But it was too late. Savannah had sliced open Teagan's face and appeared next to Alexa.

This is where your sharp shooter training comes into play. It's all or nothing here, big guy. You can do this. With a keen eye steadied down the barrel of the gun, he took aim and shot.

Savannah spun like a cyclone and caught the dart. Before he could take aim again, she had him by the throat.

With uncanny strength she lifted him off his feet. "What is this?" She held the dart up.

He coughed and gagged. She decreased her grip on his throat until he could speak. "What the fuck? You can talk?"

She dropped him to his feet and kicked him in the chest. He landed in a soft patch of grass with an 'oomph'.

"Holy hell. Where'd the wrecking ball come from?" When he tried to sit up, the pain in his chest increased by a thousand as Savannah landed on him.

Razor sharp claws pricked into his throat. "The object you shot at me. It's not the same as what the other weapons fire. What is it? I will not ask again."

"It's a tranquilizer. We're trying to capture one of you alive." He hoped she'd fall for his lie.

"Why?"

"We need to know what you are and why you're here."

"And how to kill us?"

"No." He struggled to breath. "How to save you."

"Maybe we don't want to be saved. Maybe we are exactly how we are meant to be?" Her claws retracted from his throat and her eyes changed color.

"Do you even know what you are?" *Jesus, how much does this girl weigh? Can't be more than a buck ten? So, why can't I move?*

She looked to the sky. "I'm not sure—yet. But the answer is out there, waiting for me."

"Are you being controlled by someone?" The line of questioning felt right to him. However, he didn't know why he bothered as she'd probably tear him apart any minute. No. This line of questioning did have a purpose—to buy time.

Her eyes closed and she breathed deep, pondering. "Not to my knowledge."

The answer didn't ring truthful to Ross. His instincts for such things usually hit spot on. And in this instance, he felt a moment of doubt. It shone in her eyes as if she had an idea of some higher being, holding her extra-terrestrial puppet strings.

"Do you have a purpose?" he asked.

"If there is a purpose for us, I do not know of it."

"I still don't understand how you can talk."

"Some I picked up listening to people talk, some I learned from the television."

He couldn't believe she'd mastered the language so quick. But other questions needed answered. "What about the males? They don't seem to be as smart as you."

"The males are supposed to be with me. The gathering has commenced."

"Why gather them to you? To mate?"

"Yes. Procreation is a must."

He sensed that wasn't the only reason.

"Why didn't you kill Teagan?"

"Teagan?"

"The girl over there." He tried to point, but was still pinned down.

"She carries one of us inside of her?"

What the hell? Teagan's pregnant?

"Why haven't you killed me?" Somewhere deep inside, the creature, this girl, she had feelings . . . purpose. He sensed she searched for these things.

"I'm thinking about it?" She shot him a terrifying smirk.

"What are humans to you?"

She licked a dribble of his blood from her finger tip.

"Got it, we're cattle. Do you drink our blood?" *Fucking vampires. Everything's about vampires these days. Can't look at a bookshelf or movie mylar without seeing something about blood-sucking fiends. Now we've created them?*

"It's palatable, but we require the thicker tissue of the heart." She licked her lips. "I don't know why."

"Why don't you eat cows, chickens, pigs, something other than humans?"

She gripped him around the throat, leaned down, and gritted her razor sharp teeth together. Then she laughed, a cute giggle, not a heinous cackle which should come from an evil demon wretch before she kills you.

"Can't you smell them? They're disgusting." Her nose crinkled and she drew in a deep whiff of his chest. "You smell . . . delectable."

Ross had been inching his hand toward the dart gun, which had landed just out of his reach. His questioning distracted her, but he needed a few more inches.

"Where did you all come from?"

"Didn't we cover this already? I don't know."

"I still can't believe how well you speak for a one week old."

"I'm confused as well. I learn everything I see, everything I touch. All I had to do was listen to someone speak and I knew the language. It's incredibly overwhelming. Then I have these urges; an urge to seek out the males and an insatiable urge to kill people, eat their hearts, wipe them out." She licked her lips and ground her hips against him.

The motion sent a twinge through his balls. Instead of a creature on top of him he became painfully aware of the young beautiful girl riding him. This made him extremely uncomfortable. For crying out loud, she seemed the same age as his daughters, maybe a little older. But her hip-grind had worked in his favor. It moved him closer to the dart gun.

A little closer. A few more questions should do it. "Can females of your kind mate with human males?"

"I don't know." She pressed her crotch against his and licked the side of his face. "Want to find out." Her tongue flicked his earlobe.

He gulped and bit down on his lip to keep his other head in check. This wasn't seventh grade anymore. He did have a modicum of control.

"Not particularly," he answered.

She sat up, but still rode him. "Human males are food, nothing more."

"Then why do your males sexually assault our females?"

"They seem to be mindless without me around. I don't think they can tell the difference between human females and their own kind, but our male reproductive anatomy is not compatible with your females. The male's reproductive system is deadly to human females. In order to control them, I have to gather them to me."

"Are you the only female?"

"No. But there aren't many. They're doing the same as me, gathering the males."

"Why . . . exactly?" There had to be a reason.

"I don't know. But I have the feeling I'll know as soon as I complete the gathering. Don't come after me. Take the dead ones for your research. But if you try to destroy us, I assure you, something bad will happen."

He grasped the handle of the pistol, but by the time he'd lifted it, she'd turned and disappeared into the dark field.

"Shit!" When he sat up, he saw Alexa standing in the street.

She hobbled toward him, her lab coat looked tattered and blood had dried to her forehead. "Why didn't you shoot?"

"I have no idea what just happened." He stood and rubbed his chest. "Bitch packs quite a punch."

She smiled, which put a smile on his face. He thought she might be mad at him for not killing Savannah. At least they had survived.

Alexa rubbed the back of her head. "The tri-alleles are strong, that's for sure."

They both found that out the hard way, but he had a lot of information to give Alexa and . . . *Oh shit.* "I forgot about Beef."

They met at the side of the road. "You're hungry?" She stumbled and held onto him for support.

"No. Beef's the firefighter we came here to rescue. He's been waiting patiently for us to come get him"

Alexa frowned. "Hopefully he's still alive."

"I'd call, but have no idea where my radio fell off." He looked around the immediate area.

50.

ALEXA LET GO of Ross's arm. "I can walk on my own, thank you." While her right foot throbbed and ached, it still worked.

"Are you sure?" He had one hand on his ribs, the other under her arm.

"You're worse than me. I'm good."

He responded appropriately by letting go. The gesture had been chivalrous and she appreciated his help, but she was used to taking care of herself and didn't require assistance. Her attention turned to her daughter.

Teagan sat with her knees to her chest. Streaks of blood poured from gashes in her cheek. The blood alarmed Alexa a little, but the blank stare of Teagan's catatonic state that scared her to death. The fact Teagan wasn't tending to her wound or acknowledging her mother's presence, petrified her.

She knelt and took Teagan's hand. "Take some deep breaths." Her sweat-filled, cool hand trembled.

Buttons shot in several directions as Ross tore his grass stained shirt off. "She's in shock." He knelt on the other side of Teagan and pressed the shirt to the wound on her face.

Alexa turned. The half clothed appearance of Ross felt surreal. The woman inside of her (the one who reared her head every once in a while) forced her to take another quick peek. Thick striated muscles rippled under a mat of chest hairs that dwindled as they arrowed toward his belly button, which would usually cause her to yearn, however, he'd told her something she already knew, as if she wasn't smart enough to think of it on her own. Not okay.

"I'm aware she's in shock!" She huffed.

"Okay. Sheesh. Don't bite my head off."

The retort had been much harsher than she had intended. "Let's lie her down here for a moment."

They both helped Teagan lie back in the grass.

Ross kept pressure on the wound with his shirt. "She's gonna need stitches."

Not only stitches, she's going to need some extensive plastic surgery. Alexa knew this wasn't a killing blow by any means. The female had commanded Teagan's attention and knew a slap to the face would get it; a way of letting the human know who's in charge.

"Ross?"

"Yeah."

"Go check on Ellie." They had gone through so much. Ellie seemed to be sleeping it off. Teagan, however, still wouldn't come around. If the formula worked and Teagan survived the child birth, therapy could help.

Ross half-jogged to the Navigator. He disappeared behind the blinding headlights. A few moments later he emerged.

"Is she . . . ?"

"No. Ellie's alive. Like Teagan, she's in shock. I put a blanket over her and raised her legs using the firefighter coats.

"We need to get them out of here. Is your car still working?" She knew the lights had been on the entire time they had been there.

"It's running. I just started it and turned the heater on."

"Good." When she hit the Trill the front end of her car had collapsed and her radiator exploded leaving a trail of greenish orange fluid on the road. Her car wasn't going anywhere.

Again Ross disappeared behind the lights.

Teagan whimpered.

Alexa looked into her eyes, still nothing. "We're going to get you out of here. You'll see. All of this will go away. Odds are you will have a viable fetus. I mean, healthy baby. We'll raise it together." An agnostic at heart, she had her opinions on life. It began in the womb and wasn't supposed to end there. Of that, she was absolutely sure.

Still looking like a man who just got his ass beat in a rugby match, Ross lumbered over. A wool blanket dangled from his right hand. He touched her shoulder. She took the hint and moved away from Teagan.

He crouched, and lifted the blanket draped Teagan. "What do you say we get the hell out of here?"

The warmth and fatherly love in those words sent warm fuzzy prickles through Alexa's body. He'd managed to save himself and four other lives. In the process he procured two fully matured Trills. Not bad for a day's work, except, he'd also put Teagan and Ellie in harm's way, and came close to losing Ellie in the process.

She followed him back to the Navigator and helped him lay Teagan down on the third row bench seat. Ellie didn't move under the blanket in the second row of back seats. Her chest rose and fell. A good sign she'd live.

In her haste Alexa had completely forgotten about the serum. She climbed into the passenger's seat next to Ross. "Do you think the serum worked?"

"The one in the field caught a couple in the chest and my shotgun finished the job. So, I'd say we had a successful field trial. What about the other one?"

Again she'd forgotten a slight detail. It had been a very long, grueling day. "You're talking about the one you killed without the serum?"

"That's the one. He's already in the back." They pulled off the road. "I'll get ya the one that still has a head. Give me a minute."

Alexa cringed at the thought of a headless tri-allele decaying in the trunk. Ross hopped out and pulled a tarp from the back, then disappeared into the field. Her head still throbbed. She felt her scalp and the many lacerated areas. Her hair had matted and successfully clotted the wounds.

Ross emerged from the dark with what looked like a large roll of tarp hanging from his shoulder. Two bare feet stuck out the front. Blood soaked down his chest and into the front of his dark slacks. He grunted as he lifted the man onto the hood of the Navigator.

Alexa stuck her head out the window. "So, we're going to strap it to the hood like a deer?"

"Nope." Ross climbed onto the hood and dragged the Trill's body up to the roof, leaving a blood-smeared racing stripe in his wake.

"Gonna tie it to the roof, like a Christmas tree." He let out a muffled guffaw.

The joke mildly amused her. She laughed and her head bing-bonged as if she'd stuck it into Quasimodo's bell at toll-time.

Metal crinkled under the weight of his feet. Even though the car's roof should be sturdy enough to hold the weight of a two-hundred-pound man, she still ducked a couple of times, thinking he might fall through.

What he'd brought her held the keys to solve this horrific, nightmarish riddle. Each drop of blood, inch of tissue, and clump of brain matter, would lead her to her goal and could save millions of lives. The most important were the lives of her daughter and unborn grandchild.

Ross climbed back in. "Look what I found." He pulled out his radio.

"That's good news?" She guessed.

"Not really. I can't hail dispatch or Beef." He revved the engine and they sped down the highway toward the lights of the downed fire truck, and probably, more human remains.

51.

SAVANNAH DIDN'T KNOW why she hadn't ripped the man's hammering heart from his chest. He'd killed her males and put her mission in jeopardy. Mission? Yes. There is a mission. Though she didn't know what the mission entailed, or why she needed to find the males and gather them to her. She had an idea the truth would be revealed to her once she'd done her part. Instinct had her headed west, toward the Oregon coast. Every step brought her closer to another male. Her heart ached for him. A literal pain in her chest grew as she closed the gap between them.

She enjoyed the feeling of the forest as she leapt over downed trees, climbed boulders, and hurtled canyons. Cars roared by when she zipped across a street or came close to a highway. Her goal had been to stay clear of those areas. She didn't want to be spotted by more men with guns.

The tree-line ended and opened into a clearing. A strange home made of metal sat in the middle. Junkyard relics littered the landscape. Spindles of nettles prickled and danced along her spine, a passionate indicator of the imminent birth of another male.

A swoosh, followed by several soft thumps came from inside the home. A woman shrieked throughout the assault. The trailer shimmered as if hit by an earthquake. On the fifth thump, she whimpered her last breath and her heart ceased to glow. The door flew open and a man stumbled out of the trailer. In one hand he held a can of beer. The other held a butcher knife. Sweet liquid dripped from the blade to the dirt below and thick globs of it decorated his coveralls.

Behind the man, through the open door, the infant's eyes lit up the shadows under the cupboards. Any minute the young one would be enjoying his first meal.

He pounced.

The man's perplexed look turned to sheer terror. He lurched forward and fell face first into the dirt. Flesh, blood, and bone flew from his back as the infant's claws tore into him. A gurgle escaped the man as the tiny hands lifted his heart through the hole in his back. Then the male sat on his haunches and feasted. Strands of blood squirt from the heart with every bite the infant took. When he finished, he looked at Savannah.

In a matter of seconds she stood in the pasture of wrecked vehicles and beckoned the infant to her. He launched from the corpse and landed in Savannah's arms.

"That's a good boy." The infant male cuddled into her bosom. "Let's find you some more food so you can grow big and strong. There is still a lot of work to be done."

Their best hope of finding ample sustenance for the boy was to go where people were; densely populated areas. Her motherly instinct took over and she realized the infant had no clothes on. With the child in her arms, she stepped over the dead man's body and climbed into the trailer.

Hoarded old newspapers lined one side of the unkempt trailer. Several plates caked with dried-up food sat in the fly-swarmed sink. A pan on the stove bubbled and splashed. At the end of a short hallway a woman, with her legs spread, slumped against a soaked bed. Multiple stab wounds surrounded the carnage the baby made tearing his way out of the woman. Through the torture of the man stabbing her, she'd squeezed the placenta out, which now hung by a strand of flesh from her ripped and tattered inner thighs.

The woman bore no consequence to Savannah. In a hall cupboard she found a blanket to swaddle the baby in. After she wrapped the child tight, she followed a long dirt driveway to a paved road and kept moving toward the coast where another male waited for her. Once she found a good place for the baby to feed, the little one would grow fast. But the other one had already reached full growth and sought his mate. He too would join her as would many others along the coast line and even more inland. Thus, the gathering began.

52.

EVER SINCE ROSS returned from the fire truck he'd been in a sour mood. Apparently his friend, Beef, hadn't been inside. He told her bloody, bare footprints led away from engine seven and he didn't want to risk following them just to find the mutilated body of his new friend at the other end. So, they had turned around and headed back to the lab at OHSU.

Alexa dozed on and off during the trip back. Ross flipped through the radio stations and found a few stations playing the President's speech over and over. When they pulled into Beaverton, Alexa couldn't say anything. A war zone. That's the best description she had for her home town.

Flames sprouted from an overturned pickup they crept past. Abandoned, broken vehicles cluttered the streets. A ripped open torso dangled from a broken window at her favorite Starbucks coffee shop.

"I guess she came through here." Ross shook his head. His knees held the steering wheel while he dropped the empty clip from the dart gun and slapped another one in. Alexa flinched.

"Sorry. Would ya look at this mess?" In a slow crawl, he steered the Navigator around several more stranded cars. "Come to think of it, I haven't heard any chatter over the radio in a while." He reached down and pulled the radio from its perch on the dash.

"Dispatch, this is Agent Harris, come in." He waited for the snotty voice to ring in his ears, but he heard only empty static. "Dispatch, this is Agent Harris, come in." Again, silence.

"I don't like the sound of this. Try calling someone on your cell. Maybe Ray." His hand grazed her left shoulder.

His touch electrified the hair on her arms. The frantic search for her phone revealed a fractured iPhone in her right side pants pocket. "Crud. The impact from the Trill tossing me across the street crushed my phone." She dangled the destroyed iPhone so he could see.

He frowned. "Shit. I think mine's in my jacket pocket, somewhere in the back seat."

Alexa unbuckled her belt and turned on the overhead light. Teagan flinched, but didn't open her eyes.

"Sorry, baby. I'm looking for a phone." She wished her soothing tone would calm Teagan.

Ross's crumpled pin-striped jacket lay in a wad behind the driver's seat. Alexa pulled it up front and found the phone tucked into the inside pocket behind the right lapel.

He took the phone from her. "Thanks."

"No problem." She smiled. "That's what I'm here for." Yeah, there for phone-fetching and motherly soothing of children and to keep the attention of the F.B.I. guy on the important stuff.

He didn't respond and tapped away at his phone. "This is Agent Harris. May I speak to Director Ranzoni?"

A tense moment went by.

"Director, this is Agent Harris .... Yes sir. No sir. Yes sir."

The cryptic conversation annoyed Alexa. She wished she could hear what the other man had to say.

He told the entire story of the Independence ordeal and the fiasco on Highway 99.

"We think the serum will at least make them vulnerable to our weapons. We haven't been able to test it completely. We have a dead male, but we need a live specimen as soon as possible. Yes, sir. Please notify me as soon as you procure a live one for us. Yes, sir. We'll keep in touch." Ross put the phone down next to him on the seat.

"Well?" She didn't want to wait anymore. Her foot tapped incessantly. The conversation wasn't going anywhere. A thorough explanation would be welcome at this point.

"The Trills have started to cluster, forming small groups." His eyes tensed.

"What is it?" She squinted her eyes at him.

He wiped his brow. "They're congregating and marching into

highly populated areas where they hunt down every human they can find. Is that it? Are you trying to wipe us out?"

She snapped her seatbelt back on. "That's to be expected, especially with what you told me about the females gathering the more subservient males to them. This leads me to believe, suspect really, that this could be some sort of invasion. They're exterminating us; wiping our species from existence."

"My God." He reached over and put his hand hers.

The sudden affection confused her, but his warm touch soothed her mind for a moment. This jar headed man had shown true courage in the midst of adversity. He'd not only saved her, he'd also saved Teagan and Ellie. These qualities attracted in every sense of the word. But she needed to remain focused. Besides, if he kept running off half-cocked like he had been, he'd end up dead anyway. Emotions should be kept out of this.

She removed her hand from his. "If my serum doesn't work, I anticipate the world being overrun by tri-alleles in a matter of months."

His hands gripped the steering wheel tight. "What makes you think they're aliens and this just isn't God's next step in the evolution of man?"

"I know things that you don't."

Ross's eyes squinted as if he wanted to glare at her, but kept his eyes on the road and elsewhere, always scanning. "Well? What do you know?"

"An Indian scientist made the discovery of a meteorite."

"Yeah," he said.

"This meteor should have passed by our sun, but it fractured into billions of tiny particles which penetrated the ozone layer and entered our atmosphere."

"Seriously? What happened? Why are all of these babies being affected?"

"Of course I'm being serious. Why would I lie about such things?"

He shook his head. "Let me guess. The particles entered our atmosphere on Halloween?"

"About an hour before patient zero; Savannah Staten, was born."

"So the Alien mojo would have a chance to work on the fetus."

"Yes. But I've isolated the Alien 'mojo' as you call it, and we can now fight back."

"If your serum doesn't work, we're fucked, excuse my language."

At this point, she didn't even care about the language. She had her highly-tuned mind wrapped around the magnitude of the entire situation. They were in the midst of a pseudo-apocalypse. The world as they knew it might never be the same.

"What a nightmare." Ross took his phone from the seat and began to text someone.

"You're correct. This is a nightmarish time. Get me to my lab where I can start mass-producing the formula. I fear it's our only hope of survival. You know texting and driving is very dangerous. If you want, I'll text for you while you watch this very dangerous maze we used to call Highway 99."

"What?" He didn't look at her, only glanced at the road from time to time as he texted someone. When he finished his text, he kept checking the phone every couple of seconds.

"Waiting to hear back from your boss?" She figured that's who he'd texted. To give them the good news about the anti-Trill agent she'd created. But his persona showed something different. Sorrow, as if he might burst into tears any moment, which definitely did not go along with his character at all: big, tough, jar-headed, F.B.I. guy. A coefficient of this man's complicated equation had eluded her.

"Nope. My daughters. I'm praying they're okay."

"I'm sorry. Where are they?"

"With their mom, on her sister's ranch, hidden. She usually gets back to me in minutes."

Then his phone chimed. He checked it again and pointed the face at Alexa. The screen had a huge cartoon smiley face on it. Guess that answered his question because he put the phone away and settled back down.

"Hold on!" Ross slammed on the brakes, bringing the rig to a sliding halt.

Alexa choked as the seat belt tightened across her chest and throat. Again she gasped and found her heart trying to make an escape from her chest via her throat. Two full-grown male Trills stood in the road. Their naked, pallid bodies, splotched with blood stains from their victims, didn't look as if they'd come to town for fun. They came to—feed.

53.

"**B**ACK UP! Back up!" Alexa smacked Ross's right arm.

"I'm going. I'm going."

Teeth barred and snarls ripped from the Trills as the SUV sped in reverse. Alexa kept her eyes on them and hoped Ross didn't wreck the car. One leapt an incredible distance, landing with a thud. The hood of the SUV crinkled and for a moment, the back tires lifted off the ground.

The SUV's rear bounced against the concrete.

"Hold on!" Ross slammed on the breaks and whipped the wheel to the side. The rig spun 180 degrees before he crammed it into drive and sped forward.

The Trill on the hood slid off.

It landed in the street next to the other one, gaining ground on them with each long stride. The speedometer, now at forty miles per hour kept climbing.

Alexa thought Ross navigated brilliantly through the automobile-littered street. The pursuit swerved them around abandoned cars, but the creatures kept coming. They flew over the tops of the obstacles, free running across building fronts and skewed vehicles.

Were they not bound to the laws of gravity? Alexa questioned herself. "They're gaining on us." She watched the creatures chasing them.

"We're almost to the highway." Ross glanced at her.

The SUV veered onto the ramp of Highway 76. The Trills leapt off the overpass landing only feet behind them.

"How fast are you going?" The Trills had made up some ground, but seemed to be falling behind.

"We just hit 65."

"Well that's good to know."

"What's that?"

"They can't run faster than sixty."

"Shit. You're right." He wiped his sweat covered brow with his bare right arm.

"Now what?" She slumped in her seat, her heart pace returned to normal.

His brow furrowed. "We're not going to make it to your lab. Not with the amount of Trills roaming around. No. We need to find a place close by. Someplace where you can do your work."

She knew only one. "Okay. I think I know just the place and should be safe enough for the girls as well." She hopped.

"Where's that?"

"My house isn't too far from here." She logged the coordinates into the GPS on the Dash. "That should do it."

A sense of calm washed over her. It didn't last long as she realized. "Oh crap."

"Now what?" He looked at her with one raised brow.

"I left my keys in my car."

Ross sifted through his hair and scratched the center of his head. "There's another way in, right?"

"There's a spare key in a lockbox on the front door. But the keys to my husband's shop are on the key chain."

"What's in the shop?"

"It's now a small lab. I have enough equipment to make the serum there. I'll call Ray, he can email me the formula and process notes. Hopefully that will be enough. If not, maybe he can bring us what we need."

"Sounds like a plan." Ross pulled off the freeway and followed the GPS.

Alexa kept watch for any more Trills. The desolation of her own neighborhood staggered her and for a moment she couldn't catch her breath. Mr. Winters, one of her daughters favorite teachers (history), lay face up in his perfect lawn. His front bay window had been smashed, blood covered his face and he had a whole in his chest the size of a cantaloupe.

"Poor bastard," Ross said as he turned onto her street.

Most of her neighbors had vacated. Front doors and garages raised and bits of luggage scattered across a few of the lawns. She looked away from a body which dangled out a two story window, entrails spilling to the ground.

"It's the white house on the left, the one with the pillars out front." She pointed at her home. At least the house remained undisturbed.

Ross pulled into the driveway and parked. "Nice house."

"Thanks." When she stepped out of the car she heard the whip, whip, whip of her neighbor's home alarm. They needed to get inside, quick and quiet.

"Should I go check it out?" Ross appeared next to her, dart gun in one hand, his own pistol in the other.

Henderson's cars sat in their driveway. Their boat took up the entire three-car garage so they would usually leave the truck on the street. They'd taken it.

"From the size of those skid marks, I'd say they took off in a hurry." Ross Put the dart gun in his shoulder holster, which looked a bit odd against his bare skin.

Somewhere in the distance a woman screamed. The hairs on Alexa's neck had a conniption as if they'd all started to wriggle their way out of their slots simultaneously. An ominous shadow passed by the Henderson's front room bay window. Alexa feared the worse for the Henderson's family of five.

Ross finished circling the car. "We need to get inside now!"

Like a church mouse she skittered to the lock box bolted to the left pillar on the porch. Once opened, she took the key and instinctively closed the box. A mistake as it made a loud click. *Oh, no.* The unwanted sound could have alerted a nearby Trill. Her hands trembled as she unlocked the front door.

Ross followed her with Ellie in his arms. The girls had both slept through the entire chase. A bit worrisome as they most certainly had shock symptoms and possible concussions, she'd check on them once she knew the house wasn't crawling with creatures.

"Put her on the couch." Alexa pointed to the living room sofa.

Ross nodded, laid Ellie down and headed back out to get Teagan.

Alexa wandered down the unsettling dark hall which led to the downstairs bathroom, the spare room, and the master bedroom. She stopped, frozen as if time ceased to exist. An ominous shadow at the end of the hall stood tall in the corner. Squinting did not help discern the entity. In her mind she made it out to be a stark naked male tri-allele. It kept to the corner, ready to strike. Her heart skipped as if tossed across a pond. Her hand searched the wall for the light switch. She flipped it on. *Nothing.* No killer human/alien hybrid just shadows playing nasty little tricks in her mind.

She retrieved several blankets from the hall closet. They included one which conjured a flood of emotions. Across the middle of the comforter, in fire-engine red, were the words 'Best Fire Chief Ever'. Brad worked hard to become Fire Chief. Even as a young Fire Fighter/Paramedic, his work ethic astonished her, but he'd work a lot. Sometimes they wouldn't see each other for three or four days, which was hardly conducive to married life, but for some reason it had worked. To her knowledge they had a perfect marriage.

The comforter floated out in front of her and drifted over Ellie. When she finished tucking the blanket around her she leaned over and kissed the girl's soft freckled cheek. She supposed it was an emotional response to the blanket since she *never* kissed or hugged anyone. Maybe this needed to change.

54.

SAVANNAH'S MALES FOLLOWED her through dense Oregon forests to the top of a shallow canyon. People in the valley below scurried about a small town. The oldest male's cobalt eyes followed a couple holding hands. They snuck from house to house. Sweat gleamed off his bald head. Froth oozed from his mouth in anticipation of her orders.

The young one had shed and now walked on two feet. His clawed hand held hers and squeezed giddily when he noticed a woman chase a child, about his height, into the street. No others had touched the area yet. Savannah claimed it with a deep low-throated growl. The hoard went to their knees.

With a simple thought, *feast;* the males raced down the mountain. The little one headed straight for the child and mother. He alternated between scampering on all fours and running on two legs. A yip came from the human child when Savannah's young one pounced and bit into the back of his neck.

A full-grown male approached the child's mother from behind. She'd fallen to her knees, and wept while the youngling tore her own child's still-beating heart from his chest. He attacked the woman like a wolf in heat.

Her scream sent a shiver through Savannah.

His claws sank into the back of the woman's neck and protruded through the front with a splash of blood and a gurgled last protest before he took her.

Savannah sat on a tree stump, turned away from the carnage. Her fingers caressed the soft tips of a bright yellow flower. Cries of terror and agony erupted throughout the town below. The people tried to hide, but their hearts could be seen through the thickest of walls. She thought of the man she spared. The human had risked his life and killed two of her males. Why had she spared him? Did she admire him? Was it his courage? Savannah frowned. When the cries below quieted for good the males made their way back to her; their work in town completed. Now they needed to move on. More coastal towns full of people needed to be eradicated and she had many more males to collect. Their ethereal pull came from every direction. From the west however, she felt something else.

55.

"**W**HERE DO YOU want her?" Ross held Teagan's rag doll body over his shoulder.

"Lay her in the spare bedroom bed, down the hall, first door on the right."

"Got it. Mind if I wash up a bit?"

Brown flecks of dried blood stuck to his chest hairs and coated his back. His pants probably had never been the color of blood, mud, grass stains, and guts before.

"Go ahead." She didn't know if the sound of the showers would alert any nearby tri-alleles.

Ross followed her direction and clicked the light off as he disappeared down the hall.

After closing the shades, she noticed Ross had left the front door open. She frowned as she closed and locked it.

Ellie looked secure on the couch. She proceeded to the spare bedroom where Ross stood waiting.

"Could you get the blankets?" He nodded toward the bed.

"Sure. Sorry about that." She pulled back the spare bed's blankets and sheets. He laid Teagan down and she tucked her in.

"The bathroom?"

"It's just down the hall on your right. We passed it."

"Great." He looked at his chest and arms. "I'm a mess."

She didn't disagree as he left the room.

What now? The fact remained that a baby with a third allele grew within her daughter's belly. This brought on the questions. How could she have let this happen? At what point did she lose control of her child? She moved a strand of hair from Teagan's face, then sat on the floor with her back against the bed and wept.

When she stopped sobbing, she kept a keen ear out for any noises other than her daughter's breath and the shower. Even though she'd drawn the shades, she looked for shadows moving about the hall. Another scream came from somewhere in the distance. The shrill of terror probably permeated all of Beaverton.

A few minutes after the sound of the shower died, Ross returned to the bedroom. His gray-dusted black hair stood in all directions. One towel draped over his shoulder, the other wrapped tight around his waist. He cinched it up and sat on the bed above her. His thick muscled calves flexes as he stretched.

"That was great. Thanks."

"Please don't do that again." Men could be so careless.

"Do what? Take a shower." He dried his hair again with the shoulder towel. Both biceps rippled and she couldn't help but stare at his wet chest hairs. Her husband had a bald chest. Every once in a while he'd grow a hair which she would pluck. A lone hair on the chest was like the last donut in a box, sooner or later someone would get it. Ross looked like a werewolf from the neck down. When her eyes trailed, she saw something under the towel she hadn't expected and quickly averted them.

"Leave the door open. It's too dangerous out there to be leaving doors wide open." She remembered what he needed lecturing about.

He scowled. "I'll try and remember that next time I save your ass."

"And fix your towel for goodness sakes. I can see, well . . . *everything*."

He stood. "Yes, your majesty." He dropped his towel in front of her and walked out of the room.

She gritted her eyes shut and ground her teeth. *How infuriating.* Had she lost all control?

Ever vigilant, she kept watch on all windows and doors and, yep, the hall. Where had he gone? Would he be coming back? Did he think she was a total bitch? She didn't care. Or did she? The gambit of emotions playing with her heart and soul overwhelmed her. She closed her eyes.

A few moments later, warm arms wrapped around her and pulled her close. The aroma of her husband's shirt and deodorant Ross now wore made her cuddle into him like she had done on occasion with her husband. He'd changed into her husband's Polk County Fire and Rescue t-shirt and a pair of his work jeans. "I'm sorry," she said.

"No explanation needed." With her ear against his chest she could hear how deep his voice really was.

"It's just . . . the Trills are out there . . . and . . . I need to get to work."

"We're all a bit wired." He lifted her chin until she could see his steel blue eyes. "No worries, I'm sorry I snapped at you."

A shiver, not from the cold, but from the twinkle of his eyes and his smile ran through her as if she'd touched two positive wires together.

The tear he wiped from her cheek glistened on his finger. She hadn't even realized she'd started crying. "I don't know if I can do this." She buried her head in his chest again.

"You can do anything. You're Doctor Alexa-freaking-Mason. You're the 'Top Gun' of your profession, the best in the entire world. I know you can do it."

"But, if I don't, then what? I lose Teagan and her baby?" The thought of losing him crossed her mind as well. Could she take that kind of heartache again? And how would Teagan handle losing another man in her life? She had to face the fact that this brave F.B.I. Agent's chances of survival were minimal, given his inability to control his instincts in dangerous situations. Had she lost her mind completely? Ross was not her husband. He was a business associate, that's all. Wasn't it?

"I'm here and I'm not going anywhere. I'll protect you three with my life, if I have to." He lifted her chin until their eyes met.

Oh my. What's he doing?

"I'll stay with you until you're no longer in need of my services. I swear it."

"You don't have to ..."

He leaned in and kissed her: soft, yet gentle. His lips trailed hers as if he caressed them with a feather. Again he pulled away.

What's the protocol here? She had no idea. He'd kissed her. Now what? *Do I kiss him back?* Her eyes darted from his eyes to his lips. She licked her upper lip. He tasted of mint toothpaste.

He pulled her close again, like he wanted to give her a hug.

Cuddling would be good. She needed to be wrapped in strong arms, safe arms. But their lips met again. His tongue probed deeper and his hands cupped her backside and began to slip under the back of her shirt.

Definitely kiss back.

In her entire life she'd only kissed one man and it never felt like this. She'd heard others speak of kisses being magical, but never believed such nonsense. This kiss felt as if the world stood still around them. Universes exploded as her usually negative ions met his positives. Like two synapses with one purpose.

He lifted her onto his lap. Lips, full and wet, brushed the side of her neck; a thrill of energy zipped through her, intensifying as they trailed to her earlobe where he nibbled for a moment. Hot, lustful breath permeated her ear.

With a forward thrust she ground her hips against his thighs. Then her nerves took over and she began to shake.

"What's wrong?" The back of his hand brushed her face.

"Nothing." She lied. How do you tell a man that you can't? You mustn't.

She looked over his shoulder at Teagan. Then realized why she was so nervous.

"We can't do this in here. But I want to."

"Are you sure?" He smiled.

The thickness between his legs pressed between her legs. He had no idea how bad she wanted to let him take her. Heat washed up her neck and across her face.

"It's okay if you don't. We can stop."

Alexa looked into his eyes and drowned in them. Was this man a hypnotist? Every part of her wanted to get up and leave. But the ooze between her thighs said otherwise. There's no way she wanted to stop. It had been too long since she had intercourse. Even if the sex was induced by a stressful situation, she could use the stress relief. Maybe it would clear her head from the night's activities and she would have some sort of breakthrough in the morning.

She kissed him again. "No way, but we can't do anything in here."

He stood and lifted her. "Which way?"

She timidly pointed to the hall. Butterflies, bees, hummingbirds, whatever insect or animal had crawled into her stomach, frenzied.

The palpable beat of her heart created a steady thump in her chest and throat. His biceps bulged as he carried her down the hall.

"Upstairs." She continued to nuzzle against his neck and could easily fall asleep in his arms. But she wanted more.

When they reached the top of the second landing he headed for the master bedroom at the end of the hall. She pulled away from his constant kiss. "Not there." A gentle finger pointed to the upstairs spare room. She hoped he didn't mind as she really didn't want to make love in the same bed she had shared with her husband. It didn't feel right. But everything else, the kissing, the touching, the love making, with Ross, felt perfect.

56.

WHIMPERS FROM RANSACKED homes filled the night. Human females bled to death, their innards desiccated by the males. The brood stood behind Savannah. Blood spattered their torsos, dripped from their mouths and oozed from their claws. Before, the human heart had called to her, beckoning her to feed. Now, it appalled her. She didn't know why, but for some reason, her appetites had changed.

From the pack emerged a large male. Muscles rippled against his tough skin. Dark hair bristled from his chest and dusted his scalp. The intent in his eyes and the mass between his legs made her cringe.

He lunged for her.

A quick step to the left and she dodged his initial attack. Flesh blurred as he circled her and grasped her from behind. His massive arms wrapped around her like pythons. She tried to pull away, but he wouldn't budge. His right arm let go, but not before he wrapped his left arm all the way around her and held both of her arms tight. His free hand grabbed the back of her skirt and lifted.

Without a second thought she reared and the back of her head smashed his face. The male let go and stumbled. She whipped around, baring her teeth. His nose and mouth had caved in. Blood poured from every part of his face.

She hissed and he cowered behind the other males. They needed to learn who led them. She wondered how many more she would have to fight. Her throat opened in a shriek.

The males fell to their knees and looked at the ground. She'd made her point. In her mind she urged them to press on. More towns along the coastline needed their attention. Soon they would turn inland where another female and her brood would meet them. Where the thought of another female came from, she did not know, what she did know was that the confrontation would not be a pleasant one.

57.

"Mom?"

Teagan's voice woke Alexa, her head still buried in Ross's chest, his arms wrapped around her. She sat up and pulled the sheet over her bare chest. Heat crept up the side of her neck, basting her face and burning her ears.

"You little slut," Teagan said.

"Out! Out now!"

"I'm screwing with you, Mom." Teagan winked.

"Watch your language, young lady." Alexa scowled. "But I'm glad you're feeling better."

"What language? God. You're so . . . you're so . . . aghhh!" She flung her hands into the air. "I'm taking a shower."

Alexa looked around the room for the clock. "Teagan, what time is it?"

"I don't know, Mom. Why don't you ask your boyfriend? He's wearing a watch."

Ross smiled and sat up. The sheet slipped to his waist.

Teagan turned her head. "Kak. Gross."

"You can leave now." Alexa pointed the way out as if Teagan wasn't standing in the doorway already.

"And shut the door!" She couldn't believe she'd been caught in bed with a man.

"Kids." Ross stretched.

Teagan slammed the door behind her.

"Teenagers." Alexa caught his hand on the way down from his stretch. He leaned over and caressed her jaw-line with his other hand. A bolt of energy raced from her face to her toes. She dove into the kiss as if she'd been kissing him her entire life. Then a sense of foreboding came to her as she remembered her husband's kiss, soft, pleasant. Ross's kiss had something different . . . chemistry . . . ecstasy . . . raw animalistic passion.

"It's three-AM," Ross said, his mouth still connected to hers.

She jerked away. "You didn't look at your watch while kissing me? Did you?" Nothing could be ruder than becoming sidetracked whilst kissing.

He showed his pearl whites. "Well. Not that this hasn't been a blast and I'd love round two, but . . . "

What did he just say? "Don't flatter yourself." She pushed him away and sat up properly. "This was stress relief, that's it. And it won't be happening again."

"What do you take me for?" Ross pulled the sheet round his waist more securely. "If we live through this, we'll talk. I think we should get you to work in that lab of yours. You have a world to save."

The thought hit her like an anvil that bounced up and landed again, sinking her into the ground. Save the world? As a geneticist she couldn't help but run end of world scenarios in her head. But the end as a reality had never even crossed her mind.

"You're right." She sighed. "Let's get to . . . "

Glass shattered downstairs.

Ellie screamed.

"Ellie," Alexa said.

Ross rolled out of bed. She couldn't help but catch a glimpse of his muscular buttocks as he pulled on his slacks, commando style. Without bothering to put a shirt or shoes on, he pulled a gun from his shoulder holster. She hadn't even seen him grab it when he whisked her upstairs for their evening rendezvous.

Another mind-numbing scream ricocheted throughout the house.

He turned to her. "Get Teagan, stay quiet. I'll get Ellie."

She nodded. "Where are the darts?"

"I think they're on the table downstairs with the gun. I'll let you know when it's clear."

Alexa slipped out of bed and threw on the bare essentials. Shirt, pants, shoes. No bra, no panties. Teagan's life could once again be in danger.

58.

Ross DASHED DOWN the hall on his tiptoes, hit the stairs and slid. He landed between flights and aimed down the Glock's sights into the dark living room.

The Trill had positioned himself over Ellie on the couch, his back arched. She'd curled into a fetal position. One clawed hand ripped at her jeans, the other dug into her right shoulder, pressing her deep into the cushion. Spittle dribbled from his mouth and sloshed over her face. She'd clenched her eyes shut. She didn't have a tire iron this time.

From his angle the bullet would hit the creature in the right temple. If it clenched down, the pressure might crush Ellie. The bullet wouldn't kill it, not until it had been dosed. But maybe it would give him time to retrieve the gun and darts from the kitchen. Step-by-step he inched down the rest of the stairs, keeping his eye on the creature poised to violate Ellie, ready to pull the trigger.

An explosion of wood and shattered glass rattled the house.

Ross skulked down the last four steps and ducked around the corner into the kitchen. Still in the line of sight of the creatures he scurried behind the kitchen counter. The shadow of a second male enshrouded him as he walked in, sniffing the air, scanning the room. The new Trill towered over the one in the living room. He bolted through the kitchen like a newly captured mare. He past Ross's hiding place and launched into the living room. Ross feared for Ellie even more.

A loud hiss, reciprocated by one of the loudest roars Ross had ever heard came from the creatures. Both creatures flew back into the kitchen on top of each other, biting and gouging. They smashed into the oak table, sending it sliding into the wall.

The darts and gun slid across the table and clinked to the ground, one on each side.

Ross took a breath and lunged across the room on his hands and knees. The Trill's vicious battle for the girl cracked and shattered around him.

Ross dove through blood and torn flesh. He rolled under the table and snatched the dart gun. Then he squirmed over, grabbed the clip and snapped it into place. Without a sound he waited for the perfect moment. Then shot as one of them rolled onto the floor in front of him.

Both darts hit their targets in the throats. The Trill's weren't fazed by the tiny needles and continued their vicious battle. Again Ross had to wait. He didn't want to, but he had no idea how long it took for the agent to take effect on the epidermis.

The larger male had four large gashes under his left ribs. One shot with a hollow-tipped bullet would explode the creature's heart; if they had the same anatomy as a human being.

The smaller of the two leapt onto the bar, back-flipped, and landed on the larger ones shoulders, slamming him into the tile. The creature began to lift himself into a push up position, his back bowed from the weight of the little one.

As good a time as any.

Ross aimed and shot. The bullet entered the bleeding flap of flesh below the large male's left pectoral muscle. Without a sound, its eyes popped wide and its body slammed to the floor.

The smaller made a glorious gesture of triumph and stomped on the larger ones head. A flood of blood and brain matter scattered across the floor. Ross scooted against the wall to avoid the stream.

The survivor stalked back towards his prey lying on the sofa. Ellie still hadn't moved. Was she dead? Or just in shock? There wasn't any time to check. With a quick flick of the wrist, Ross tossed his gun from his right hand to his left and shot the Trill in the back several times. First it fell to its knees, then face first onto the living room carpet.

Ross took a minute to make sure the bullets had killed the creature. He then crawled out from under the table and jumped over the pooling blood. He scooped the unconscious girl into his arms and carried her upstairs two steps at a time.

Teagan and Alexa stood still. Their eyes and faces asked the question for them.

"She's alive." He laid Ellie on the bed.

The girls collectively sighed.

"Thank God!" Teagan rushed to her friend's side.

"Did you kill it?" Alexa raised her brows.

"God, I hope so." Ross slipped the clip out from his gun and snapped a full one in from his shoulder holster.

59.

ANOTHER FEMALE, THAT'S what she felt. At least she thought she did. Headed toward Savannah and hers. The males sensed danger as well. Heat rose from their skin. They sneered. Growls ripped through the night and their eyes turned to wet lumps of coal. A confrontation lay ahead. What exactly that confrontation entailed, Savannah didn't know. But it couldn't be good. Maybe the two leaders of the groups would fight to the death and the winner would take over the dead one's brood? Savannah didn't want to fight. She'd seen enough bloodshed, why fight her own kind as well? She didn't even know what her kind was. People had referred to them as creatures, monsters, abominations, genetic anomalies, a new evolution of mankind and aliens. Truth be told, she had no clue, just a vague purpose.

She turned her brood of males and headed east through the mountains. Maybe this would cause the other female to go another way. Crisis averted.

Savannah urged her brood to follow as she sought out the next city full of humans to annihilate. An image flashed in her head of another female. This one had long straggly red hair and many more males with her. She turned her brood to match Savannah, creating a head on collision. Again she turned her males another direction, but the other female sensed her. She sensed Savannah's compassion for the cattle called humans. The confrontation was now inevitable.

60.

SWEAT DRIPPED FROM her brow as she extracted the concentrate from the beaker and ejected it into the synthesizer. After keying in the proper code the machine whirred in circles. The data scrambled across the computer monitor and she hit send. The info would fax to Washington where several top scientists waited to mass produce the compound. Still, she hadn't come up with a way to reverse the genetic response and knew in her heart, it might not be possible. The thought made her cringe. If that did indeed end up being the case, she would have to help Teagan abort the baby. That's the only conclusion she could come up with to save her daughter's life.

"Try it again." Alexa's Blue Tooth headset dangled from her ear.

"Same thing Doc," Ray said over the line. He'd been running different equations while she created the anti-Trill compound. His tests should be yielding positive results.

"I don't understand." She tapped away, entering the specs from the samples through the computer program once again. "Why won't it reverse the process?"

"Couldn't tell you boss," Ray said over the speaker phone.

She stamped her foot, baffled. Why can she lower their defenses, but not reverse the mutagen? It didn't make sense.

Ross stuck his head in the door. He'd been patrolling the perimeter of the house.

"Any luck?"

"Nothing. It's one of those things that if we put a period in the wrong spot, we'll have to do the entire formula over again."

"Well, keep trying. I have faith in you."

She didn't have faith in things anyway, so having someone have faith in her rang illogical. "I'll do my best."

Alexa turned back to her computer screen, but quickly whipped her head back around before Ross left her sight. "Did the girls find something to eat?"

He stopped and backed into the doorway. "Teagan's making eggs, I think. You hungry?"

Famished, is more like it. "I could use something to keep me going."

"Coffee it is." He smiled.

The room swayed again. *Ughh. Why now? Under these particular circumstances? Convenience? Probably. True love? Improbable.* But her heart told her different. "Coffee would be great." *A one night stand Alexa, that's all it was. You could never be with a guy like him. No way.*

"You got it." He shut the door behind him. Even though they had plenty of darts and Ross carried around his cannon of a gun, they still needed to be quiet. If they happened to be attacked by a pack of Trills, well, the romance would be gone, that's for dang sure. If romance was being swept to her room and made love to for a couple of hours in the first place.

"Is the love fest over?" Ray asked. "Could have sworn I heard a smile in your voice just then. What's going on with you two?"

"Get back to work, Ray."

"Fine. Boss?"

"Yes."

"You better not make a love child. Not till we get this thing figured out."

White lightning struck, nearly knocking her over. "You're brilliant!"

"What? Ah . . . you finally recognize."

"What you said about the love child. I think you figured out what we need."

"What's that?"

"DNA from one of their females that's pregnant." This had to be the breakthrough she'd been looking for. But where on earth would she find a pregnant Tri- Trill female? Someone needed to go hunting. "I'll talk to you later, Ray. I might need to make some calls."

Before Ray could say anything else, she pressed the button on the headset, cutting him off.

"Ross!" *Crap. Too loud.*

A moment later he jogged through the door, dart gun in one hand, shotgun in the other. "Where is it? Are you okay?" His eyes took inventory of everything around him.

"When the female attacked, could you tell if she was pregnant or not?" Alexa folded her arms.

"Guess that means all's well out here?" He scowled and hung the shotgun back over his shoulder. "I'm not sure. It would have been a good question to ask her. Sorry I didn't. But she was different. Seemed like she wanted to talk more than fight, maybe it was because she had a bun in the oven."

"Did she say why she wasn't going to kill you?"

Ross leaned against the doorjamb. "I'm not really sure. Something behind her eyes held . . . I don't know. Maybe you could call it, humanity? I don't think she wanted to kill me. Or anyone for that matter."

Teagan snuck up behind Ross.

Alexa shook her head.

Teagan frowned. "You ruined the surprise. Sheesh." She had a plate in one hand and a glass in the other. "Sorry to interrupt."

Good. Manners. One thing which could either drive her insane or make her happy was manners. "That's okay."

"Made you some eggs. Over easy with toast and glass of OJ." Teagan squeezed past Ross. "Excuse me."

More manners. That's my girl.

He smiled at her in a fatherly way. "Not a problem."

Teagan set the plate and glass on the desk next to Alexa. That's when Alexa noticed the bulge in Teagan's belly.

"Oh my, Teagan. Your stomach." She reached over and felt the large lump. This wasn't the tummy of a person only a couple of weeks along in her pregnancy. Alexa figured at least seven months. A ripple slithered underneath Alexa' hand and she yanked it back.

Tears welled in Teagan's eyes. "It's been doing that all morning. Mom . . . I want it out. Get it out now. Please."

Alexa stood and wrapped her arms around her daughter. Something she had seldom done since Teagan was a youngster coming in with scrapes on her knees or having fights with girls at school. The wriggling beast in Teagan's stomach writhed against her own flat belly. "I think I figured it out. We'll fix this. Go back into the house and tend to Ellie. How is she anyway?"

"Scared. Just like the rest of us. But she's strong, she'll pull through."

Teagan left and Alexa looked at Ross. The sadness reflected in his eyes did her in. She dropped to her knees and sobbed.

He sat on the ground next to her and cradled her. The warmth of his love wrapped around her. Not love for her. Love as a father of twin daughters who he may or may not ever see again. After a few minutes of uncontrolled sobbing and silence, she looked up.

"We need to find the Staten Trill. If the males are truly looking to mate, she's bound to be pregnant by now. If she is, I need that fetus. And we need to do this now. At the rate the Trill is growing in Teagan, it will be born in a couple of days. Save my baby, Ross. Please—save her." She hugged him again.

He kissed her on the lips, soft, compassionate. "I'll do what I can." His goodbye hug scared her. Would she ever see him again? She hoped she hadn't sent him to his death.

61.

Ross BACKED OUT of the driveway. After fishing through the glove box and finding his spare phone, he'd contacted his superiors who had acknowledged his good work. They had begun the process of shipping the recipe to weaken the Trills around the world.

Mike told him that the government had already developed bullets, like tracer rounds, to introduce the agent into the Trill's system. However, even with a ban on pregnancies, baby Trills kept being born.

Hoards of them gathered the world over, hundreds of thousands marched on larger cities. Smaller groups took to the outskirts. They tore through cities, killing every human. They seemed to hunt by heat signature, but tests with cold blankets and cooling the body did not work. The President had called it an E.L.E or an Extinction Level Event. Usually they reserved the acronym for such things as dinosaurs, annihilating meteors, and nuclear war. Nonetheless, the human race had been targeted for extermination. But by what, no-one knew.

The cell phone went off. "Harris here."

"Harris, this is Major Bingham at Hill Air Force base in Utah."

"Hello Major. Any intel for me?"

"Yes. We picked up your group of Trills headed from Waldport Oregon; they're making a beeline for Corvallis. We satellite tagged your female and have her on GPS for you. I'm uploading the info to your cell phone now. Good luck."

"Thank you, sir." Ross thumbed through the programs on his phone until he found what he needed. The GPS showed the female Trill near the town of Philomath. Driving wasn't going to get him there fast enough and he didn't have the firepower he needed to take on an entire pack.

Time to call in a few favors.

Ross called his superiors and set up a rendezvous with a Coastguard helicopter at Tigard High-School. Also, the Air Force would be dropping a package for him with guns and the new ammunition. They asked if he wanted any help, but he'd turned them down. He needed to get close to Savannah, build on the trust a little more. If he came in with a swat team or soldiers, she'd be out of their in a heartbeat.

Before he arrived at the football field he saw the parachute in the sky fall from the C-17 soaring high above. The package came to a sliding halt just outside the fence.

Ross scanned the sky for the helicopter he'd requested, but found only billowing Oregon storm clouds. He pulled the rig next to the large army issue duffel bag with the parachute waving in the wind behind it, hopped out and tossed the bag into the back seat.

Inside he found a plethora of guns and ammunition: two 9mm pistols, two 9mm sub-machine guns, an M16, a sniper rifle (with infrared scope) and two bags of the new ammo for each. He hoped it would be enough. If he took out the males and isolated Savannah, he could probably get her more easily.

The deep-orange helicopter buzzed overhead and made a wide arc in the sky before it swooped down and hovered above the center of the football field. Ross pulled the bag of weapons from the back seat and threw the strap over his shoulder.

"Holy shit this is heavy."

He waited for the helicopter to land. Instead, they dropped a rope ladder.

"Sonofabitch." *They expect me to climb this thing with two hundred pounds of weapons and ammunition on my back?*

Without hesitation he latched on. One of the occupants leaned out. His helmet with dark visor reminded him of one of the pilots in Star Wars. His arm stretched out with a thumb up. Ross reciprocated the gesture and felt the rope start to rise. Good, at least he didn't have to climb it with the pack on.

He tightened his grip as the ladder ascended towards the open side-door of the helicopter.

A burly Guardian leaned out and pulled Ross in. He handed him a headset and motioned for him to sit in one of the empty seats. Ross strapped in.

"Welcome aboard, sir," he heard, but wasn't sure which of the four men had said it. Then the pilot turned to him. "We should be over our destination in about fifteen minutes."

"Thanks. We need to beat this group to Philomath." He handed the pilot the GPS.

"Shouldn't be a problem."

Ross gave him a thumbs up. "Appreciate the help fellas."

He unzipped the bag and started loading the weapons, slapping in clips and setting safeties on.

The pilot turned again and held up the phone. "They're close. You might have ten minutes. "Where do you want us to drop you, sir?"

Ross took the phone. His fingers danced over the screen as he searched for a satellite image of the area. When he found one, he combined the image with the location of Savannah on his grid.

"If you drop me on the roof of the Philomath Fire Department, I should be able to intercept the female before she gets to town."

"You got it." This time, the pilot didn't turn around.

Savannah and her group had picked up their pace, as if she knew they were coming for her. If he got lucky, he might have five minutes to set up before she came into range.

"We're here, sir." The stocky Guardian gathered a rope. "We'll lower you using this line."

"Sure thing." The man wrapped a harness around Ross's chest and secured it before he opened the door.

"Just step out and we'll do the rest."

"Thanks again fellas, wish me luck."

"Good luck," they all said in unison.

He smiled at the men, strapped the weapons bag over his shoulder and stepped into the air. The helicopter grew smaller as they lowered him on the pulley. Ross thought it might be good to have some help, but he had to do this alone. Time to use some good ol' fashioned charm and expert marksmanship.

62.

SAVANNAH WATCHED FROM her perch on the roof as her males ransacked the house below. The home owners had already vacated the premises, unlike the unfortunate people in the restaurant they hit a few minutes earlier where they had caused serious damage.

A barricaded bunker of sorts below the restaurant held several families' women and children. The determined males found a door on the outside which led to the basement. A withered old man with a shotgun made an attempt at a stand, blasting one of the males in the stomach several times leaving barely a blemish. His brothers made short work of the man. They'd clawed him so many times his face and skull split into multiple sections down to his jaw and flapped away like the petals of a wilted flower.

She'd supervised while the males tore out the man's heart and wrestled each other for pieces of it.

An elderly woman and a young mother gathered their children and cowered in a corner. Their teenage brother held his own with an axe for a while before two of the brood latched onto his arms and tore him in half.

This time Savannah tried something different. When they started their assault on the human females, she simply said, "NO! Feed only."

She'd left as her males heeded her words and feasted instead of accosting. For some reason, the ravaging of human females nauseated her. Now she knew she could stop the males from the senseless torture of humans.

The whap, whap of rotor blades had her scanning the sky. In the distance she saw the machine fly over the next town. She lunged across the street, landed on a parked car and sailed onto the roof of another house.

The helicopter hovered above a building. A human male descended from a rope. She twisted her head in bewilderment not understanding what the intentions of the man on the roof might be. Perhaps she would pay him a visit and ascertain the nature of his arrival before her males could get to him.

She signaled for her brood to stay put. The males obeyed, save the largest of them; the one who looked most human. His unruly behavior had started to grate on her. With a growl and barring of teeth, she attempted to back him down. His intentions remained the same. Again she snarled and hissed, though something inside of her wanted this male in the worst way.

An ethereal trigger in her mind pulled, leaving her libido as the only sane element in her body. Every cell in her body wanted this male. She needed him. His barbs flexed and spun sending shivers up her spine. Her thoughts beckoned him. A moment later his warm breath cascaded against the nape of her neck. A tight prickle of pleasure raced down her spine. She walked deeper into the forest behind the house, leading him with her mind.

When she could no longer see the others, she pulled up her skirt. The male followed her lead. She pulled her shirt off. The cool evening hardened her nipples like daggers.

He spun her around. His tongue flicked out and trailed down her neck, between the pert mounds on her chest.

She scooted her legs further apart and leaned against a tree. With a grunt, he plunged as deep as he could. Chirps of pleasure escaped as he drove himself into her. Over and over until she screamed out in ecstasy and he exploded inside of her.

After he finished convulsing, he stepped back, awaiting her orders. Savannah knew one of her own grew within her. This new life would live. She'd protect and nurture him.

The father would do everything in his power to protect her and her baby. She motioned for him to return to the others and wait for her to return. With some hesitation, he turned and went back to the group.

Still, she needed to know why the lone human waited for them. She had no other explanation for why he crept along the roof of the building ahead, other than ambush; a suicide mission, if nothing else. She beckoned her brood to wait until she called. While her males stewed in the background, Savannah headed for the roof of the building to pay the mysterious human a visit.

63.

Ross LAID THE weapons across the rooftop facing west. Each loaded gun had the safety catch off and an extra three clips lying next to it. The sniper rifle, with a 100X infrared scope, sat on a tripod; its silenced barrel jutted from the building. The GPS showed Savannah on the move toward him, at an incredible speed.

The sun dipped on the horizon. Its multicolored hue blasted up from the Pacific Ocean, like blood spatter from a rainbow's slashed throat. Ross lined up the scope of the rifle with the direction of the blip on the iPhone. He clicked the infrared sights on and took aim into the distance.

A streak of yellow slurred between two trees about three hundred yards away. He didn't have a shot. A short clearing between two farm houses lay to his right. If she stayed at the same speed and direction she'd come into the clearing in about 15 seconds. He aimed into the clearing and laid down a blanket of fire right to left across the field.

The dosed tracer rounds flew toward the blur he believed to be Savannah. She slowed for a moment, not losing much momentum. She turned and headed straight for him. This time he caught a brief glimpse of the shape of a young woman. Again he fired the sniper rifle in her general direction, but she zigzagged, avoiding every shot. She leapt onto a convenience store, then bounced from building to building like a giant grasshopper.

The rifle clicked empty. Ross rolled to his right and picked up the 9MM Uzi and showered the roof tops with a blanket of bullets, sure he'd hit her again.

Savannah ducked behind a Chevron gas station.

Ross scooted back to the sniper rifle, re-loaded and aimed at the nearest gas pump and squeezed the trigger. It took two shots to penetrate. The explosion ignited the pump and spread to the other six. All of the pumps exploded. A plume of black smoke and red-hot flames shot hundreds of feet into the air. Ross covered his from the flash of light.

"Holy shit." The only place Ross had ever seen such an explosion was the movies. He'd never caused one and thanked the Lord the gas station had been evacuated. He scanned the area with the infrared scope, searching for a body

"You missed," a soft female voice said from behind.

Ross depressed the trigger of the Uzi, whipped around and sprayed bullets across the fire station's roof. Some of the bullets had to have hit their target.

Savannah dropped under the onslaught of bullets and slithered forward. Before Ross could aim down, she popped up in front of him and snatched the weapon. With her right hand she tossed the Uzi over the side of the building. Her left hand grasped him around the throat. Her finger nails extended. A flame of pain shot through his collar.

He grunted. "Kill me if you're going to."

A snarl ripped from her and she bore her teeth. "Why would you risk your life like this?"

Ross gagged. "Because your fetus . . . " He coughed.

"What about it?" She placed her free hand over her stomach.

A rush of heat washed up his face as he felt her squeeze down to where he could barely take a breath. He sipped in some air. "It's the key."

"Key? Key to what?"

"To . . . to save my friend's daughter, her baby, and . . . and to preserve the human race."

The intensity in her eyes softened. Her grip loosened, claws retracted and she lowered him until he felt the roof once again under his feet. She dropped her head and covered her stomach with both hands. "I can't let you do that."

His gaze followed hers to a plump, near full term pregnant stomach. It stretched against her blood stained Hard Rock Café t-shirt. "It will end this madness. This war you're waging on mankind. Do you even know what you're doing?"

The disdain in her eyes dissipated into a pain. Then sorrow fell across her face and shone in her eyes. "This is the first." She patted her belly.

"The first of what?" The thought of going for his pistol crossed his mind, until he realized he'd left it next to the bag of guns before he set up the sniper rifle.

"I'm not sure, but I know she's important and that I have to complete my task."

"She? You know it's a girl?"

"Yes. Doesn't every mother know?"

"No. They don't. We use machines to tell us what sex the child is." Ross mused.

"They'll all be female." She continued to look at her oversized stomach.

"Why would they all be girls?"

"I'm not sure." She turned away and looked into the sky.

A wet spot on the flank of her shirt caught his eye. One of his tracer rounds with the anti-Trill agent in it had penetrated the skin just under her left arm. She was hurt, vulnerable, but also very smart. She'd positioned herself between him and the weapons, save the sniper rifle behind him. Though he'd emptied one clip, he had another sitting next to it on the ground. He'd never be quick enough. Not with her speed and agility. He needed to keep his conversation going until a moment presented itself.

"You're looking up. Do you think you came from space?" He scratched his chin.

The movement must have startled her because her eyes left the ponderings of the universe and settled on him. They began to darken from the corners in, as if some invisible artist decided to fill her eyes with a black magic marker.

"I guess that's a no." Frantic. Desperate. He considered all possibilities for an out. Could he roll back and get to the rifle before she strikes? Maybe. If he anticipated her lunge he might be able to roll under her and get to the back of weapons. Again, he needed to stall. "So, what now? You gonna to tear my heart out and eat it?"

"The thought had crossed my mind." She flashed a sinister smile which settled into a flatness he hadn't seen from her. A face he might put on when interrogating a prisoner.

"I regret to inform you that the answer, sadly, is no. I won't kill you. But you can't have the one I hold inside of me." She covered her stomach again. "Agree to walk away without my child and I'll let you live, if you can get through the males surrounding us at this very moment.

"I'm not a threat to you anymore." A ruse to throw her off-guard.

"I wouldn't say that. You've already injured me." She touched her left side. "I feel pain in my side and a strange tingle in my feet and hands."

"Shit."

"What?"

He looked at the blossom of blood covering her shirt and watched as it ran under her skirt and down the side of her leg. "You're bleeding to death."

"How do I stop it?"

"I can help. But you have to help me in return."

"By giving up my unborn?"

Ross didn't know if his idea would work. The alternate, however, meant death to both of them.

64.

A SILENT ALARM of sorts went off within her mind. White-hot streaks of fear coursed through Savannah. She'd told the human too much. Instinct would have her rip his heart out. But she'd promised to let him live if he helped stop the bleeding in her side. She'd also promised him some of her afterbirth, which he thought he could use to create a cure.

A cure for what? Was her kind diseased? Maybe he could stop the babies from being born? No matter, they were no longer necessary. Enough males and females had been born to carry out their innate cause, which seemed to be the annihilation of the human race for an unknown purpose.

Savannah followed the human male from the roof to the fire station's garage. She held up the side of her shirt while he worked on her side. He climbed into the ambulance to get the equipment he needed to help her.

"This is going to sting a bit."

With a pair of pliers, he dug into her skin. There was a little pressure, but no pain.

"Got it." He held up the pliers and showed her a chunk of metal between the needle-nose beak.

"So small, yet causes so much damage." She felt the weight of the tiny slug as he dropped it into her hand.

"You have no idea. A shot in the right place could have killed you." He tossed the pliers onto the seat in the back of the ambulance and pulled out some bandages.

The only knowledge she had of such weapons came from the television and people trying to kill her. One thing she knew . . . her immunity to the weapons wasn't there anymore.

A whistle of wind brought the stench of death. The other female and her brood had arrived.

Ross must have sensed her anxiety. "What is it? What's wrong?"

"Quiet." She no longer felt her males, nor did she feel the other brood, just a torturous jagged pain in her left side and—her. "We need to get back to the roof. You'll need your guns."

Ross finished wrapping an elastic bandage around her ribcage, securing the pads covering her wounds bandages. "Why's that?"

"They're here." She tugged his arm and nearly tossed him out of the ambulance.

He stopped and folded his arms. "Who's here? What the fuck are you talking about?"

"Shhhhh. Be quiet so I can listen." She didn't have answers for him. Only the fact that she no longer had control of her brood and the bitch waiting for her on the roof wouldn't leave until one of them died. Maybe the other sensed her injury and vulnerability. Nonetheless, protecting her baby became the priority.

65.

SAVANNAH'S ANGST WORRIED Ross. "Wh . . . who . . . are you talking about?"

"The other one." Her nostrils flared as she sniffed the air. "Her stench is unbearable. We need to go. Now!" Jagged nails tore through his skin as she yanked him toward the exit door.

"Whoah . . . take it easy. Remember, I'm human." She didn't stop or pay any attention to his pleading and led him outside.

The sun sank into the depths of the Pacific Ocean. A full moon ignited the evening with a baneful glow cast across the horizon. Ross couldn't believe this beautiful, pregnant Trill needed his help. She'd loosened her grip once she realized he wasn't going to try and get away. Outside they stood next to the ladder going up to the roof. He reached for the first rung and she stopped him.

"It's too late she's already here. You'll be dead before you get to the top."

His insides rolled at the thought of being decapitated as he reached the top rung of the ladder. "Any bright ideas?"

"I can get you closer to your weapons." She looked up.

"What are you . . . ?"

Before he could finish the sentence her dainty, yet firm hands gripped him under his arm pits and she jumped.

A stinging sensation shot from his underarms to his shoulders as his weight settled into her clawed hands. Warm trickles of blood raced down his sides.

They landed on the roof with a thud. Small shocks of energy bolted through his feet, ankles, and knees. He cursed high-school wrestling for giving him weak joints. He'd only had three arthroscopic surgeries, though he'd eventually have to have total knee reconstructions on both.

She nodded toward the row of guns on the ground. "Guns." With a whisk of air she leapt to the side of the building and peered into the dark, taking huge whiffs of the evening air.

Ross raced to the line of weapons. He slapped a clip into the Uzi he'd used earlier, locked and loaded the M16, sniper rifle and his own semi-automatic pistols.

Savannah moved with the grace of a wild cat as she paced the four corners of the building, crinkling her nose at whatever stench wafted about. Ross couldn't smell anything other than a cow pasture somewhere upwind from them.

She walked over to him. "We're surrounded."

Ross scoped the countryside with the sniper rifle. The infrared picked up multiple images headed right for them.

"You mind if I call in some help?"

A slow growl rumbled inside her throat. "Do what you must. But I doubt either of us will live through this. She has too many males."

He took his phone out and clicked the number for the big guy. A few seconds later he heard. "Go."

"Boss, this is Harris."

"I said, go. What's your situation?"

"I need whatever resources you can send me at this location and make sure they're armed with the new tracer rounds. They work. I hurt one of them, bad."

"You got it. Be careful, kid. We gotcha in about ten."

"Thanks Boss." Though Ross knew resources dwindled, he welcomed anything they could spare.

He tossed the cell phone into the duffel bag. *If I live through this, at least I'll know where that is.* With his right hand he swung the M16 over his right shoulder. His knees crackled as he crouched to pick up the Uzi's; one in each hand. When he turned around, ready to fight, his heart sank to the floor as if pounded by a sledge hammer.

Male Trills lined three sides of the roof. An attractive young woman with strands of straight dark-auburn hair pulled into a tight ponytail, stood in the center of them. They frothed at the mouth, snarled, growled, and sneered.

Savannah held a hand up like one of the Supremes. Instead of

'Stop in the name of love', this tune said, 'stop moving and don't shoot for the sake of your life.'

Ross took her advice, but still made sure he had his weapons locked and loaded. He tightened his grip on the M16.

From her perch on a metal fan, Savannah dropped onto the roof without a sound. The other female stepped off the ledge onto the roof and stalked toward her. Those fearsome razor-sharp claws extended like switch blades. She growled, revealing several rows of fangs.

Ross thought Savannah had a height and arms length advantage on the other one, though the other female had twenty or so rapid males at her back.

To his astonishment, the two females began to talk. Like civilized human beings.

"What do they call you?" The redhead's hair ran down her back in perfect curled rows, flipped up at her hips.

"Savannah. And you?"

"The humans at the hospital called me Maleia."

Savannah relaxed, which gave Ross a reason to let out a sigh and peek around at her deadly entourage. All eyes had fixated on the girls. A few males became overly excited.

She searched Maleia, her eyes darted up and down the girl's body as if weighing all of her options. "What are we to do now?"

Maleia placed one foot in front of the other as if to brace for impact. "I kill you and take your human's heart." Her expression remained emotionless.

It reminded him of his old partner's interrogation face. Emotions can mean the difference between a conviction and the perp walking and every time she had interrogated someone he had been emotional with, her face didn't move a muscle. This also came in handy on poker night as she used to kick the crap out of the rest of them. So stoic.

"Now." Savannah gestured, her arm forward as if she had called her own platoon into battle.

Ross didn't hesitate. *Now means . . . now!*

He squeezed the triggers on the Uzi submachine guns.

Non-tracer rounds dented the male Trill's skin and bounced off. Though, when a tracer hit, it exploded and release the anti-Trill serum into their systems. Most of them leapt from the building. Others took the shots as if they didn't know bullets could harm them. Several fell dead. Ross sprayed bullets at anything moving other than Savannah.

The two females met in the middle of the roof. Savannah flipped over Maleia. Long gashes appeared down her back and soaked her shirt with blood. When she landed, one of the males attacked. Her fist entered his chest and burst through the skin of his back with his crushed heart held tight in her grip. His eyes closed as she retracted her hand. He and his heart hit the ground at the same time.

A bald male launched over the two girls, his claws extended, aimed for Ross's chest. The second Uzi clicked empty and he tossed it to the side while he pulled his Glock from his side holster. Ross emptied the clip into the creature's chest.

He side-stepped as the Trill hit the ground in front of him and slid to a blood smeared halt.

The deadly battle unfolded in his peripheral vision. Savannah needed help. The males had stopped attacking him and fled from the building. Four had died at his hand, another three by Savannah. Ross picked up the M16, took aim at Maleia and shot. Even with bullets tearing up her back, she continued to claw, bite, and kick Savannah. From the side Ross barely saw the streak of white flesh before it slammed into him.

He and a very large male rolled to the edge of the roof. The M16 strap broke and the gun clinked to the ground between them and the girl's. The male reared up and bit into Ross's shoulder. When he pulled back, a chunk of Ross's left shoulder and shredded shirt went with it.

Ross clenched his teeth as the pain seared down his arm and into his neck. His left arm wouldn't move and he didn't have any weapons left near him. The Trill stood in triumph and swallowed the chunk of meat. More males gathered around him, ready to sink their teeth into whatever he'd left behind.

A bright light drew the creature's eyes to the south. The stealth helicopter hovered.

"Stay down Agent Harris. I got you," a voice came over a PA system.

"Savannah, get down!" He hoped she heard him in the midst of her fight.

An onslaught of heavy machinegun fire came from the helicopter. Thousands of tracer rounds pelted the males around him. The 50-caliber bullets tore through them like they would any human at eighty meters, turning them to minced meat.

Several rounds hit the one standing above Ross. Its head scattered in several different directions. A downpour of blood and brain matter covered Ross.

"Jesus." He wiped chunks of something out of his face and looked over to see what happened to Savannah. The other female wasn't in sight. Savannah laid flat on her back with her head turned toward Ross. Bullets whizzed inches above her face.

"Clear," the voice over the PA system said.

Ross stood and witnessed the carnage of twenty shredded males. Did the tracer rounds work? Hell yes they did and proven by one kick-ass-positive field test.

66.

HEAVY MACHINEGUN FIRE drifted into the night and away from the fire station as the hunted down the fleeing males. Savannah heard Ross tell her to get down and she had. But she'd been riddled by bullets.

Ross staggered forward. Blood poured from a wound on his left shoulder as he thumped down next to her.

Pain blazed across her chest and the left side of her face. She tried to sit up, but couldn't.

His eyes roamed over her wounds, assessing the damage. "You're pretty fucked up." Genuine concern reflected in his eyes.

"Look who's talking?" She gestured toward his shoulder.

"You gonna be okay?" he asked.

"I'm not sure." She had so many gashes, gouges, and holes in her she couldn't even see them through her blood covered clothes.

"Where'd the other one go?"

Savannah looked around. When she had ducked, she saw Maleia get shot several more times then she had closed her eyes. "I'm not sure. I think she jumped or fell off the roof."

"Hopefully we got her." He panted and rubbed his hand across his forehead, which smeared blood on his brow.

Savannah admired his courage. "I did quite a bit of damage before the bullets ravaged her. I'm not sure I could have beaten her without the help."

"Oh. I'm sure you would have given her a good run for the money." He smiled, but she didn't really understand the reference.

A twinge of pain shot through her belly. She slowly lifted her shirt from pregnant belly. Two long gashes tore through the elastic bandage he'd wrapped her belly earlier with. Multiple bullet holes in her stomach oozed with blood. An overwhelming sadness consumed her as she realized the child within her no longer moved.

"I'm sorry." Ross took off his blood spotted shirt and pressed it against her wounds.

"Looks like you're going to get what you need after all." She coughed and black liquid sprayed from her mouth.

"Can you heal from this?" His hand pressed firm against the blood soaked bandage.

"I don't think so."

Life flowed from Savannah like the swift waters of the Willamette River she'd jumped over earlier, the current more urgent with every beat of her heart.

"I'll wait to take the baby's body." His sincerity and sorrow showed in his eyes even as he winced from his own pain.

"She was going to be the first." Tears filled her eyes. Ross held her hand tight. Blackness darker than the darkest night caved in on her. But, before her short life washed away, her eyes went wide one last time in horror as Maleia crept up behind Ross.

67.

ROSS TOOK SAVANNAH'S non-verbal hint from the fear reflected in her glazed over eyes. Her respirations ceased, pupils dilated, and with a last exhale, the incredible being he'd fought side by side with gave him one last gift, a chance to live. It wasn't only a chance for him to live, but a chance for all of humanity.

He'd left all of his guns behind when he came to aid Savannah, all except for one. The pistol in the front of his jeans pressed tight against his belly as he crouched next to Savannah's body. Before he could pull the Glock, Maleia grabbed him by the neck and tossed him away from Savannah's body. Her only care seemed to be whether or not Savannah lived.

Still in the air, Ross pulled the gun and shot Maleia four times, two times in the back and twice in the back of the head.

Maleia's body launched forward and slammed against the air conditioning unit. Her body slid to the side, next to Savannah.

The report of gunshots echoed from somewhere below. Ross figured the soldiers had landed the helicopter and had some straggler males to take care of.

He struggled to stand and fell twice before he staggered to his feet and headed for his bag. He'd seen a sheathed combat knife in the duffel bag of weapons. It would do the trick in retrieving the dead fetus from Savannah. When he knelt and began rummaging through the bag of weapons, he no longer had any feeling in his left arm or hand. "Shit." He'd avoided looking at it, but when he did, it looked like minced meat with bits of bone sticking out of it. He couldn't worry about a non-lethal wound. The bleeding wouldn't kill him, what he needed was the fetus.

"Sir. Let me take a look at that," a young man's voice came from the other side of the roof.

Ross pulled the knife from the bag, turned and saw a large soldier standing with an M16 in his hands. He wore a flight suit with a visor-less helmet. A soft, pudgy, baby faced boy, no more than eighteen or nineteen years old, smiled within.

"What's your name, soldier?"

"Reynolds, Sir."

"Your first name?"

"Gavin, Sir."

Gavin had a fanny pack on his hips. He unzipped it and pulled out a large strip of gauze, some tape and scissors. Ross couldn't help but think of his friend Beef. Gavin and Beef had a lot in common, though it seemed like Gavin had a few more cylinders pumping.

Ross gritted his teeth as Gavin worked on his shoulder. "Boy scout, eh?"

"Yes Sir. Eagle Scout. USAF military police and Nationally Certified EMT Intermediate."

"Didn't mean any offense."

"I didn't take any, sir."

"You can call me Ross."

"Yes, Sir. I mean, Ross."

"Hard habit to break."

"Sure is, *Ross*."

Ross stood as Gavin pressed the gauze into his shoulder wound, wrapped it with the tape, and made a sling from a bandanna he had in his pouch.

"Feel okay?"

Ross swung his arm up and down in the sling. The shoulder ached as if he'd chopped several cords of wood, but nothing more. "Great job, Gavin. But I need my hands for a few minutes. I'll just slip out." When he dropped his arm, the pain engulfed his entire left side. He couldn't let the pain detract him from his mission.

He swiped the knife off of the ground where he'd left it while Gavin patched him up.

"What are you doing with that?" Gavin asked.

"You don't wanna know kid . . . don't wanna know."

"Can I give you a hand? You're in need of one. Plus, I've

performed an emergency c-section in the field before. I could be of some use."

Smart. "Sure thing." He pointed the knife at Savannah's body, an unspoken question in its blade.

"Yes, Sir. I mean, Ross. Damn."

"It's okay." Ross knelt on Savannah's right and Gavin across from him. Gavin used his scissors to cut Savannah's shirt up to her breast line, where he modestly laid the cut flaps of cloth across her bosoms; a true act of chivalry in Ross's book.

"Make the incision here." Gavin used his finger to draw an imaginary line from just below her navel down to the pubic bone. "Don't cut too deep. You'll need to make a horizontal line when you get to the uterus. Then we'll pull on each side and push at the same time until the baby pops out. This will get kind of messy." He reached into his bag and pulled out a pair of latex gloves for Ross. "Can never be too careful." He smiled the whitest, largest, toothiest grin Ross had ever seen.

Ross struggled with the knife.

"Forget it. Give me that." Gavin took the knife from Ross and made the first incision.

With all the blood loss from the bullet wounds, the incisions didn't bleed much.

"There's the uterine muscle." Gavin felt under the skin with his finger and then made the horizontal incision.

"Okay. Now we both grab onto a side and pull and push until the baby's head pops out, the rest is a cake walk." Gavin counted to three.

Ross pulled and pushed with his right arm while Gavin used both of his hands. The baby's head popped out first.

"There's a good sign we're doing it right." Gavin pushed again and the baby popped into the big guys arms.

"Sad story for that little one." Ross shook his head while running his fingers over Savannah's lifeless forehead, stroking her hair. As if he'd just delivered one of his own daughter's babies.

"Um, Sir. This kid's bucking for air."

"What?" Ross leaned over and saw the baby attempting to breath, her tiny chest heaved.

Gavin turned the baby over and made a sweep into her mouth with his index finger.

"I wouldn't do that if I were you." Ross flinched. He assumed the baby would bite off Gavin's finger.

A glob of something fell onto the roof with a soft splat.

"Don't do what?" Gavin smiled.

"Smart ass. You've seen what they can do."

"Felt like a baby's toothless mouth to me." He vigorously rubbed the baby's chest.

First she gagged slightly and then cried loud and clear.

"Don't have a blanket in there, do ya?" Ross nodded toward the fanny pack. "You know those went out in the 80's right?"

"Don't you know, everything comes back in style, eventually? And, no. However, those ambulances in the bay have blankets."

"I'll snag one." Ross stood, his knees buckled for a moment and he sat back down. "Lost a little more blood than I thought."

"Here. Take the baby." Gavin handed the baby girl to Ross.

Memories of holding his daughters for the first time brought tears to his eyes, and for some unfathomable reason, that same love flowed for this child.

Gavin jogged to the edge of the roof and climbed down the escape ladder.

The baby looked normal. Like a regular human baby, other than her green eyes. A color of green Ross had never seen before. They glowed in the soft light of the moon. The baby had calmed and stuffed her thumb into her mouth. She didn't seem to have the same homicidal tendencies as the other baby Trills. An interesting development Alexa would love to hear about before she slices and dices the little thing. Which he wouldn't allow her to do, she'd have to find another way of getting the specimen she needed.

"Hey Gavin!" The bay doors were open, so he was sure Gavin could hear him.

"Yeah!"

"Grab me a cooler, would ya?"

"Need ice in it?" he hollered.

"No. Just the cooler!"

A few minutes later Gavin returned with a blanket and a cooler. He took her from Ross and swaddled her tight and handed her back.

"Can you do me a solid, Gavin?"

"Sure."

"Put the afterbirth in there. I think we only need the placenta and umbilical cord."

"Not a problem." Gavin knelt next to Savannah and pulled the placenta from the hole they'd made in the abdomen.

After he slapped the hunk of meat inside the cooler and closed it, Ross handed the baby back and they headed for the helicopter. Ross knew what they had could save Teagan's life, her baby, and possibly the world.

68.

ALEXA HAD ALMOST completed the formula. Ross's call had her ecstatic. He'd told her of the horric battle and sacrifice the Savannah Tri-Allele made for him. But what excited her the most had to do with their precious cargo. They had a pure blood Tri-Allele child and the afterbirth. The answer to the mutagen DNA would be in her palms in a few minutes.

It surprised her how Ellie had gone from catatonic to nursemaid. Like a switch flipped inside her head, making all the bad stuff go away. Alexa thought this would be a good way for her to block out the terror she'd been through and the awful sadness of losing a best friend. She wiped a tear from her eye.

The sound of tires locked on pavement drew Alexa from her computer to the door. Through the glass window she watched Ross step out of a large black pickup truck parked halfway on the driveway, the rest on her grass. A tingle climbed up her spine as he retrieved a white cooler with a red top from the back. From the other side of the truck emerged one of the largest men she'd ever seen. Ross stood a good six-four, but this kid made him look half the size. Best guess, around six-foot-seven or six-foot-eight. He wore an army uniform and held a baby swaddled in a blue blanket in the crook of his left arm.

Alexa met Ross at the door. "Good work, Agent Ross." She didn't know whether or not she should hug him or kiss him. She did the next best thing and shook his hand.

Without hesitation he pulled her into him. "Kind of a dull reception, don't you think? This is what I risked my life for? No way." He smiled and kissed her. It felt like two roses had drifted against her lips.

Alexa wanted to push him away. No, she wanted to be in his arms. She really didn't know what to do.

The biohazard cooler swung back and forth in his right hand. "Better." He set the cooler on the ground.

She didn't think after one night together she would have any feelings for this man. At least she hadn't intended to. But he kept amazing her and if this worked and saved her daughter, then the kisses were well worth it, even if he didn't reciprocate her feelings. His smile pushed buttons that hadn't been pushed in a long time. Odds they would last weren't in her favor, but . . .

Ross kissed her again and pulled back. "You wanna do something with this so we can get on with our normal lives?" He handed her the cooler. "Hope this is all you need. We've got the real deal in the house if you need to get any blood."

She opened the cooler and saw the perfectly intact placenta and umbilical cord. "This should do it." The umbilical cord in its self would hold the DNA code she needed, but having a female uterus, this opened up a whole new opportunity. She may be able to extract stem cells and this could reverse the process. She didn't know if she had enough time to make an antidote as Teagan's baby had come full term and would tear its way to freedom at any moment.

"Thank you." She took the cooler into the lab and went to work.

69.

Ross stood around like a nervous father before the birth of his first baby. After the longest fifteen minutes of her life, Alexa had extracted what she needed. The stem cells and Ray's whining on the phone helped more than the DNA itself. She filled the syringe from the beaker and tapped it, releasing the bubbles by letting the clear fluid drip from the tip of the needle. The anti-Tri-Allele serum had to work. She didn't have much time before . . . she didn't want to think about what she could lose. Now her daughter would be the first human trial. The idea didn't sit well with her at all.

"It's done?" Ross's eyes brightened.

"I hope so." In her right hand she held the key to saving her daughter's life.

Teagan screamed, "Mommm!"

Ross bolted out of the garage and beat Alexa to the front door and opened it for her. They hurried to the pull out couch covered in her good 800 ply double-thread sheets. Teagan wasn't there.

"Teagan! Ellie! Where are they, Ross?"

"We're in here," Ellie called from the spare bedroom down the hall.

Alexa and Ross dashed down the hall. Inside the room Teagan's legs dangled from some sort of homemade stirrups using bath towels a couple of trashcans and her good shower rod.

Ross patted Gavin on the back. "Wow Andre McGuyver."

Gavin laughed. His sweet, childish face and deep laughter made Alexa feel better.

"Name's Gavin, ma'am."

A polite giant.

"Nice work." Ross examined the make shift birthing center and seemed pleased.

Alexa watched Ellie hobble over to Ross. He offered his arm for balance. She took the offer and steadied herself.

"Thanks."

It looked to Alexa as though Ellie had died and came back to life. She had bags under her eyes and her mascara smeared down both cheeks. No doubt grieving for Alissa and dealing with her own double mauling's at the hands of a Trill.

"No problem." Ross escorted Ellie bedside.

Alexa also examined the crude operating room. It didn't look half bad.

"Gavin told us to get her off the couch and into a bed. Gavin carried her in here. Little Lesa's sleeping in the other room."

Ross's brow lifted. "You named Savannah's baby?"

"No. Gavin did." Ellie let go and sat down in a rocking chair next to the bed, near Teagan's head.

"Lesa's my sister's name." Gavin listened to Teagan's stomach with a stethoscope and timed her respiration. "And my Grandma and her Grandma's and I'm not sure after that." His voice boomed through the room.

Gavin didn't turn around. "How about we test that stuff in your hands and see if you're really the genius your daughter tells me you are."

"Yeah, Mom. Stick me already. It's coming. Now!" Teagan had a contraction and screamed.

A wriggle against the skin of Teagan's stomach sent Alexa into panic mode. If Teagan died, she didn't know what she would do. She'd no longer have a family. At that moment the pain and anguish of her husband's death a year earlier hit her. She went to Teagan's side and gave her a hug. Tears cascaded down her face. "I can't lose you. I know this is going to work," she whispered into Teagan's ear. "I love you."

Teagan's eyes had burst blood vessels in them from the intense contractions. "Love you too, mom. Now get this fucking thing out of me!"

A tiny nail poked through the skin, sending a stream of blood down Teagan's bare belly.

"Mom!"

Gavin grabbed some gauze out of his fanny pack and put it on the small wound. "I've never seen anything like that before." His eyes looked concerned more than shocked.

She'd procrastinated long enough. *It's time to test this stuff. God help us.* Alexa followed the lump of the child until she felt what might be the baby's rear end. It wasn't hard enough to be the head and she couldn't be sure without proper ultrasound equipment, but she drove the long needle through the skin until it bumped into the hard uterine muscle. She then put more force on the syringe, praying it wouldn't snap the needle. After a second of the heavier pressure, the needle punctured through and hit something rock solid.

"Oh shit!" She wasn't sure what she'd hit.

"What is it?" Ross came to her side.

She whispered into his ear, "I can't get the needle through the Trill's thick epidermis." How could she be so stupid?

Two more claws ripped through the skin in the upper left quadrant. Teagan screamed.

"Press harder." Ross took hold of the syringe.

"No. The needle could break and I don't have another one."

"I got it!" Ross turned and ran out the door.

Where the heck did he go?

A minute later he swept back into the room with something between his fingers. "Will this help?"

Alexa smiled. He'd brought her the one thing that could penetrate the baby's skin. She couldn't believe she hadn't thought of it. She took the anti-Trill serum filled dart from him and extracted her needle.

Ellie had hold of Teagan's hand as she screamed. "A little help here."

Gavin had Teagan's other hand. "You can squeeze my hand as hard as you want sweetie."

Ross pulled the dart apart and broke the vial. "This going to work?" He handed the broken vial to her.

"Pray to your God it does."

"I am."

She took the dart from him and the needle out of Teagan. Blood blossomed in different parts of her stomach and poured down her belly. Gavin wiped away the blood and put pressure and bandages on the wounds. She didn't have much time left.

Alexa extracted a small amount from the dart. Her biggest worry was that the two serums would have a deadly chemical reaction. She did a couple of quick calculations in her head and it wasn't probable, but it could be possible.

Once again she poked the needle into Teagan. This time through one of the holes the baby's claw had made. The baby moved around inside. She hit its tough outer layer and depressed the syringe a little, to work the needle into the skin.

"Is it working?" Ellie asked.

"Give it a minute. C'mon baby, work with me."

Then she felt the baby's skin give and the needle popped through the hard exterior epidermis. She depressed the serum and pulled the needle out.

The baby writhed around and made one large gash in Teagan's stomach, before it stopped moving all together.

"OH FUCK!" Teagan screamed as another contraction hit.

"Breathe." Ellie wiped her head with a washcloth.

"You fucking breathe. I want it out now. Take it out!"

Gavin took control. "She's fully dilated. We could do this naturally or finish cutting, but we don't know where the baby's at health-wise. It's up to you." His huge brown eyes met Alexa's.

"Why's he delivering the baby?" Teagan glared at her mom.

Ross moved and sat next to Teagan. He took her hand. "He's a medic. He's done this many times in the field. Let him do what he's good at, okay."

"But mom's a doctor."

True she was. "I'm not that kind of doctor. We'll let Gavin here do his job."

"Okay." Teagan grunted as another contraction hit.

"It's time for you to push this baby out. You're a strong girl, you can do it." Even under intense pressure, Gavin's deep voice soothed Alexa.

Alexa's wiped the tears away from her cheeks with her sleeve. In a few moments, she'd either be a grandma, or they would all be dead.

Ross smiled at her from his perch next to Teagan. She didn't know if she should go over there or not. He answered her question by holding up Teagan's hand. She followed his lead and went to Teagan's left side and knelt between Ross and Ellie.

"It'll be done soon, Kiddo." Alexa hadn't called Teagan Kiddo in years. Not since she was in Kindergarten. Teagan gritted her teeth, but managed a smile and bore down hard.

Ross put his arm around her. She squeezed into him. Her heart raced harder than she'd ever felt it before. It wasn't her nature to take a stab at something and hoped it would all work out for the best. The Trill inside her only child had left her no other alternative.

70.

ALEXA HELD BABY Lesa in her arms and rocked her back and forth in the recliner.

Teagan cooed at her son. "That's a sweet boy. Is Adam a sweet boy? Yes he is." Adam kicked his legs and flailed his arms. "It's starting, Mom." Teagan turned up the volume on the remote control.

The president stood at a podium, collected his notes and began to speak. Alexa hugged and kissed her new adopted daughter. Lesa's bulbous, florescent green eyes seemed to change color with her mood. Bright-green meant happy, forest-green she needed changed and when they went black as night, she was angry. So far she hadn't exhibited any of the destructive behavior the other Trills had, but yet again, she was a new species. Not quite human, but with a DNA sequence unlike anything Alexa had ever seen in her career as a geneticist.

Lesa had also taken to the bottle and loved formula, the fluorescents in her eyes danced as she drank. A good sign she wasn't a carnivorous creature about ready to tear into someone's chest any minute.

Alexa caught the gist of the president's speech. New beginnings, the lift on martial law and ceasing mandatory termination of pregnancies, new laws regarding immunization during pregnancy and what the governments of the world had in mind for the relocation of any captured Trills. The females seemed re-trainable and there could be a possibility of them becoming civilized. Even being integrated with mainstream society, but not before extensive testing had been completed. The males were a different story, carnivorous, mean and unruly unless one of their females had control of them. The government hoped the females would cooperate in this manner.

Alexa sighed. Content with the fact her daughter and grandson had been spared. She'd once again found something in a man, maybe it was love, but she'd have to see after Ross got back with his daughters; affectionately called the M&M twins by Teagan. She might date him and see where it goes from there. Her husband stayed in the recesses of her memory where he belonged. The time had come for a new beginning. Her new mission in life was to be a new mother, a grandmother, hopefully a wife again and to continue her research with the first pure blood Tri-Allele born on Earth.

71.

LESA'S EYES RAN from creature to creature. One stuffed something in her mouth, forcing her to drink a vile fluid. Large glowing orbs within the creatures called to her. A rumble ran in her stomach. The tasteless muck oozing down her throat would not satiate. Those morsels . . . the pulsating ones, those would sustain.

BIBLIOGRAPHY:

http://ourtownlive.com/ourtown/?p=2376 (Orville Roth Quote)
http://www.businessballs.com/elisabeth_kubler_ross_five_stages_of_grief.htm
Human Molecular Genetics second edition:
   http://www.ncbi.nlm.nih.gov/books/NBK7585/

ACKNOWLEDGEMENTS:

This book is dedicated to my family and fans, whose feedback is detrimental to the success of this novel. I love you all.

Special thanks to my publisher Page after Page Press, editor Sakina Murdock, cover artist Monique-Cherie Snyman, weapons procedural adviser Detective Mark Harkins, inside designer Lori Michelle, and my readers David Burleigh, Josh Parker, Maleia Hubbard, Christine Burleigh, Hemi Burleigh, Rebekah Coffman, Stacy Bolli, Jason E. Rolphe, Tommy B. Smith, Tania Valdez, Franklyn and Lloyd Bowman, and Nat Robinson,—I couldn't have done it without the help and insight of these wonderful people.

ABOUT THE AUTHOR

Nate D. Burleigh is an author of speculative fiction whose work includes the novels *Sustenance, Nasferas: The Be-gotten*, and now *The First*. Nate is a widely published author with short horror stories in multiple ezines, magazines, and book anthologies. Please visit him on his Facebook page and follow his work at www.natedburleigh.com and twitter @natedburleigh.

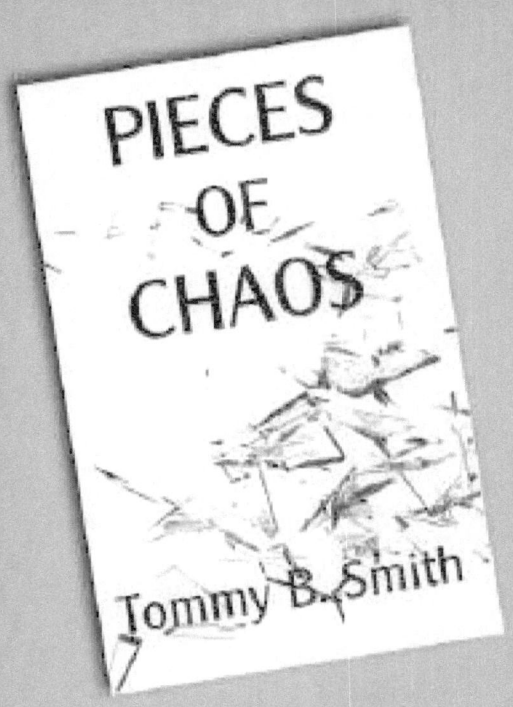

www.ingramcontent.com/pod-product-compliance
Lightning Source LLC
Chambersburg PA
CBHW022109240626
47153CB00007B/2297